BLURRED LINE

A. D. JUSTICE

BLURRED LINE.

A CROSSING LINES NOVEL.

Copyright © 2019 A.D. Justice.

Cover photo by Wander Aguiar.

Cover model is Jacob Cooley.

Cover design by Sommer Stein, Perfect Pear Creative Covers

PROLOGUE

Silas—Moscow, Russia

"I'm surprised to see you. I didn't know you were coming." He narrows his eyes and stares at me suspiciously. He's a large man, formidable back in his heyday, but that was many years ago. Today, he'd sooner reach for his gun and blow a hole in my gut than spar with me. Can't say I blame him.

My Russian contact is leery of surprise visits, especially when I haven't been here in quite some time. That's what happens after living in a military-ruled country that still leans strongly to Communism and enjoys torturing citizens for information. Sure, to the rest of the world, they're now a republic. But that's just the face they wear and the front they show. Walk a mile on the wild side of Moscow then tell me that bullshit party line is real.

The KGB would haul Dmitri away right now if they thought it would gain them an inch. The cold war may have ended years ago, but there's a secret war still raging with no signs of slowing down. And they're playing for keeps, though most of the world has no idea what's going on behind the iron curtain. And that's exactly how they want it.

"If you'd known I was coming, it wouldn't have been a surprise." I purposely keep my hands visible. I mean him no harm. I'm here for answers only he can give.

"What do you want, Silas? I'm in no mood for fun and games. It's been a long day, and I'm ready to get out of here."

I walk farther into his office at the government's fortified complex in the heart of Moscow. There are cameras and voice recorders all over the building; I'm not stupid. But then, they knew I was here the second my plane touched down on the tarmac. My visit here is for unofficial business, but if it turns out to be even remotely what I suspect, the NSA and CIA will duke it out for investigating rights. Good thing I've already assembled a team of three highly skilled and able officers to handle just such an investigation.

Two of them will be starting their training next week with a significant advantage over their classmates because of their previous experience. Now they're learning the spy and asset component, the psychology behind turning a loyalist to a separatist, along with how to blend into a crowd, to become unrecognizable, to become invisible when needed. Very special skills when "sharpshooting assassin" is added to the curriculum vitae.

Glancing over his shoulder, I rest my gaze on the only personal item I've ever known Dmitri to display in his office. It's a picture of his twin daughters—beautiful girls with long black hair, eyes almost as black as coal, straight, thin noses, and perfectly bright complexions.

"I'm here as a friend, Dmitri. How about you and I go find the bottom of a Chernobyl-poisoned bottle of vodka and catch up?" Friends in our business are hard to come by. Dmitri knows this better than anyone, I'm sure of it.

"Your Russian has improved since the last time I saw you. Have you been practicing on someone?"

"No, my Russian has always been impeccable. You were just too drunk to notice when I was here the last time."

Dmitri laughs, the smile reaching his eyes and showing he's warming up to me at last. That's no small feat in the bitter cold of Moscow, even in early spring. "Okay, let's have a drink and regale each other with tales of the good old days."

We walk silently through the corridors until we're well outside the building. There's a time and place for everything, but his office inside the Moscow Kremlin complex is not the place for idle chitchat. And especially not for the questions I have for him. The beauty inside the walled compound—the five palaces, four cathedrals, and the Kremlin Towers with spires reaching to the sky

—masks the true inner workings of the secret government operations. To the public eye, most of the government's work is handled at the Moscow White House, a few miles away. But to those of us in the trade, we know the Kremlin is where the clandestine operations begin and end.

We walk along the Moskva River, then cross the bridge to head to Gorky Park. Despite the cool evening temperature and the time it takes to reach our destination by foot, I'd rather walk the entire distance than chance getting into the wrong car. Besides, traffic in Moscow is terrible, and driving would probably take longer than walking. The time out in the cold air gives me time to think and breathe. Being back here isn't exactly easy for me, but with the high stakes involved, I don't have another choice.

The odds of someone from the KGB following us are high, and I'm not keen on being snatched into an unmarked van and whisked away for questioning. On paper, the KGB as it once was doesn't even exist anymore after it was disbanded and split into two units. But as the powerful regime leader declared, "There's no such thing as a former KGB man." That same leader has worked behind the scenes to reestablish his elite police force, full of henchmen, assassins, and ruthless torturers.

Dmitri and I are careful and take our time before deciding where to stop for a drink, leisurely strolling in the old section of the park until we find a pub tucked away on a side street. We choose a booth away from the other patrons, one that allows a view of the front door and anyone who may try to get too close. The music playing in the background is enough to drown out our conversation on any external listening devices their government has in their arsenal.

My toys are slightly more advanced and higher tech. If the tables were reversed and I were spying on them, I'd have their every word in my ear, clear as a bell. Thankfully, they haven't quite caught up with our advanced gadgets yet. However, their medieval torture methods to extract information are top of the line, and I prefer to avoid them at all costs.

Dmitri orders shots and beer for both of us before turning his keen and penetrating gaze on me. "Silas, why are you here?"

"Tell me, Dmitri. How are your daughters, Mira and Kira?"

He strikes a match, lighting his cigar and taking a few drags on it before hardening his eyes and staring me down amidst the smoke swirling between us. The blunt end of his cigar glows in an angry red shade, much like the coloring overtaking his face at the moment.

"I told you I'm in no mood to play games. Speak your mind or get the fuck out of my sight. I'm giving you this one warning because we've been friendly in the past, but don't mistake this pass for weakness. I will gut you like a fucking fish and dump your body in the river, never to be seen again."

The waitress sets our drinks down in front of us, then

pauses to take our orders. Dmitri dismisses her with a simple wave of his hand. I wait until she's out of earshot to continue.

"Calm down, Dmitri. I'm here to help you and your daughters. But I need you to level with me about what's really going on. What has happened to them?"

"You're not only asking me to commit treason against my country, you're asking me to put my family's lives in real danger. This I cannot do. Go home. Mind your own business. Forget you know me." He throws his shot back then chases it with the entire pint of beer before slamming the mug on the table.

Before he has an opportunity to slide out of the booth, I stand and toss enough rubles on the table to cover our drinks plus a hefty tip. He cuts his eyes up at me, distrust and murderous contempt shining in his eyes.

"You know, your daughters are very beautiful. I know you've always been very proud of them. Their picture is the only personal memento you have in your office. That's a very telling sign, one I'm sure your superiors also picked up on and used as leverage against you. But I assure you, I'm not the guilty party in this. It seems there's something awry in your own government. A blurred line is far too easy to cross—and that's exactly what they created when they used your children against you after all your years of faithful service."

I begin to walk away then stop and look back over my shoulder. "There are slight differences in your girls, even though they're identical twins. For one, Mira has a much softer expression in her eyes than Kira does. Mira's a considerably gentler soul, isn't she? Not quite as fierce and resilient as Kira."

Before I reach the plane for my return flight home, I predict Dmitri Petrov will desperately want a meeting to resume our conversation.

And I'll be waiting for him.

Outside the pub, I pull my heavy overcoat tightly around me, flipping my collar up and pulling my hat down lower on my head. The wind whips around me, and the setting sun makes the air even colder. Without Dmitri's help, I'll have to go off my own assumptions and start directly with the source. I'd hoped to have a little more intel in my back pocket first, but his lack of answers is telling enough.

"Silas, wait."

That didn't take as long as I thought it would.

I stop and turn sideways, casting a glance at Dmitri over my shoulder. The primary reason I'm here is to help make sure a friend doesn't get caught in the cross fire of whatever covert operation the Russians have underway. The fact that I've known Dmitri almost the entire time I've worked in the CIA is a distant second. Our friendship, loosely labeled, is one of convenience and mutual benefit. The moment I'm no longer of use to him, he'd throw me under the bus. As it turns out, we can both help each other this time.

"Suddenly feeling chatty, Dmitri?"

"Do you really think you can help?" The pleading in

his eyes isn't fake, but that's about the only fact I'm certain of right now.

"Do you really think you have any other options? I have an idea of what's going on, and if I'm right, you're the one who's playing games—very dangerous games."

He nods, not so much in agreement with my jab that he's behind the duplicity, but that knowing and doing nothing about it makes him complicit.

"Come to my house tonight. You can stay in our guest bedroom, we'll talk, and I'll drive you back to the airport in the morning."

"When you say airport, you don't really mean Siberian prison camp, do you?"

"Not this time. Next time, maybe."

He calls his driver to come pick us up, and we wait inside the pub, throwing back shots of vodka and snacking on caviar, until he arrives. The black sedan idles alongside the curb, and we walk out together. A moment of hesitation hits me before I slide into Dmitri's car, but I'm banking on his love for his kids to overrule his love of Mother Russia.

Our conversation on the way to his house in the suburbs is benign—nothing the driver or any other prying ears can use against us. When we arrive, his wife Natalya waits for us in the doorway, wringing her hands. The telltale sign of excessive worry gives me comfort—that I'm not walking into a trap.

"Silas, hello, it's been a long time." Natalya greets me with a wary expression despite her warm words.

"Don't worry, Nat. I'm here to help if I can." I kiss both of her cheeks, trying to reassure her of my intentions. She visibly relaxes, dropping her hands to her sides before inviting me in.

"This house is clean. I do my own bug-proofing so Nat and I can have private conversations. We can talk freely here." Dmitri sits at the dining table and begins filling his plate. Nat grabs another plate for me, and I join them for a full meal.

"Dmitri, tell me what's going on. I know you know, so don't bullshit me. And don't leave anything out."

He lowers his fork and levels me with his keen glare. "Will you save both of my girls? No matter what you find?"

"You know I'll do my best, Dmitri. That's the only promise I can give you."

"They were taken to America...by the GRU."

So Russia's largest foreign intelligence agency is hard at work on US soil.

CHAPTER 1

Kira—Eighteen Months Later

*G*oing through the motions day after day and pretending to give two shits about the man sitting across from me is exhausting. He's droning on endlessly about his golf game, as if his commentary on the sport is the most exciting topic ever. As if I care one bit about golf or his swing or how close to par he was during his last game. Close to par is still subpar, that much I know about him. It's winter, for crying out loud. No one golfs in the snow.

But it's my job to pretend I care. He must believe I'm hanging on his every word, dying to know his next magnificent revelation—like a new fucking golf glove he's trying out or something else equally as asinine. We're sitting in a bar that's only a couple of blocks from Capitol Hill, chatting over drinks and flirting as if we're really into each other. The sad thing is, he honestly thinks I want to go home with him tonight. He has no clue I'd rather stab myself in the eye than spend one second longer than I have to with him.

"David, you make it all sound so easy. But I've tried hitting that tiny little ball before, and it's so hard, especially when you have to chase it all over the course. What else do you do for fun?" I pick up my vodka and orange juice, intentionally holding the stirring straw provocatively between my lips. On cue, his eyes drop to my mouth, his lips part, and his breaths increase. He's so fucking predictable. Not that he has a snowball's chance in hell of getting anything from me tonight, but he doesn't need to know that yet.

"I'd love to show you all kinds of things we can do for fun. Your satisfaction is guaranteed."

And I guarantee there's no fucking way that will ever happen.

"Aren't you always working, though?" I stick out my bottom lip, pouting like a child while trying to get him back on topic.

This demure act is slowly killing me inside.

"Well, yes, that's true. My job is very, very important, and it requires a lot of my time. I'm on call twenty-four seven, in case the senator needs me to work on an urgent matter for him. You know, he gets all the glory while I do all the hard work behind the scenes. He only takes the information I give him and argues the points in our favor. I'm the backbone of his entire office. He'd completely fail at his job without me." David raises his glass and downs another shot of bourbon then signals the waitress for another.

That's right...keep drinking. The more you swallow, the looser your tongue becomes.

"That's so not fair. You should be sitting in the Senator's office instead of him. He'd be lucky to sit in your chair. Maybe you can show me his office one day soon. I bet he has a huge...desk." I run my fingernail along his forearm, driving home my insinuation.

He shrugs one shoulder and smirks, clearly trying to be nonchalant but failing miserably at it, as the waitress sets a new glass in front of him. "We can go tonight, if that's what you want. You know, I have keys to the office and can go in there whenever I want. What do you say, baby?"

Baby. Inwardly, I cringe every time he calls me that little pet name. It's not the term of endearment as much as it is the irritating man behind it.

"I say we have a couple more for the road, then go make exciting use of that huge desk." I pick up my glass and make a show of the lack of alcohol. "Can you get me a shot of vodka from the bar? The waitress is busy, and the bartender serves you faster than he does me."

"Of course, baby. I'll be right back. Ronnie, the bartender, knows me. I come in here a lot."

When he leaves our booth, I pull the small vial of tasteless, odorless liquid from between my breasts and empty it into his glass. It mixes with his bourbon instantly, undetectable to the human eye or tongue. The first real smile of the night crosses my face. Soon, I'll be rid of this loser and on to better marks.

He returns with two shots—the straight vodka I requested and another I recognize instantly. I literally force myself not to roll my eyes at his blatant attempt to be cute. My inner voice tells me to stab *him* in the eye, steal the keys, and get this over with as soon as possible.

"Here's your vodka." He sets the shot glass in front of me, and I smile appreciatively, as expected, before I toss it back. "Now for a little something sweeter. Here's your first screaming orgasm of the night, and here's to many more."

When he lifts his bourbon for a toast, I happily raise mine to clink our glasses together. "To many more, indeed."

Just not with you.

The contents of his glass disappear, sliding down his throat before a devious smile crawls across his face. My response is more relaxed, knowing by the time we reach the congressional offices, he'll start to feel the effects of the extra kick I slipped him.

With the tab paid, we leave the bar and walk hand in hand the two blocks back to the office building. By the time we reach the south side entry doors, David is already feeling the effects of all the alcohol he drank plus the extra sedative. We should have just enough time to make it through the security checkpoint and up to the eighth floor before he becomes too sloppy drunk to manage.

The open, airy interior of the Hart Building is much more modern than the older Senate offices. The halls teem with people at all hours of the day and night, especially when significant bills are on the cusp of passing and those involved want to stake their claims. This evening is no different, with staffers rushing back and forth between offices and conference rooms. Their attention is focused on their specific assignments, so they don't even bother glancing in our direction.

David throws his arm over my shoulders as we walk down the spacious hallway together, leaning his face close to mine as he whispers loudly. "You are so fucking beautiful. I can't wait to bend you over the desk, pull your long blond hair, and smack that perfect ass every time you scream my name."

"Let's hope the office is empty, then. What a sight the others would see if they're still working."

"The Senator hasn't been in the office all week. His daughter is getting married this weekend, so he's overseeing the huge tent going up in his backyard. The other staffers left before I did today, so his office is all ours."

The office doors are solid glass, allowing natural light from the central atrium to illuminate the external spaces. Walking past the aides' offices and desks in the outer area, we stop in front of a thick, wooden door that conveys the opulence and prestige of the position without the need for further explanation. He retrieves his keys from his pocket, unlocks the door, and lets me step inside first.

The senator's inner sanctum is two-stories high, and every bit as lavish as I imagined it would be. The rich mahogany wainscoting wraps around the bottom half of the room, and the masculine, dark-green walls stretch up to the ceiling. Large works of art adorn the high walls, each one costing more money than I've made in my entire life. The hypocrisy is astounding—they don't serve the people here. They help themselves while riding on the backs of the people.

He moves behind me, wrapping his arms around my waist and burying his face in my neck. His body sways back and forth, unable to steady himself with the room spinning so fast around him. "Are you ready to have some real fun?"

"Absolutely."

His arms drop from my sides just before his knees give out, and his body crumples to the floor in a heap of drunkenness. I step over him and walk behind the big desk, the one that holds all the information I need to copy before I can leave here. The docking port for the senator's laptop is empty, but his desktop computer is still on. The encryption on his password is strong, but not enough to prevent my portable brute-force attack software from identifying the letters, numbers, and special characters in milliseconds.

After I make myself a system administrator, nothing stops me from copying the data I need to a flash drive.

Rifling through his computer files gives me extra ammunition. He apparently believes his computer is safe from any prying eyes, if the very personal pictures and documents he has "hidden" under a folder entitled "Personal Folder" are any indication. Those, I conceal in a special folder on my flash drive. I may need them later.

After I've copied everything that could be used as leverage against him, along with the highly classified files on the server that I still need to comb through, I replace the folders with a spyware program renamed to match each one. No matter which icon a user clicks on, it'll open another door to the network that won't be detected for some time.

When I finish my job, I make sure everything in the office appears precisely as it was before I entered. The chair is back in place, and the monitor is turned off, nothing showing I was ever here. With the exception of the aide still passed out on the floor, of course. I'll never see him again since my cover is that I'm only a tourist here in DC and I'm heading back to San Diego soon. But if I ever have the displeasure of his company again, my reason for leaving him here to sleep it off is explained easily enough. And it'll be all his fault since he drank too much and left me alone in a strange place.

As I leave the office, I don't bother to close the heavy wooden door to the senator's private office behind me. If anyone walking by sees David and wants to help him, more power to them. But no one seems to notice anything when I step out into the main corridor.

Everyone is anxious to get home after working extra-long hours on a Friday, well past the time average workers have already gone back to their families. I step into the thick of the passing group, easily absorbed by the masses as we make our way down to the lobby level and out the east side of the building. After I step out into the crisp, night air, I hail a taxi and ride away from the scene of the crime, leaving no trace of my real self.

When I reach the interior of my small home in Alexandria, Virginia, I reset the alarm, kick my high heels off, and pull the blond wig off my head. In the summer, the wig and the net holding my long black hair in place can get uncomfortably hot—close to the point of feeling as if a heat stroke is imminent if I'm not careful. But January in Washington, DC, is cold enough not to notice I'm wearing it for the most part. Before I even make it to my bedroom, my phone starts ringing, and I know who it is before looking at the screen.

"Hello?"

"Hello. This is Erika with HairBenders Salon. I'm calling to confirm your appointment on Wednesday morning at 9:15 at our Cameron Station Boulevard location."

"Thank you for the reminder, Erika. I will be there."

We disconnect, and I grab my laptop out of the safe. Before I hand this flash drive over at the designated drop Wednesday morning, I want to memorize everything that's on it. I'll also make my own copy. The information I nabbed could come in handy one day if I

play my cards right. Every move I make must be calculated, weighed, and measured first. Every step I take
must be plotted and coordinated. The dangers are too
real, and the odds are stacked against me, but sometimes there's no choice but to roll the dice and hope for
the best.

I'll have to face the consequences of getting caught
red-handed with the classified information if my cover is
somehow blown. Sometimes the risk is worth the gamble.

With the jump drive inserted into my laptop, I open
the folders and mentally prepare myself to go through
the highly classified data, document by document. My
near-photographic memory is both a blessing and a
curse, but right now I'm going with a blessing. It helps
me connect the dots when I have to recall information
from something I read ten documents ago, but my
memories can't be admitted as evidence the same as
physical documents can.

Some of the files contain information I already know.
Nothing too exciting—the Americans are watching the
Russians who are watching the Americans. The ones they
know about anyway. My name still isn't on the list, so I'll
survive another day. Time gets away from me the deeper
I dive into the senator's files. My stomach growls,
reminding me I haven't eaten anything since this
morning.

My cheap-ass date only sprang for the alcohol
because he thought he'd get lucky tonight, but the joke's
on him. I stand and stretch before walking to the refriger-

ator to stare inside until something I want to eat magically appears.

I'm still waiting…and staring.

After I quickly calculate the time it takes to cook something from scratch versus the time it takes to order delivery, my decision is made. Chinese food delivered hot to my door, it is. The shower calls my name, mainly stemming from my need to wash any remnants of that loser off my skin. But the truth is I've grown weary in my bones of this job and how much it demands of me every time I step out the door.

This is not the life I'd planned when I was a child. If there were any way I could wash it all away, watch it flow down the drain with the bathwater, I would take that shot in a second.

CHAPTER 2

Silas

Kira walks down the hall to the bathroom and leaves the door standing wide open behind her as she adjusts the water. Telltale sounds of her undressing before opening the shower door help me visualize her every move. Before leaving the safety of my hiding place in the shadows inside her home, I wait another few seconds, listening intently to verify she's actually inside the tub.

As a fellow spy, she would know the tricks of the trade already. Our number one offensive move is confusing the enemy by making him believe we're doing one thing when we're actually using misdirection to gain the upper hand. When I hear the water falling in waves, I know she's washing and rinsing her hair, letting the water pool in her long black hair before releasing it with one large splash. Now that I'm confident she didn't sense my presence inside the house with her, I move silently toward her laptop.

She's obviously not on her game tonight. No spy worth his—or her—salt leaves a computer unlocked, the flash drive plugged in, and the stolen documents still open on the desktop. With a few clicks, I erase all evidence of their existence from her computer and eject the flash drive. Just as I slip it into my pocket, the sound of water coming from the bathroom falls silent, then the shower door opens again. The noise of the hairdryer covers my exit from her house, just in time to avoid the teenager delivering her food.

From my vantage point outside, I wait and watch the exchange. Usually, I'd be long gone from the scene, but not this time. Not with this case. Nothing about this situation fits the conventional mold, from the person I'm watching to the reasons why I'm doing it. Even Kira's actions don't match the typical spy patterns. She's all over the board—unpredictable and difficult to follow one minute, to downright sloppy and amateurish the next.

After she pays the delivery boy and closes the door, I watch with a smirk I couldn't contain even if I wanted to, which I don't. She hasn't yet realized both the drive and the data she saved are gone, but she will as soon as she sits down to eat and finish perusing the pilfered classified documents. This is where her predictable response will kick in—she'll run to the door, fling it open, and rush outside, straight into the cold January air, without protection or checking her surroundings first. All mistakes even rookies at The Farm don't make during their initial training.

She is an enigma wrapped in a contradiction.

Thankfully, she can't hear the chuckle that escapes from me when she reacts exactly as I suspected she would. The front door stands wide open while she rushes around the perimeter of her house in nothing but her bathrobe and slippers. When she makes it back around to the front, she stands on the porch, her eyes scanning up and down the street in front of her house. But she can't see me from where I'm watching at the moment.

In fact, she hasn't seen, heard, or felt me watching her at any time in the past year and a half since I returned from Moscow. Standard GRU training should've refined her skills and honed her senses to be able to identify a tail with barely a second glance, even one carried out by a seasoned agent like myself. She can get an invitation into a senator's office, maneuver through secure areas, and steal information from a secure system, and yet, she has tunnel vision where her own safety is concerned. Like not covering the keypad when she enabled the alarm, giving me a full view of her four-digit code. The inconsistencies in her skills and deeds don't make sense to me.

Her shoulders droop noticeably when she releases a defeated sigh. She drops her head back, closes her eyes, and curls her hands into tight fists. If she could kick her own ass right now, she most definitely would. But there's more than anger in her body language. A pained expression crosses her features before being quickly replaced with almost paralyzing fear. She knows she fucked up and there's no way to explain it away, no way to reclaim the data now— from either her computer or from Senator Hunt's. When I wiped hers, I made sure it was wiped CIA clean.

Even I couldn't retrieve it now if I wanted to.

This surveillance is throwing me off my game. I've never been one to show my hand like this, and now she knows without a shadow of a doubt she's being watched. She knows someone was in her home. She knows the data she stole earlier tonight was taken right out from under her nose as soon as she let her guard down. If I'd revealed myself to anyone else in the trade, I'd be a dead man by morning. But with Kira, I'm betting on another angle.

The desperation she so easily displays—from the way she covers her face with her hands before running her fingers through her still damp hair to the way she keeps glancing up and down the street, as if the flash drive will mysteriously appear out of thin air—tells me I've hit the jackpot with reading this peculiar Russian spy.

She'll be reckless enough to try to get back into the senator's office. The same senator who just happens to be on The United Senate Select Committee on Intelligence.

When she turns and walks back into her house, I remain in place for a while longer. Now she knows her cover is blown so she'll be watching for movement, looking for any vehicle that seems out of place in her quiet little part of the neighborhood. I'm guessing that dinner she ordered isn't looking too appealing right now, with her stomach in knots and her nerves set on edge. She has plans to make to try to find a way back into the secure offices now, especially since she burned her bridge with the aide tonight.

An hour after the house is completely dark and still, I stroll over to the next street, slide behind the wheel of my car, and make my way back to my apartment. There's only one viable prospect for her now, and I have my own preparations to make to attend the black-tie political fundraising event, where the buy-in for a plate easily costs $1,000, but that's lowballing compared to the individual donations of $30,000 or more. This is the life in DC— someone is always fundraising for something, and someone else is always more than willing to donate to it for a favor in return.

I need to dust off my tuxedo and get an invitation to the party for myself. I have a hot date all lined up for tomorrow night—she just doesn't know it yet.

Back inside my apartment, I sit down with my secure CIA laptop to check out the contents of the flash drive. At first glance, it seems she copied everything she could find in hopes of finding anything of use. It'll take time to go through all the documents and identify any significant national security risks we're facing as a result of this breach. That research will have to wait until later, though, when I can give it to one of my sidekicks. It's already been a long day and night.

Stick a fork in me, I'm completely done.

WHEN I STEP INTO THE ATRIUM OF THE RONALD REAGAN Building on Saturday evening, my undercover training immediately kicks in. The room is as tall as it is long, with a rounded glass dome that adjoins the third-floor ceiling. Both upper floors are wide-open promenades, providing an excellent view of the grand room below. Flowing rolls of white gossamer fabric are draped all the way from the glass above to the floor below, gathered strategically to create the ambiance and rich tone of the gala. The music from the jazz band on the stage at the far end of the room carries on the room's acoustics, adding to the overall mood and vibe.

A waiter approaches with a tray full of champagne flutes, so I take one to sip on as I begin mingling with the crowd. Saying hello to complete strangers as I work my way through the party, acting as if I know them and I belong here, keeps suspicious eyes from staring too long. They return a polite greeting and quickly resume their conversations. Listening for tidbits of information as I pass by is second nature to me now. It comes as naturally as breathing. I'm just waiting for the right conversation to catch my ear.

When I slow and turn, taking a lingering perusal of

the people at the party, my gaze locks on the sexiest woman in the entire room, standing regally at the top of the stairs, unaware of her beauty and allure. Kira's long black hair shimmers, catching the soft white twinkle of the lights and reflecting them like tiny bursts of starlight. In a sea of black cocktail dresses, she stands out even more in her pure-white, floor-length gown that leaves one shoulder bare and clings to her every curve, beckoning every man in the room to her beauty.

Then it hits me. That's precisely her intention—mesmerize and hypnotize the men with her exquisiteness, then knock them on their ass with a hidden syringe or a tiny vial of liquid sleeping medicine. The congresspeople, aides, and other staffers in the room have the access she desperately needs. Experience tells me she's meeting someone soon to turn over the information she stole—someone who expects nothing less than success. Whichever unwitting victim falls into her web will do, as long as she can use him to get back into the secure office and on the secure servers.

I have other plans for her, though.

She's descending from the top of the wide, runner-covered stairway, three stories up, so I have plenty of time to drink her in while formulating my approach. After dropping off my champagne glass on an empty table, I weave through the crowd with my sights set on her, watching her every move to coordinate my own to match. She reaches the bottom of the steps just as I reach the edge of the crowd and enjoy an unobstructed view of her.

She starts by assessing every individual to find the perfect mark—who's here, who's vulnerable, who's alone. She takes a step into the crowd but quickly realizes her task won't be quite as easy as she thought. Most people don't show up to these elaborate fundraising events alone, and for a good reason. They're here to rub elbows and tap shoulders to get their own politicians more funding. Every connection in this circuit only helps the cause in the end—the more lips flapping and hands extending for handouts, the better.

When she identifies her target, her facial expression changes, and she morphs into character. She's on the prowl now, stalking her prey as she moves past the elaborately decorated round tables and the throngs of people laughing and chatting each other up. Following her line of sight, I realize which victim she's chosen for tonight's performance, and I instantly recognize him.

She's in way over her head, but she doesn't have a clue.

Moving quickly and silently through the crowd, I slip around all the obstacles in my path until I'm directly in front of her. The tables line the walls, leaving enough room in the middle for a decently sized dance floor. Several couples are taking advantage of the slow, sultry jazz sounds carrying over the air. When she raises her arm to touch the man's shoulder, I grab her hand just before her fingers have a chance to graze his jacket.

With my other arm wrapped around her waist, I walk her backward a few steps, surprised expression and all, until we reach the dance floor. We begin swaying to the music, our feet moving naturally to the beat, our bodies in sync without conscious effort. As if we've danced together our entire lives. Her intoxicating perfume fills my nostrils, making me want to bury my face in her neck and inhale every bit of her essence. She keeps her dark eyes glued to mine. The shock is still registered in them, but it's now mixed with a little excitement and a little leeriness.

I'm curious to see which emotion wins in the end.

"Not that I don't appreciate the dance, but I have to ask. Do I know you?"

She doesn't know me—that's not her real question. That's merely a polite way of saying, "Who the fuck are you?"

"We've never met." That's not a lie. "But you were about to make a huge mistake, and I felt a strong need to save you from yourself."

"I was about to make a huge mistake? What do you mean?" Waves of suspicion churn in her eyes.

"The man you were about to flirt with? I know him, and he's not someone you want to double-cross. He's not an unsuspecting senator's aide who's too scared to report he was outwitted by a young lady he snuck into his boss's office. The man behind us has the means and the determination to hunt you down and kill you for much less."

Her confusion clears, giving way to clarity. The angry

red tinge creeps up her skin, starting at her neck and disappearing into her hairline. I tighten my arm around her waist, holding her against me before she decides to scale my body like a beautiful little spider monkey and choke me out with her bare hands.

"You. Son. Of. A. Bitch!" She hisses the insult at me in an irate whisper, enunciating each word with marked aversion. If we were alone, this would be a very different scene. She's a bit of a wildcat when provoked. This may be an inappropriate time to tell her how fucking sexy she is when she's mad. "You're the one who broke into my house!"

"To be fair, you broke into my government first. Now, there are a lot of things I can sweep under the rug and pretend I didn't see, but that's not one of them. On top to that, you're a Russian spy, and our countries historically haven't been the best of friends. The only reason you're not in custody right now is because of your father. Try that shit again, though, and you're headed for Guantanamo Bay, where they'll hold you for interrogation for as long as they want. I'm not *that* tight with your dad."

"That's a ridiculous accusation. I'm not a spy. But it's very convenient for you to claim to know my father when I have no way to verify it. Especially since I don't even know your name. Maybe you're the Russian spy, trying to work me and turn me against my country. Maybe I should call for security right now."

"Now, Kira, don't try to bluff me. Dmitri is a friend, and he's beside himself with worry about you. I gave him my word I'd help you as much as possible, but I won't help you steal top-secret information from my country and hand it over to yours. I've done enough favors for you over the last eighteen months, tracking you down and keeping you out of prison, or worse—out of the real bad guys' hands. And my name is Silas."

She glances nervously around the room, her eyes jumping from one spot to another. I chuckle, mostly to myself, but I can't hide my amusement.

"What's so funny?"

"You're looking for an escape route. Do you really think I would've revealed my upper hand if it was my real ace in the hole?"

"There's nothing you could possibly have on me, Silas. You have nothing to hold over my head to threaten me with. My laptop is completely clean. Thanks to you."

"You may be surprised by the things I know. May surprise you even more when you realize you didn't even have a clue about the truth of the matter. But I do have a few questions—a few holes in the story you can help fill in. So why don't we call a truce—broker our own peace treaty right now—and help each other out?"

The music continues, we keep swaying, and the wheels keep turning in her mind. She has been trained to work assets, turn them to support her country, or give her the information she wants in exchange for something else. She hasn't been in this situation before—where she's the one being worked and giving up the information to the enemy. No time like the present to learn on the job.

"What do you know that I don't? You have to give me something to go on other than you know my dad's name."

"I know more than your dad's name. Your mom, Nat, knows me too. She even cooked for me the last time I visited their house—the one Dmitri sweeps for bugs himself so they can have private conversations. He also keeps a picture of you and Mira on his desk in his office at the Kremlin. It's the only personal item he has there— the only one he's ever been proud enough of to show others. I'm guessing he assumed his KGB days would keep his family safe, though he should've known his own government better than that. Communists aren't known for their friendships or loyalty to anyone."

"Haven't you kept up with current political affairs? Russia hasn't been a communist country for a very long time."

"Ah, yes, of course. United Russia. Because the last election wasn't rigged at all, right? Come on, Kira. I've given you enough information to prove I know you and your family. I also know that you secretly like me, even though you don't want to admit it."

Now she laughs, a genuine one that reaches her eyes and lights up her face. "And why would you say that, Silas?"

"Because you're still dancing with me, without even noticing the music stopped a couple of minutes ago."

CHAPTER 3

Kira

$\mathcal{T}$all, dark, and handsome. Fit, muscular, and stealthy. Not prone to following the rules, making plans up as he goes, and approaching life-and-death decisions as a game to be won.

Definitely CIA.

FBI agents follow the rules to the letter, never veering off the beaten path. They're much more serious and don't negotiate with outsiders. Silas is an officer who can change to fit his environment. The chameleon who can never be caught. He was invisible last night, leaving no trace of being in my house, other than his deliberate acts of stealing my flash drive and wiping my computer clean. Now tonight, he's dressed in an Armani tuxedo, tailored to fit his massive frame in an all-too-appealing fashion.

His easygoing disposition is no doubt meant to subdue and disorient his victims, never seeing the runaway train that hit them until he's long out of sight.

He's not wrong about one thing, though. Once he started talking and I got lost in his deep blue eyes, everyone else in the room faded to black. His air of authority is innate. It's in the way he moves, the way he speaks, and the way he commands respect with no effort at all. His dazzling features disarm me with barely any struggle. His thick arms enveloped me in a comforting cocoon, and his alluring cologne pulled me even further under his spell.

We were still dancing, our bodies aligned and swaying in time to our own song, and I didn't even realize the band had stopped playing. He infuriated me and scared me and concerned me, but he also made me feel protected. I've never felt simultaneously so powerless and powerful in my life, and that is the very sensation that finally brings me back to my senses. The flashing red "warning" sign in my mind reminds me that spies can't be trusted no matter how enticing their promises are. They're trained to lie, steal, cheat, and kill to get what they need.

I should know.

What he needs from me is yet to be seen, but admitting my subterfuge right off the bat isn't fucking happening, no matter how charming and dashing he is.

"I'm still dancing with you because I'm still entertaining this ridiculous theory you're working on that I'm a Russian spy. Do you even hear the slightest bit of a Russian accent in my voice?"

"No, I don't. You're very good at what you do. And your English is perfect. That's all part of your training. You'd be surprised how well I can speak Russian."

He leans down, and his lips brush the shell of my ear. The deep and sensual timbre of his murmur makes goosebumps fan out across my bare skin.

"You look beautiful tonight." He speaks in perfect Russian, giving away no hint of an American accent.

"That sounded very seductive in your gravelly whisper. If I spoke or understood Russian, I may have liked what you said, but we'll never know."

He laughs and rolls his eyes, clearly knowing I'm lying through my teeth. "Tell you what I'll do. If this doesn't prove it to you, nothing will."

We walk to the edge of the dance floor, and he pulls out a chair at one of the empty tables for me to sit. He releases my hand, slides into the chair beside me, and reaches into his pants pocket, retrieving his cell phone. After a few clicks, he presses the phone to his ear and begins speaking in Russian. "There's someone here you need to convince to let me help her. She's being very stubborn, seems to be a strong family trait."

Then he hands the phone to me.

"Hello?"

"Kira?" My mom's voice fills the line, relief and fear

fighting for first place in her tone. "Is it really you? Please listen to Silas. He's our friend—he's only trying to help you."

I push the phone back into his hand as fast as I can, as if it's a ticking bomb about to explode. Everything about this situation runs counter to my training, to what's expected of me, to what's keeping me alive. Speaking to my family back in Russia is expressly forbidden. The traced phone calls would absolutely blow my cover and put my entire family in grave danger.

"Hey Nat, she's a little shy to talk right now. Probably afraid my phone calls can be tracked. I think hearing your voice did the trick, though. We'll talk again soon."

"You shouldn't have done that." I glare at him, ready to kill him with my bare hands and take my chances in this crowded room.

"Relax, Kira. My phone is secure, untraceable, and undetectable. No one except you and I know about that call. I had to show you I'm not bullshitting so you'd believe me. I'll help you get on a plane back to Moscow, but then my part in any of this is over. If you step foot on American soil again, you'll be detained immediately and indefinitely."

"Why would you help me like this at all? What do you owe my father?"

"Nothing. This isn't for him, exactly. He benefits from my interference, but I'm mainly looking out for a friend."

"I don't understand. How do I know your friend?"

"You don't. But your sister Mira does."

"Mira?" I'm so confused. Silas acts as if I should understand his explanations and reasoning without questioning him, but none of this makes sense to me in the least.

"She's a good person, and I don't want to see her end up in a supermax federal prison, or worse, because you refuse to comply with the laws of this country. Years of living in a soundproof isolation cell would be worse than death for her. I'm only trying to spare her from trouble with immigration, interrogation, and prison time for as long as I can." His charming smile and easygoing personality instantly change, revealing the lethally serious man underneath.

"But..." I pause, trying to connect my thoughts and words coherently. "Mira's already in prison. Are you saying you can get into the prison where she's being held?"

He tilts his head to the side and the corners of his eyes contract. Then he lifts his eyebrows and immediately lowers them again, putting his own pieces of the puzzle together. "Someone told you Mira's in prison, huh? My guess is they're using that cover story to make sure you keep toeing the line."

I sit up straighter, instantly more interested in what Silas has to say. "Don't play games with me, Silas. Do you know her? Is she okay?"

"She's perfectly fine. She's safe, she's happy, and she's living with a very loving family."

His answers are intentionally vague regarding where

she is, I understand that. He's doing his job, getting ready to put me on a plane back to Russia for stealing top-secret and other classified documents from a secure server in a controlled-access government building. But she's my twin—and I've felt like half of me has been missing without being able to talk to her. All this time, I've believed my handlers—and they lied to my face every fucking day about my sister. What else have they lied about? What else do I not know?

My throat starts to clog, burning with tears that I force back down and refuse to let fall from my eyes. So many emotions run through me at once—but the most prevalent feeling of them all is regret. Because if Silas has his way, I'll never see Mira again.

"Can we go somewhere a little quieter and more private so we can talk? I'd like to hear more about Mira."

"We can talk on the way to the airstrip. There's a private jet waiting to take you to Moscow tonight."

He stands and extends his hand to help me up. I robotically accept his offer while trying to formulate how I'll ditch him once we step outside the building. If I get into the car with him, my life as I know it will be finished. There's no way I'm going back to Moscow. Not ever. Not even to see my parents, as much as I miss them. He has a job to do—I respect that. But his succeeding at his job would mean certain death for me. Had he been captured in Russia under the same circumstances, no one would give him the second chance I'm hell-bent on taking for myself.

We move through the crowded room, and I try to keep my expression neutral. All I can think is I'm being marched out to face the firing squad. My every step is harder and harder to take until my feet feel as if they're weighted down by concrete shoes.

A large crowd of interns—judging by how young they appear to be—with huge smiles on their faces and nearly empty glasses in their hands, weaves between the tight spaces around the tables and chairs, heading for the dance floor. At least some people are having fun at this party. A few of the girls start dancing well before they've moved out of our way, obviously a little tipsy and ready to have a good time. One of them grabs my arms and urges me to dance with her.

The unwitting stranger pulls my hand loose from Silas's grip.

Then I realize I'm free—and I allow her to pull me farther away from him while her friends fill in the space between Silas and me. He starts to push his way through the crowd, walking toward me, but the young studs in hot pursuit of the pretty girls prevent him from getting closer. The easygoing man I first met is long gone, replaced by the serious officer underneath. His facial features turn to stone. His eyes are as sharp as an eagle's and as cold as a marble slab—and he's determined to have me in custody.

But this is my chance, the only one I will have in the foreseeable future since my cover is blown and my real identity is out. While the horde of young revelers enjoys the upbeat music coming from the band—jumping, dancing, and forming a human wall separating me from Silas—I make a run for the exit door at the back of the room. If the alarm sounds when I run through the door, so be it. Maybe it'll create more of a diversion and give me extra time to get away.

When I push the door, I'm relieved to find it's unlocked. No extra bells and whistles are going off, so I can only assume it's because the enormous space is packed with people for tonight's fundraising event. Whatever the reason isn't important now that I'm in the clear, so to speak. I can still almost feel his hot breath breathing down my neck. In my rush, I left my coat in the cloakroom, and the thin material of my evening gown doesn't offer much protection from the winter winds whipping between the buildings. Running in heels isn't exactly graceful, but the line of taxis dropping off passengers along the sidewalk provides a modicum of cover, making it seem as if I'm only hurrying to reach an open cab before it's gone again.

When I slide into the back seat and slam the door closed behind me, I give the driver my address. "There's an extra $50 tip if you get me there in less than ten minutes."

"You got it, lady."

He guns the engine, and the tires squeal as he pulls away from the curb. I turn to look out the back window and realize how narrowly I escaped Silas's grasp. He was reaching for the door and just barely missed the handle when we sped away. He lowers his chin and narrows his eyes, watching intently with the expression of an assassin who just accepted a direct challenge. That's not what gives me chills, though. He hasn't moved from his spot on the sidewalk despite the distance the cabbie has already put between us.

How long has Silas been watching me?

What else does he know?

The only option I have now is to reach my house, change clothes, and throw an extra set of clothing into a bag in record time, then clear out of there before he shows up. My heart is running away in my chest, pounding so hard, my skin is visibly jumping with each beat under the thin fabric of my dress. I know I should be planning my next move—where I'll hide out now that I know the rest of the government agencies will be after me—but all I can think about is what Silas said while we were dancing.

Mira isn't behind bars. She isn't being held in a dark, cold cell somewhere, being tortured for information. She's happy and healthy and being taken care of by an American family.

But Silas is a spy, too. He's trained to tell lies for a living, to make others believe every word that falls from his lips. I have to consider his story about Mira could be a carefully constructed scheme to get information from me. Maybe they broke her and that's how he found me, intending to finish the job by finishing me.

My mother wouldn't be in on a scheme like that, though. She'd die before she'd help anyone hurt us. In this entire confusing and maddening situation, that's the only fact I can cling to and not second-guess.

She said Silas would help me.

However, she doesn't know what I've discovered. And with that damning information in my head, I can't leave. If only I could convince Silas to help me instead of just throwing me on a plane back to Moscow. But that would've been a highly unlikely "if," even before I ditched him at the gala.

True to his word, the cab driver ran every red light and stop sign between the Reagan Building and my house to get the promised extra tip for getting me home in record time. I discreetly slide the $100 bill out of my bra and hand it to him. "Keep the change."

"Hey, thanks, lady!"

His night is made. Mine is falling apart. Story of my life.

I rush to the front porch, retrieve the hidden spare key, and head straight for my bedroom closet. After I kick off my shoes and leave the beautiful gown in a crumpled pile on the floor, I pull an oversized black hoodie over my head, slide black leggings over my legs, and complete the blackness of my mood with matching socks and boots. Extra jeans, sweaters, undergarments, and sneakers are shoved into a duffle bag, along with a stack of hidden cash and new identification, before I rush to the living room to grab my laptop and phone.

Everything else I've accumulated will have to stay. There's no time for sentimental attachments to material things when I live my life on the run day after day. With my electronics safely stashed in my bag, I turn from the table and take two steps toward the front door…before two strong arms grab me from behind. One muscular leg wraps around mine, hooking my ankle and preventing me from fighting back. Wrapped in a blanket of thick muscle and hard body, I can't even move.

My front door swings open, and Silas steps inside the frame, taking up the entire space with his enormous size. He crosses his arms, lowers his chin toward his chest, and glares menacingly at me. One thing I've learned about the men in this business—they don't care if the enemy is male or female. The same treatment is doled out regardless of sex, strength, or circumstances. From the way Silas is burning holes through me with the anger in his eyes, I'm not looking forward to the next few minutes.

"Kira, that was an incredibly stupid move." Silas moves inside and closes the door behind him. "As I recall, I offered to help you leave this country without being captured and sent to Gitmo for being a Russian spy and stealing top-secret government documents."

He takes the duffle bag from my tight grip with no effort at all and makes a point of looking it over. Then he cuts his eyes back to mine, barely hiding the anger seething just underneath. "And yet, this packed getaway bag makes me believe you were planning to disappear and continue your attack on my country."

When I don't reply, he shifts his eyes from mine to the man behind me. After a barely perceptible nod from Silas, I feel the tight coil of muscles encircle my neck a split second before I slip into complete darkness.

CHAPTER 4

Kira

I begin to rouse to the gentle rocking of a moving vehicle. Instinct nudges me before realization sets in, and I sit straight up with a start. We're well outside the city now, and everything is pitch black. Silas is driving; I can make out his silhouette from the back seat. Two large men flank me, leaving me very little room to move between their hulking forms. In fact, I think my cheek rested on one man's shoulder before I woke.

"Which one of you choked me out?"

A dark chuckle rumbles through the chest of the man to my left. "That was me, but I didn't choke you. It's a special technique that just helps you go right to sleep with no fuss."

I don't know this dickhead from Adam, and I have no

idea where they're taking me or what they're planning to do to me once we get there. Years of training kick in, and I react violently, regardless of the massive men sandwiching me in the middle of the back seat, regardless of the moving vehicle, and regardless of the dark streets with no discernable landmarks to tell me where I am.

When my elbow connects with his nose, the familiar pop of bone and cartilage giving way echoes through the vehicle. His eyes shut involuntarily, and his hands fly to cover his face on pure reflex. I lunge for the car door on the other side of him, ready to tuck and roll before disappearing into the night, far from these men. Just as my fingers wrap around the door handle, two strong arms grab me from behind and haul me across the seat into his lap.

"Calm the fuck down. We're not here to hurt you—unless you make us."

"The fuck you say. He just knocked me out, and you three loaded me into a vehicle against my will. Now we're in the middle of Bumfuck, Egypt, and you think I should just go along and trust you?"

"I think you just broke my fucking nose." The other man glares over at me while wiping the blood from his face. The man holding me suppresses a chuckle, while Silas's deep laugh rumbles through the car without apology.

"And? You're lucky that's all I broke. What would you do if you woke up in a car with three strangers? Who the hell are you guys anyway?" I try to get a look at his face, but the lack of light works against me. I'm sure that is part of why they're taking me somewhere into the countryside of Virginia, if I had to guess.

He's silent, but Silas speaks up from the front. "That's Roman. The man on the other side of you is Nick."

"Well, I would say it's nice to meet you, but considering the circumstances, it's not." All three men laugh even though I didn't actually mean it as a joke. "Where are you taking me?"

Nick moves me back to my seat in the middle then secures the seat belt around me, pulling it tight across my body until it locks me in place.

"We're going to a safe house to talk." Silas is being especially tight-lipped and more reserved than he was at the gala. I realize that's my fault. He's punishing me for running away from him, but he'd do the same if our roles were reversed.

"Is that CIA code for you're taking me out to a remote field to kill me and dispose of my body?" I did mean that as a joke to lighten the mood in the car, if possible, but there's no reaction for a few seconds.

"What makes you think we're CIA?" Maybe Silas doesn't have a sense of humor after all.

"Because you bend the rules to suit you. Other agencies with three initials don't do that—they follow the rules to the letter. CIA officers only follow rules that benefit them."

Nick smiles, and I see a slight nod of his head. He knows what I said is true. I'm not judging since I obviously make decisions on the fly, all depending on the circumstances and pressures I'm under.

The car begins to slow, then Silas makes a right turn onto a long, darkened driveway. The gravel crunches under the weight of the tires as we creep toward the house hidden among the trees. Their idea of a safe house is vastly different than the city apartments and homes the GRU has. This location is more like the places we use to question traitors—isolated, secure, and soundproof. This situation doesn't bode well for me.

When we park, Roman gets out and turns to take my arm. Rather than exiting on the opposite side, Nick moves across the seat toward me, keeping me securely between the two of them. There's no way I can outrun all three of these men anyway—even if I knew where I was and which way to run. Once we're all out of the car, Silas walks behind us as Nick and Roman walk beside me, each gripping my arms until we're inside the house and the door is locked behind us.

The entryway opens directly into a large living room to the left and dining room to the right. After seeing the modern floor plan and comfortable furnishings, I now realize this house is newer than I initially thought. The unpaved driveway conjured images of an older dwelling —one other people wouldn't often visit.

"Have a seat." Silas walks through the dining room into the kitchen, and I sit on the plush leather sofa. While he's in the other room, I take the opportunity to glance around the fully decorated home. If this is a place for torture, they don't leave any evidence of it behind. "Here. This will wet your whistle and help you talk all night if needed."

He extends his hand to offer a bottle of cold water, so I take it from him and twist the cap, noting that it hasn't been opened before now. No unknown additives to help loosen my tongue. With his other hand, he swings a chair around to sit directly in front of me, our knees touching from the close quarters. Nick and Roman remain standing, guarding the exits with their large frames. I cut my gaze between the two men before rolling my eyes at them.

"You two can sit down. I won't try to run as long as we're only talking. But I'm not getting on an airplane. The only way I'm going back is if you shoot me and send me back in a casket."

They ignore me and maintain their vigilant stance instead.

"What were you looking for in the senator's office?" Silas pulls my attention back to him.

He's such a handsome man, still in his tuxedo, but now without the bow tie. The top couple buttons of his crisp white shirt are undone, hinting at his finely tuned body underneath. He stands a full head and shoulders taller than me, with a fully muscled frame perfectly proportionate to his height. I've caught glimpses of the different facets of his personality. His suave and debonair side and his playful nature.

But right now, he's in all-business mode, impatiently

waiting for me to explain my actions. This man is very different from the one I danced with just a short time ago. That man was warm and inviting, but the man sitting in front of me is cold and calculating. There is no line he wouldn't cross to neutralize a threat.

What he doesn't understand is how volatile the bomb I'm about to drop in his lap is. He doesn't realize that in order to defend the country he loves, he'll have to cross the line he never thought he'd have to face. He'll have to betray his country in order to save it.

My silence stretches a little too long, and his patience is wearing a bit too thin. He leans forward, puts his forearms on his knees, and pierces me with his deep blue eyes. I've noticed they change with his mood. When he's friendly and accommodating, they're a warm, inviting shade of blue. Malleable and friendly, they draw others in on the premise of trust, honor, and duty. When he goes into interrogation mode, like now, the warmth completely disappears, replaced by an iciness that chills me to the bone. I have no doubt this man is a trained killer and has no misgivings about using his unique skills.

"We're doing this the easy way at the moment, Kira. But this is the last time I will ask nicely. You think you've pegged CIA officers so well. So, believe me when I say this. If I don't get a complete and honest answer right now, you'll find out firsthand exactly what I'm capable of doing in order to protect and serve my country. I know what you are and why you're here. You've been here illegally, silently observing but not actively conspiring against us. Until tonight. Now that you've stepped up your game, I want to know why—what prompted the change in your behavior. And you will tell me everything."

I'd like to have the warm and flirty Silas back now. But he's long gone, and I'm afraid he won't be back anytime soon.

"My sister and I were brought here against our will twenty years ago. We were only ten years old when we were ripped from our mother's arms, Silas. You say you know her? Then you know she doesn't exactly wear her heart on her sleeve when it comes to showing her emotions. So imagine seeing her have a complete breakdown, right in front of you, while men you don't know, have never even seen before, drag you away from the only home you've ever had. All they would tell us was that we'd have a new family soon and to forget about our old one if we knew what was good for us.

"We grew up here in America, taking English lessons until we were fluent, and all traces of our Russian accents were gone. We went to school here, just like every other American teenager. But we had extra lessons after school—learning fighting skills, staying up-to-date on the latest technology advancements, and training how to get in and out of buildings undetected. We didn't know what we were being prepared to do throughout our teenage years, only that we had to keep everything a secret from everyone else. We were one person by day and a completely different person at night. Then we turned eighteen and were forced into this life—no questions of what we wanted to do with our lives, no options to go off to college somewhere, and no mention of our future. Nothing we've done since we were ten has been our choice. You have to believe me."

I'm fully aware all my blurted confession is entirely off topic, even though he already warned me about not answering his direct questions. But this is all information he needs to know, nevertheless. I need him to understand what occurred in the past, so the path we should take in the present and the future is crystal clear.

"That's a very touching story. I'm perplexed, though, because you told me everything except what I asked." With a menacing expression covering his face, he starts rolling up his sleeves, revealing his muscular forearms.

"I'm trying to tell you everything—so you'll get the big picture and understand what's happening. Just give me a chance to explain."

"By all means, continue." He waves his hand in front of him, but the skepticism in his voice is loud and clear.

"There are more people like Mira and me planted here, waiting to be activated. They've been here for years, working in every walk of life, rising to the top of corporate ladders, or just hosting new recruits in their homes. They're also in the government, from a secretary in the FBI to a staffer in a congressman's office…maybe even a senator himself. They're doing their jobs normally and living their daily lives until they hear from their mentor. Then they cross that line and become a spy again."

"Are you saying the senator whose office you broke into is a Russian asset?" His expression matches his voice, wholly skeptical and ready to toss me into a cell then forget I exist.

"I don't know what his exact capacity is, but I do know he's important to whatever the current project is. He has ties to the Academy and the GRU somehow. That's part of why I had to get into his computer—to find out what he's doing and why."

"The Academy?"

"The training center that runs all of our operations."

"How do they do that—get your orders to you? What's their process?"

"They send the encrypted orders to our handlers, but never directly to the operative, and no one here has all the information about any single op. The information is divided up between several players, only giving each person the information about their specific job. There's also always at least one layer of contact between everyone—the GRU and us, and between the activated operatives."

"How do you know the senator is involved?" Silas's expression doesn't change, but something in the air around us makes me think he's starting to believe me. The twenty-questions game is a one-way street, and I understand why, but we're wasting valuable time.

"Have you ever heard pieces of different conversations, picked up on various tidbits of information, then put them all together, and they made a perfectly clear picture?"

He nods without verbally confirming, but at least he's giving me that much.

"That's exactly what I've done. You probably expect me to point to one specific detail or give you one concrete shred of evidence to prove it. I can't do that without going through everything on that flash drive."

"Yeah, that's not happening. Do you think I'm gullible? Do you really think I'd just hand that over so you can memorize every top-secret detail in there and pass them on to your superiors? Try again. That's almost more of an insult than your stealing from my country. You really think I'm that stupid?"

"What? No, I don't think you're stupid at all. I don't want to give that information to my superiors—I wanted to use it to save my sister! I was going to change the documents before handing the flash drive off to them at our drop site Wednesday morning. They told me my sister was sitting in a prison cell at a black site because of me, Silas. They said she was being tortured and would eventually be killed—all because they thought she was me when she was caught. I've only continued working with them to get close to the senator. They said they'd find a way to get Mira out if I did this, even if it meant they had to do a prisoner exchange."

"They're open to an exchange, huh? Who do they claim to have to exchange?"

This conversation just took a very unexpected change in direction, and I'm not sure how to answer that question. If the name I give him is a high-value asset, he'll trade Mira and me in a heartbeat. If not, I've just inadvertently given up a valuable leverage opportunity. After a quick glance around the room, I confirm all eyes are on me, and if possible, they would burn holes through me with the intensity of their stares. They all want to hear the answer to that question—which tells me I need to sit on that information for as long as possible.

"Is my sister really okay?" My voice cracks at the end, but I push the emotions clogging my throat back down.

Remember your training.

I hear Olga Vladimirovna, my instructor at the Academy, in my head, relentlessly pushing me to train longer, fight harder, and show no weaknesses.

Silas doesn't move, doesn't flinch, doesn't even seem to breathe for far too long. Then he nods again. His shoulders lift as he inhales deeply then releases his breath in a resigned sigh. "Mira is fine. I wasn't lying when I said she's living with a family who loves her very much. She's working as the nanny for their children now. The three of us are the only ones who know about her past, and her former employer has no clue how to find her." He motions toward Nick and Roman as he speaks, but I can't look away from him. "And I plan to keep it that way."

"I want to see her. Please, just take me to her."

Silas shakes his head. "You can forget about that."

CHAPTER 5

Silas

"What do you think? Do you believe her?" Nick eyes me, carefully watching my every reaction. He has more skin in this game than anyone, so I understand his concern. Kira's sister lives in his house, helps care for his babies, and has become a best friend to his wife. An international incident would take both ladies down with one fail swoop.

"I don't know, man. On the one hand, I'd say she's telling the truth. On the other, I know she's a trained GRU operative—and they're not far removed from the KGB days. Same trainers. Same expectations. Same results." I shake my head, more irritated with myself than anything else. I'm too close to this case to make rational decisions. There's way too much at stake in this game. The blurred lines are not part and parcel of my usual method, and I don't like it.

Nick nods, understanding my confused state, and heads back into the living room to babysit our guest.

"The great Silas Steele can't decide if a Russian spy is lying to him or not? What the hell is going on here?" Roman glares at me as if I've lost my mind. Maybe I have. "What the fuck, man? You got the hots for her?"

"What? No, of course not. Fuck off."

"You fuck off. You're lying to me right now. You've been compromised—either fuck her out of your system or step aside and let us do our job. We don't have time to wait. We need to know what time and where her dead drop is so we can get eyes on it right now."

I know Roman is right about part of what he's saying, but my gut is conflicted for a reason. That doesn't mean his words don't thoroughly piss me off, though. I've listened to my instincts and stayed alive in much more dire circumstances than this. Not trusting my senses now would be a huge mistake—but that's about all I'm sure of at this point.

"Back off, Roman. You have no idea what you're talking about." I cut my glare to meet his and watch him instantly relax his rigid stance. "I know how to do my job —and that's exactly what I'm doing. If this senator is selling our secrets or in any way working with a foreign government under the table, we need to find out every detail so we can shut him down."

"You're right about that, of course. But it's not like

you not to know if someone is lying to you or not. What gives?" He isn't letting this one go after all.

"I think it's because I know her sister so well. When I confronted Mira about her previous employer, she didn't even try to deny it. She admitted everything, answered every question, and gave me more information that any informant ever has in my career.

"Kira, on the other hand, started out being deceitful to me, running from me, trying to ditch me. Lying about one of our senators and claiming she only wants to save her sister would be a good stall tactic. But if she happens to be telling the truth, sending her back to Russia would be a huge mistake. I don't want to make any rash decisions about her fate I'll regret later."

"Well, they do look exactly alike. I can see where that could be confusing."

"They may look alike to you, but not to me. They're complete opposites. Kira is hard, cunning, and adventurous. Mira is soft, sweet, and prefers the sidelines. I could see the differences in them in a picture their father has of them when they're maybe eight years old. Their personality traits make them as different as night and day, even in their appearance."

"That may be—to you—but not to me. From where I stand, they're the spitting image of each other, which is probably why the GRU wanted them so badly. I hear your objection, buddy, but your vision isn't clear on this one. That girl in there has your head spinning, whether you want to acknowledge it or not. She's exactly your type. I'm betting none of your other liaisons with other CIA officers over the years hold a candle to her." Roman flashes a shit-eating grin, confident in his ability to profile me, and walks off before I can object.

I slide my cell out of my pocket and dial my deputy director to fill him in on what we're facing and advise him of my plans.

"Graves."

"Chuck, this is Silas. I need to apprise you of a situation."

Over the next few minutes, I give him the rundown of the night and the accusations Kira leveled against a sitting senator. As usual, he's quiet while listening to all the facts, then gets straight to the point with his directive.

"Get to the bottom of it, Steele. Find out if she's lying or telling the truth. Don't let her out of your sight for even one fucking second. If she needs to take a piss, you'd better be right beside her, handing her the fucking toilet paper. You have two weeks to prove or disprove her allegations before she's on a plane bound for Russia."

"Two weeks? Sir, this will amount to a full-scale investigation. Two weeks isn't much time to collect intel and make a definitive decision."

"It's all the time you're getting, Steele. She's a known, admitted Russian spy. On American soil. I'm doing you a favor by giving you two weeks at all. She should be on the tarmac, headed back to her Mother Russia right now. I suggest you keep her on a very short, tight leash, because if she fucks us, it's your ass that'll feel it."

"Understood, sir."

When I start to rejoin them in the living room, I hear Kira questioning Nick about her sister. I watch her for a few moments before she realizes I've stepped back into the room, studying her movements, the words she chooses, and the information she's trying to get out of him.

"Can't you just tell me where she is?" Kira's pleading has no effect on Nick.

"No." Nick's stoic expression nearly makes me laugh out loud. I haven't seen any signs that she's an assassin, but then again, I wouldn't put it past her.

"They told me she'd been caught and was being tortured at a black site because of me. She took an assignment I was supposed to run, and then she never came back. I've blamed myself and tried to find a way to get her out for the past year. I miss her so much. She's the only family member I've been able to hold on to all these years. They let us talk to Mom and Dad on the phone twice a year, but never more than that. Mira's the only real family I have."

Tears slide down her cheeks, but I have to question if they're crocodile tears—it's part of my training and part of my job. I just don't know her well enough yet to read her real emotions. She's kept them repressed longer than any normal person, and from such an early age, so she has impressive control over them. All the more reason why my guard is up, and I'm leery as hell of everything she says.

"Can I talk to her on the phone? Will you call her? Let me just hear from her that she's okay." The desperate pleading in her voice now is genuine. She's unsure if we've told her the truth about Mira.

"Nick, why don't you go pick Mira up and bring her here? Roman and I can entertain Kira for a while. Maybe you can bring Brad back with you too." Nick hesitates for only a second before reading my mind.

"Sure, I can do that. Call if you need anything else while I'm out. We'll be back here very soon." With that, Nick leaves us alone with a very apprehensive prisoner.

Roman locks the door and resets the house alarm once Nick is off the porch. The motion sensors around the house will alert us if anyone unexpected shows up. The doors and windows are set to remain locked unless the deactivate code is entered. The only way out is if she breaks a window or someone rams the door. From the frightened expression on her face, she knows all too well she's trapped.

When she lifts the bottle of water to her lips, I notice her hand shaking as she takes a drink. Is that from nerves or an extra dump of adrenaline as she readies herself for the flight-or-fight response? At this point, I'm going with nerves. She's made no move to get up from the couch. Her eyes aren't focused on anything in particular. She's merely staring off into space, lost in her own thoughts while she attempts to make sense of everything.

Her world as she knew it was thoroughly and completely upended. The truths she based her life and actions on turned out to be lies, all designed to use and manipulate her. The people she trusted revealed their true character. Now she's clinging to the one hope she has left in the world, and that's her sister—the only genuinely loyal person she has ever known.

"I will be very upfront with you, Kira, as long as you're honest with me. If at any time you lie to me or try to run from me again, you'll be forcibly removed from my country. Do we understand each other?"

"Absolutely."

"We've been given two weeks to get to the bottom of this allegation. If we don't have indisputable and irrefutable evidence by then, I've been ordered to put you on a plane bound for Moscow. This is normally a full-scale FBI investigation that could take months and teams of agents to complete. We have a team of three, plus a couple of Russian spies, to accomplish an impossible mission in record time."

"I'm up for it if you are." Her eyes meet mine, and I see the fire and determination ignite in them again.

"I reviewed all the documents on your flash drive. Nothing in there directly implicates Senator Hunt in any type of espionage ring, unless they're using very sophisticated ciphers." Roman folds his arms over his chest. The accusation in his tone is heard loud and clear.

"That's not my fault. I copied as many documents from his office computer as I could, hoping I had the ones that would be useful. Silas knows I didn't have time to delete or alter anything before he stole the flash drive from my house. If you'd let me review them with you, I may be able to put two and two together easier."

"I am not sharing classified documents with you for any reason. Now, if the damaging evidence isn't on his computer in his office, exactly where do you think we'll find it, then?" Roman is testing her, seeing if she'll take the bait.

"You don't really think the only place he works is in his office, do you? I'm sure he works on his laptop at home or on his phone whenever he travels. His docking station was empty, so he must've taken his laptop with him. He's one of the last men in the world to carry a briefcase with actual papers in it. I'm sure at least some are classified, top-secret documents."

"You didn't complete surveillance on him before you worked your way into his office and into his files, did you?" Roman pins her with a look of utter disgust.

"No, I took a calculated risk, betting that the information would be on his computer in his office, where he'd most likely access the Intelligence Committee files."

"Wow. We really are starting from scratch on this case, aren't we? How are we supposed to wrap it up within two weeks?" Roman looks at me for answers, but I don't have them yet.

"We'll work this the same way we work any other case. One blind leap of faith at a time. We'll start with the basics, weed through the garbage, and hope we come out smelling like roses in the end. There will be a lot of surveillance, little to no sleep, and being spread very thin since we won't have a lot of help." I shrug my shoulders, not knowing what else to say to make him feel better about our odds.

"What happens at the end of that time? What if we find incriminating evidence but not enough to prove his involvement?" Roman asks.

"You, Nick, and I will probably keep working the case until resolution, but it'll be without Kira's help."

"What about Mira? Will she be sent back with her sister?"

"I didn't tell the deputy director about Mira."

Roman's jaw drops, and he stares at me in utter disbelief. "Better watch out for those blurred lines, Silas. They'll trip you up every time."

"I hear you. But I think I crossed that line about a year and a half ago when I recognized Mira and didn't turn them both in immediately when I found Kira. Something about it just never felt like the right thing to do, though."

"For all of our sakes, I hope you're right."

Off the record, I hope I'm right, too.

CHAPTER 6

Kira

$\mathcal{T}$wo weeks?

That's all the time they're giving us to find hard evidence against a heavily involved politician? How is that even possible?

If that's true, we're wasting time sitting in this house, hashing out who trusts whom instead of just getting the job done. We need to move with what we already know and figure out the rest as we go. If I'm sent back to Moscow, I'll be executed within days. They'll interrogate me first for any information that could possibly help them, but they'll get rid of me, nonetheless. Mira will have to spend her life in the shadows, always looking over her shoulder out of fear someone will find her.

"Silas, we should go to his house in the DC area and check it out. Right now. We can slip inside, get his briefcase, and check the contents right there while we're in his office. He'll never know we were there. Maybe we'll get lucky and find the documents in his possession. It's entirely possible he keeps them at home instead of at the office. His aide said the senator's been out of the office all week because his daughter is getting married at his house this weekend. Maybe he took the evidence home with him."

"I've never found working by luck to be…lucky." Silas slowly cocks one eyebrow at me, as if my idea is the craziest suggestion he's ever heard. "We need to stake out his house, check his security system, note their schedules —along with their neighbors and any rent-a-cops. He could also live in a gated community. There's a lot more to this job than just a simple B&E. Plus, if the wedding is at his house, too many people will be going in and out for us to slip in undetected."

We don't have enough time for a full-scale stakeout approach. I start to voice my objection, but the motion sensor alarm catches my attention instead. The front door slowly opens, and Nick enters first. He stops in the doorway to glance around before fully stepping inside. Standing directly behind him is my sister, Mira. When she sees me, her bottom jaw drops, and her eyes remain wide and unblinking. Her hands fly to her face, covering her mouth as her eyes start to water. She shakes her head, disbelief clearly showing in her features.

When I stand, I extend my arms out to either side, and she rushes into my embrace without saying a word.

We hold each other, not moving other than to squeeze each other tighter and tighter. Mira's sobs break free, tearing through her body and making her shake uncontrollably in my arms. I've never seen her react so intensely before, so I'm naturally concerned by her outburst. I slide my hands to her shoulders and push until she's an arm's length from me.

"Mira…talk to me. What is it? What happened to you?"

"Kira, I can't believe you're actually here. My last assignment went bad…very bad. When the explosives detonated in this old building, the structural integrity was worse than we'd anticipated. All that was left of the two-story structure was rubble. That's when I realized I finally had a chance to get out. They'd think I was still inside until the debris was cleared, and by then, I'd be well hidden away.

"So, I ran straight to a women's shelter, where I knew men weren't allowed and they wouldn't find me. But I found ways to check the message system without being traced. I intercepted one of the messages they sent back to Moscow. They reported you were dead, Kira. They told Moscow I was missing in action, presumed a deserter, so they interrogated and executed you when you didn't tell them where to find me. All this time, I've believed you were dead because of me, and that I was all alone. I'm just so happy you're alive."

She throws her arms around my neck again, squeezing tighter this time, while softly chanting "thank you" over and over again. Since we were little kids, I've been the one to help Mira stand on her own two feet, show her she is more than capable, and encourage her to keep fighting. She was never cut out for the life we were forced into living, and I've always felt it was my responsibility to keep her alive. Over the last year I've been looking for her, I've questioned if she withered up and died, or fought and blossomed like the magnificent rebel I know she is deep inside.

"I'm fine, sissy. They never interrogated me. They never hurt me in any way. They asked me several questions about you, but that was nothing. That communication was sent to draw you out because they had no idea where you were. I'm just so thankful you didn't fall for their tricks. You found a good hiding place, because I've been looking for you for the past year and a half and didn't find a single trace of you."

"I'm not living in the shelter anymore. I met the most wonderful woman while I was there. Her name is Savannah and, when you meet her, you'll love her as much as I do. You'll see." Mira's smile lights up her face and reminds me again how much I've missed her. She has always been the bright sunshine that chases away the gloomy gray clouds in my mind.

"As much as I'd love to meet her, I'm not sure I'll get that chance, sis. Silas caught me stealing top-secret information from a senator's office, so I'm to be returned to Moscow in two weeks. We have until then to get the proof we need, or they'll shut down the investigation as a false accusation. There's a lot to do and not a lot of time left for socializing."

Mira's smile fades as her face drops, and it breaks my heart to see the amount of pain in her eyes. Realization of what will happen soon sets in, and she starts shaking her head. "No. Silas, no, you can't send her back now. You know what'll happen to her if you do. They'll execute her and dump her body in a landfill without a second thought. You have to do something to stop this."

As he's a man who has lived his life in the shadows and under the cloak of anonymity, the uneasiness of being thrust into the spotlight is painfully obvious in his expression. On the one hand, he doesn't want to let Mira down by telling her the hard truth. On the other hand, I don't think he agrees with what his superior ordered him to do, so his heart isn't in it, but he knows he can't shirk his duties.

"This decision wasn't up to him, Mira. It wasn't his call to make. He tried to argue against it, but he has to follow orders or face the consequences. It's not fair of us to ask him to do anything other than what's right. I took those documents for a good reason, and I wasn't going to give the information over to the GRU, but what I did was illegal, regardless."

"What's right? How is giving you a one-way ticket to your own execution anywhere near right? If they send you back, they'll have to send me back too. There's no way I can live with myself knowing what's happening to you in Moscow while I'm here, living the comfortable life in Virginia."

"And I can't let you do that. You're not paying for my mistakes." I kiss her cheek, knowing the only thing we have in common besides our appearance is our stubborn streak. Neither of us is good at backing down once we've made up our mind.

But there's no sense in arguing the point any further now. There's too much to do and not enough time to do it the way I'd prefer—and definitely not enough time to handle it the way Silas insists. I can only hope to change their minds once the solid proof is in my hands, and I fill in the blanks with the knowledge in my head. Maybe throw in an extra measure of information that I have hidden up my sleeve—in case of a rainy day…or a life-or-death emergency.

"She's telling the truth, Silas." A man I didn't notice before now speaks up, his head popping up from behind a thick metal case. He's tall with a lean build, but he's not scrawny. His muscles simply aren't as bulky as the other men in the room. He's unassuming yet attractive with his short brown hair and green eyes. He's definitely one of them, blending in, gathering intel, not drawing attention to himself. "And there's no way in hell I'll let you go back to Russia, Mira. You know that."

"Kira, this is Brad." Mira moves to stand beside him. She has an obvious affection for him if the shy smile and stolen glances are any indication. From the way he looks at her, I'd say the feeling is more than mutual. "Brad, this is my sister, Kira."

Brad takes her hand in his before walking over to me. He extends his other hand, and I accept it as we exchange greetings. "Have you known my sister long?"

"Savannah introduced us soon after they met, so about a year a half ago now."

"You're a friend of the mysterious Savannah, too? Seems everyone knows her except me."

"She's my wife," Nick says. He's visibly still leery of me—unwilling to share more than the most basic information. The very least of what he's absolutely required to share with me.

"Oh, okay. Well, hopefully I'll get to meet her one day. My sister seems very taken with her. So, Brad, who was telling the truth and about what?"

Silas nods, giving Brad permission to explain. "You, Kira. You were telling the truth about not planning to give the classified documents to the GRU. The results were a little fuzzy when you said the decision wasn't up to Silas, but emotions can alter the results of the scan. Or, it also could be that part of you blames him for the situation. Either way, you have a strong reaction to him. More focused questioning would tell me what the truth is."

"Or you could just ask me directly."

"The answer to that question isn't really germane to the investigation." So, Brad is obviously the tech guru of the group. Direct, unemotional responses when he's focused on the problem at hand.

"But it could give us insight into her state of mind overall. Maybe we should ask her." Silas smiles, making me question if he has an actual playful side after all.

"I don't blame you, Silas. What I did is not your responsibility. Do I wish you hadn't caught me? Of course. But it is what it is." I turn my attention back to Brad. "How did you know I was telling the truth?"

Before Brad can reply, Nick interjects. "We have access to advanced technology. That's all you need to know about it."

"Fair enough. So, what's the plan, then? What's the next move?" I look at Silas and find him staring at me intently.

"The next move...is to go back to your house, get whatever you need to get ready for a black-tie affair, and show up for the wedding being held in the senator's home tomorrow."

"How will we get in at this late date? RSVPs have to be sent weeks in advance for events like that."

"We've already got that covered. Don't worry."

"Won't his aide be there? He could still recognize me, even without the blond wig."

"No, he's too low on the totem pole to be invited to an important event like that. The senator's only daughter is getting married then leaving the country for six months. They only want the cream of the crop at the reception. There will be so many people moving in and out of the house and the huge event tent set up in his backyard, they won't notice a couple of guests lost in their enormous mansion."

"Are you asking me to be your date for a wedding, Silas?" I try to lighten the somber mood of the room with a little humor, but the heated look in his eyes makes my heart race instead.

"Absolutely. And you know what the standing rule for wedding dates is, right?"

Years of training taught me to suppress my feelings, not to get emotionally involved in any mission, and view sex on the job as a necessary means to an end. No man has ever affected me while I was working in character, using him to get what I needed. Come to think of it, even the few men I dated as myself never really knew me. They never actually affected me enough to elicit real feelings.

So how, after being captured in the act and subsequently questioned by this man, do I have butterflies fluttering in my chest from a single flirtatious question?

"What rule is that?" I finally find my voice.

"You can't wear white and upstage the bride. We'll have to find you another dress because you'd definitely steal the show in that white dress you were wearing earlier."

I've never felt so stupid before in all my life. I completely misread the meaning behind his question.

CHAPTER 7

Silas

*B*rad, Nick, and Roman have escorted the ladies back to Kira's place to pack her belongings since she won't be living there again anytime soon. Or ever. Looks like she'll live here with me for the next couple of weeks while we sort through the accusations to determine if she's stalling, lying, or telling the truth.

Even though Roman has already checked the documents and I trust him with my life, I decide to take a look at them myself while they're gone. He's a good man and a great soldier, but after years in this game, there may be hidden keys I'd notice that he wouldn't. I'm leaving no stone unturned in this operation. The first few are run-of-the-mill internal sharing of information, nothing exciting or eye-opening about the content.

Then one catches my eye, making my spy senses tingle all over. Even as part of the Intelligence Committee, the senator would have no need for this information. It was classified "eyes only" when the case was opened years ago, meaning only a specific set of people have clearance to see it. And I know for a fact that he wasn't one of them, because I was.

"Now why would you be interested in this?" I steeple my hands in front of my face and let all possible, even improbable, situations run through my mind. One thing I've learned from working with all types of people all over the world—never underestimate your opponent. Or your coworker.

When the front door opens, I hear Brad, Nick, Mira, and Kira all laughing—at Roman's expense, from the sounds of it. That makes me smile. He's excellent at his job...but not so much with personal relationships. Forcing him into close quarters with others who acknowledge their feelings is good exposure for him...and good entertainment for me.

Before anyone walks into my office, I shut down the application and close my laptop. The words on that page are ingrained in my memory, though, and none of the possibilities of why Senator Hunt pilfered that specific investigation are good.

I step into the living room and see why everyone is laughing at Roman. He has multiple duffle bags draped over his arms while trying to maneuver large suitcases through the front door. But Brad's, Nick's, Kira's, and

Mira's arms are empty. Multiple straps slide off his shoulders, falling to his forearm and making him release the suitcases. He looks like a one-man vaudeville show, juggling multiple items that were never meant to be juggled.

"Did you lose a bet, Roman?" I can't help but laugh after I ask.

"He's actually in the process of losing said bet. He was bragging, as usual, saying he could carry everything she owned and then some without any help from us. So, we're letting him prove his worth. We're not convinced yet." Nick folds his arms across his chest, his smug expression intact, and continues watching Roman struggle alone.

"For fuck's sake, give us a bag, Roman, and let us help you." I grab one of the large suitcases from his grip and pull it inside the house before also taking the one in his other hand. Then I turn my attention to Kira. "Did you find anything to wear to the wedding tomorrow evening?"

"No, sorry. The only thing I have that's formal enough is the white dress I wore earlier, and we both know that won't work."

"That's not a problem. There are plenty of places nearby that'll have something appropriate for you to wear. We'll have time to go tomorrow since it's an evening wedding."

"Who gets married in January in the DC area anyway? It's too fucking cold. Why not wait until the cherry trees are in bloom and everything's beautiful again?" Kira shakes her head and takes a couple duffle bags from Roman.

"Senator Hunt's daughter is marrying a doctor who's volunteering with Doctors Without Borders. They wanted to get married before they leave the country for the next six months so their families can witness it." I had the same question and did a little research while they were away. The weather is too cold and snowy for a traditional wedding, but it seems Hunt's daughter is marrying a genuinely good man.

"Sounds like you need your invitations now." Brad boots up his unique laptop—the one specifically designed for him by the best of the best in the CIA technology center for all his high-tech needs.

With a few simple keystrokes, Brad updates the attendee list with the pictures for the aliases Kira and I will use to get into the exclusive event. I'm counting heavily on the mother and father of the bride to be too busy and overcome with emotion to notice us roaming around their home unsupervised. Good thing I can think of a distraction or two should we get caught coming out of one of the bedrooms. Being caught in the act of rifling through their drawers would be a little harder to explain, though.

"We've accomplished as much tonight as we possibly can, so everyone should head home, get some rest, and be ready to go again first thing tomorrow. Kira needs a dress, we need comms, and I need an up-to-date blueprint of the house so I can get a feel for the layout and where he'd possibly hide valuables. We still have a lot to do and no extra time to do it in."

"I'll have the blueprint for you first thing in the morning, Silas. Check your email when you wake up." Brad places his hand on Mira's lower back, giving her a silent cue that she has to say goodbye now.

Mira wraps her arms around Kira's neck and holds on for half a minute or more. Tears stream down both of their faces, neither wanting to be the first to let go after being apart for so long and not knowing the other's fate.

"Mira, why don't you plan on going shopping with Kira tomorrow? It'll be a good outing for you two to spend more time together without actually making you a party to this operation."

"Thank you, Silas. I appreciate that."

As Nick, Brad, and Mira are leaving, I tell Roman to head home, too. We have a long day tomorrow, and Kira isn't going anywhere else tonight without me. With the house locked up and protected by the best alarm system available, we'll both be able to rest for the remainder of the night without any extra security shifts. Plus, now that she's assured her sister is close by, safe, and still accessible to her, she doesn't seem too keen on leaving anymore.

"It has been a long day and an equally long evening. I'll take your stuff to your room for you." I pick up her suitcases and gesture toward the hall. "Do you need anything else for now?"

"No, I brought everything I need from my place. Thank you, though. Are you going to bed too?"

We reach the guest bedroom, and I open the door for her then place her bags beside the bed. "No, I've lived on much less sleep than I'll get tonight for many years. I'll be fine. The bathroom is right through that door over there. Plenty of closet space for your clothes over here. You're not confined to this room. If you want anything from the kitchen, it's yours. No need to ask. If you want to hang out in the den and watch TV for a while, you're welcome to it. Make yourself at home."

"Thank you for this, Silas. Sincerely. I'm drained, so I think I'll just go to bed now. Like you said, we have a lot to do tomorrow, and we need to get an early start."

"Until tomorrow, then."

ROMAN AND NICK AGREED TO TAKE BOTH KIRA AND Mira shopping while Brad and I finish working on the logistics of getting lost in the senator's mansion while scores of workers are milling about. To clarify, Roman didn't exactly agree—but he complied with direct orders, regardless. He had a few choice words to call me before he left on his mandated shopping mission, but spending time with the ladies will do him good. He thinks he's such a player, but I know where his head and heart are. Even if he's still clueless.

"Brad, I've been given permission to read you in on

this case so I can share the details of this document with you. This was listed as 'eyes only,' and I was one of the few people allowed to know the details of the investigation. I remember the case vividly, because I was going back and forth to Moscow at the time, chasing ghosts that made me look like an incompetent fool. By the time I figured out one clue to their hideout location, they'd already moved somewhere else, and I had to start all over again. My failure on that case is something I've never forgotten, and what I saw still haunts me to this day.

"The thing is, not one single US official was ever identified as a potential target—no one even with any distant ties to the suspects. But we knew there had to be someone with connections helping them because they were always one step ahead of us, and that shit just doesn't happen. Senator Hunt was not part of the special committee appointed to review the details, and our director made a decision to intentionally keep it out of the Senate's reach."

"So how did Senator Hunt get it, then? It's not like Langley's server is on a cloud." Brad's question is rhetorical, knowing I don't have that answer yet.

While he reads the entire document, his question echoes in my mind. There's only one way that document got out of Langley...and none of the possible scenarios gives me any peace. When he looks up from the screen, he wears a perplexed expression.

"This information is very high level. What am I missing? What's in the fine print?"

For the next thirty minutes, I walk Brad through every detail of the case. How it began, where it took us, and why we were never able to bring it to full closure. Every officer has one case that haunts him, gives him nightmares, and makes him second-guess his place in the agency. This one has been the thorn in my side for years, knowing there had to be a piece of the puzzle missing but driving myself crazy trying to find it. Now that I've caught a glimpse of it, I have a sick feeling in the pit of my stomach and an acute desire to ignore the truth. Because there's no going back once I've crossed the line drawn in front of me.

"What are you going to do, Silas?" The concern in his eyes is evidence of the danger we're walking into. This doesn't affect only me—the lives of our entire team are now in jeopardy.

"I'm going to do my job, even though I know exactly what that means if I'm caught before I have irrefutable proof. Even that may not be enough to get me off the hook."

"What does that mean, Silas?"

"It means I think the senator is in some very shady shit, and in order to prove it, I'll have to read Kira in on the case, too. She may not know what this document means, but she may have some insight into Moscow's involvement from the past. If I can get information out of her, it may help us figure out why he has this document at all."

"But that's treason, Silas. You can't do that—there's

no coming back from betraying your country, especially since you're a career CIA officer. Everything you've ever done to protect and serve will be dissected and questioned. Every mistake you've ever made, even if you've corrected it since then, and every judgment call you've made that falls outside the lines will be put on trial for the world to be your judge, jury, and executioner."

"Trust me, Brad. The CIA won't allow it to go that far. It'll be covered up, along with my body in the middle of the Sahara Desert where no evidence will ever be found. It'll be a miracle if I can pull this off, so I completely understand if you want to walk away now."

"I'm not going anywhere, man. You and your brother have never let me down, and I'm not about to turn my back on you now. I'll keep all eyes off you as long as I can."

"Thanks, Brad. I'm glad to have you on my side. I still have a shit-ton of other files to read through first, but this is the only one that has raised huge red flags so far. Let's see if there are more before I tell her anything about it."

The driveway alarm chimes, alerting me to an incoming vehicle. After a quick check of the monitors, I verify it's Nick and the gang returning from their shopping excursion. A pan of the camera rewards me with a closeup shot of Roman's face. His expression screams he's disgusted, disgruntled, and displeased, making me burst out laughing at his expense. I can almost feel his eyes burning straight through me when they land on the camera. Then he flips me off, holding up his middle finger all the way up the driveway.

The ladies are chatting up a storm when they walk into the house. If I didn't already know them, I wouldn't have pegged them for Russian spies. They sound like the normal, average American woman. The dress, the shoes, the hair, the makeup—every detail every other woman I've ever known has focused on when dressing for a black-tie affair. Part of me wishes I'd never recognized Mira that day I met her in the women's shelter when she was hiding from her handlers under an alias. But her fake name wasn't too far off from her real name. She used the name Miranda Petrovia to hide in plain sight.

Kira is holding a long garment bag in one hand and a shoe box in the other. Her makeup has been professionally applied, and her black hair is expertly styled in a sweeping updo. She's beautiful with her long hair worn down and flowing across her shoulders, but I have to say this new style is doubly appealing, exposing the soft skin of her slender neck.

"Well, it's not white, but I can't guarantee she won't upstage the bride, Silas. This dress was made for her—no one can wear it like she does. Even I have to admit she looks sinfully sexy in it." Mira raises her eyebrows, driving her point home.

After hearing that, I know I'm probably in for a long night.

CHAPTER 8

Kira

Shopping and getting made up at the salon took longer than I had anticipated, so by the time I got back, Silas and I only had a couple of hours left before we had to leave for Senator Hunt's estate. Silas greeted us as he usually did, made small talk for a few minutes, then disappeared into his bedroom. And closed the door. At first, I assumed he was getting dressed in his tuxedo, so I retreated to my bedroom, and Mira helped me put on my dress and not mess up my hair or makeup in the process.

That was forty-five minutes ago, and Silas still hasn't emerged from behind his closed door.

"Stop worrying. You look beautiful, exactly like you fit in their world. No one will question your presence there." Mira grabs my shoulders and holds me in place, making me look her in the eye. "Let loose and have fun on your date with Silas tonight every chance you get."

"It's not a date, sis. We're actually working and just pretending to be on a date." I shake my head at her. I know she only wants me to be happy, to drop my walls of steel and let someone in besides her for once.

"Deny it all you want, but we're twins. I've known Silas for a while now. When he could've turned me in and sent me to an actual black site, he showed me mercy instead. I didn't know until recently, but he also followed you since the day he figured out who I was. He made sure you were safe and stayed out of trouble. Even when he caught you breaking into the secure servers, he fought to keep you on the case with him. He's a good man, and he's a good match for you. I'm making it my personal mission to make sure you two realize how perfect you are for each other."

Her enthusiasm would be contagious if I didn't already know I'll be forcibly removed from the country in less than two weeks now. "Mira, I'll be gone soon. We don't exactly have enough time to date, marry, and live happily ever after in that time. In fact, we couldn't even finish a round of antibiotics in that short time. I appreciate why you're trying to do this, but there's no sense in pursuing something that can never be."

The door to Silas's room opens, and he comes strolling out, wearing his tailor-made tuxedo and looking far too sexy for the female population to take. One look at me and he stops in his tracks. His jaw is slack, and his eyes are wide, slowly dragging up and down my body. My cheeks burn, and my heart races from the heat in his gaze.

The dress I picked out is the most gorgeous formal dress I've ever seen. The glamorous silver-beaded and sequined bodice has a sweetheart neckline, dipping in the middle to reveal just enough cleavage to be stunningly sexy. The long, sheer, off-shoulder sleeves are beaded, continuing the sparkling sheen of the top, while the skirt is pure peach satin, showing enough thigh to carry off the sultry vibe. The train begins from the material gathered at the waist, long and sheer in the back and is also covered in beads and sequins. The entire ensemble catches the light as I move and twinkles like stars in the dark skies.

"Kira, you look absolutely ravishing. I mean, I thought you were beautiful before, but now I can't tear my eyes away from you. Your sister is right—you could wear a burlap sack, and you'd still upstage the bride. There's no way to avoid it." Silas keeps staring at me, caressing my exposed skin with his gaze, touching me with the desire in his eyes, and heating me from the inside out.

He clears his throat, breaking the trance we're both under, and extends his hand toward me. "We should leave now, so we're not fashionably late."

I slip my hand into his, marveling at how mine seems to disappear in the size of his, yet there's no fear associated with it. Only security and safety. These hands would never harm me; that much I already know about Silas. "Let me grab my coat on the way out, and we'll be on our way."

"Wear the long coat—the thick wool one. That way, when you take it off in front of everyone, I'll hear all the gasps and moans when they get a look at you. Every man will be jealous of me as it is, but it'll be like unwrapping a present in front of an audience." Silas's smile covers his entire face. He nods enthusiastically, urging me to accept his request.

"Gasps and moans? You can't be serious."

"I am deadly serious. Gasps from the ladies, moans from the guys. It'll be beautiful. Trust me."

"Famous last words." I turn to head toward my bedroom to grab the coat but stop in my tracks. "Hang on. How do you know I have a long wool coat? I haven't worn it around you."

"I may have watched you a time or two in the last year or so." He shrugs, completely unashamed.

"Stalker." I shake my head and walk off, smiling to myself while listening to his laughter echo down the hall.

As asked, I grab my long coat on the way out and wrap it around me. Actually, it works perfectly because it shields me from the biting winds, and it has plenty of hidden pockets in the inner lining to hide documents, pictures, flash drives, or anything else we need to smuggle out of the senator's home. Silas opens the car door for me, and I slide into the luxurious leather seat then watch him walk around the front with his confident gait and smooth swagger.

When we arrive at the senator's mansion inside a gated and private-security-patrolled community, just as Silas called it, the valet parks the vehicle while we walk up the steps to the enormous front door. On the ride over, we reviewed the plan and discussed what we'd do in case of an emergency. Now the game is afoot, and the strategy is in motion. My fingers are crossed, and my silent prayers are going up, hoping we find what we're looking for here.

Once inside, I understand why their daughter chose to get married here rather than in a church or at a destination wedding. The entrance is unlike any house I've ever seen. The large circular entryway alone is close to the size of a ballroom. The stairs curve around the right side of the room, leading up to an open second-floor landing. The arched openings and decorative black wrought-iron railing will provide a perfect view of the bride as she descends the steps toward her husband-to-be.

The reception tent has been erected in the backyard, just off the veranda directly behind where the wedding is being held. Once the guests start to move toward the reception, the temporary bottleneck will give Silas and me a chance to get lost in the shuffle of the crowd.

Staff dressed in full tuxedos, complete with top hats and tails, check the invitations before escorting us to our assigned seats. We're not high enough on the guest list to warrant a place in the front of the room, but that's better for us and our reason for being here. Sticking to the shadows and avoiding any spotlights are paramount to our success tonight. We sit patiently, quietly chatting with each other, while we wait for the main event to begin.

"You look familiar. Have we met?" A man stops beside Silas and eyes him suspiciously.

"No, Chuck, you don't know me at all. So, move on before you blow my cover and have to explain to the agency exactly how that happened." Silas speaks in a hushed voice, but his words are clear. What I can't figure out is how he did that without moving his lips.

"You look just like one of my employees. Spitting image of him, actually. Tall guy. Popular with the ladies. Working on a case that could end his career for good with one misstep. I'd hate to see that happen to him. He's been with me forever."

"If he's such a good guy, then maybe you should put a little trust in him and back him up when he needs it. I'm sure he'd appreciate your help. And your faith." Silas cuts his eyes up to Chuck, making the other man smile broadly.

"Maybe you're right. If he were here tonight—which he isn't—but if he were, I'd tell him to check out the senator's office on the second floor, behind the master bedroom. The senator is so proud of it that he took a few of us on a tour a while ago. You wouldn't believe the hidden wall safe or the secret drawer in his desk."

"I'm sure your employee would be very interested to

hear all about that home office. It sounds like the perfect setup since I've wanted to remodel my home office for a while now. Do you think the senator would mind if my date and I took a peek at it after the ceremony?"

"His daughter has so many activities planned for her reception that I doubt the senator would ever know if you took a stroll upstairs. He's more focused on spending every minute he can with his daughter before she and her new husband fly off to Uzbekistan for six months. The father-daughter dance is high on his list, as is watching her cut the cake. I wouldn't linger, just in case, but I could've sworn I saw someone tampering with the security camera for that part of the house."

"What a shame. And this looks like such a nice neighborhood, too. We'll keep an eye out for any nefarious characters."

Chuck raises his eyes to meet mine after that comment, revealing his real impression of me. "See that you do. We wouldn't want them roaming loose in our country, would we?"

"You know, my boss has told me on many, many occasions that I'm the best judge of character he's ever met. He's even written commendations for me on my interviewing skills, saying I'm better than a polygraph test because no one has ever beaten me with a lie. With all those compliments over the years, you'd think he'd listen to me now and then. I could make him look so good to his superiors—if he'd just get out of my way and let me do my job."

Chuck's expression changes right before my eyes. "You're right. If you've worked for him that long and have received that many compliments, he shouldn't worry you're about to make the biggest mistake of your life. I guess if you're willing to gamble with your life, then he should let you play Russian roulette until the game is over…one way or another."

Silas inhales a long and deep breath, drawing his spine up completely straight and rigid until his lungs are fully expanded. Chuck takes the hint and walks off to his seat, leaving the conversation on that somber note. I watch Silas for a moment, taking in his handsome face, his wide shoulders, and his broad chest. I'm sure he does have a way with the ladies, and I'm sure he's had his way with plenty of them. He's easy to talk to, with a wicked sense of humor and quick, witty comebacks. But his intelligence is even more impressive. With one look, he can definitely gauge friend from foe, and he already has a plan in place to outwit his opponents before they even know they're in the game.

But right now, he's fighting against his temper. He usually keeps it under firm control, never giving anyone the upper hand by making him react instead of act. Chuck seems to hold that power over him, though.

"You need to breathe. You've been holding that breath for a long time. If you pass out, I can't pick you up off the floor. You'll just have to lie down there and watch the wedding from an odd angle when you wake up."

He slowly turns his head to look at me, a deadpan expression on his face. But I see a small twitch in the corner of his mouth. He wants to smile, but he also wants to stay mad for a little longer.

"Silas, that man is your friend, whether he told you what you wanted to hear or not. He wouldn't have said those things if he weren't trying to help you get in and out without getting caught and if he didn't care about you successfully completing this mission. I have a feeling this isn't exactly sanctioned, so if you're caught, you go down alone. He can't shield you from the repercussions of your actions. He trusts you, or he wouldn't have said one word to you, especially knowing you're here under-cover. It's me he doesn't trust—the Russian roulette comment wasn't exactly subtle—but you can't blame him for that. You don't trust me either."

He finally releases the breath he's held since Chuck walked away and nods, wordlessly telling me he knows I'm right.

He leans over toward me. Our faces are so close, we must appear as lovers to everyone else around us. His voice is soft when he whispers to me, mirth sparkling in his blue eyes as he stares into mine. "Would you really have left me on the floor?"

"You're damn right, I would have. Try it and find out, big boy."

He chuckles and slides his arm around me, pulling me into his side. "Remind me to make you pay for that comment in some subtle way later."

"I'll put it on the list."

AFTER THE CEREMONY IS OVER, WE INTENTIONALLY WAIT for the other guests to file into the line for the reception so we can be in the very back. Just our luck, we can't sneak up the stairs because the staff stands on both sides, giving each guest a wedding favor bag and ushering us through the French doors at a brisk pace. The bridal party will be waiting for all the guests to settle in before making their toasts, after all.

Why I didn't realize the event tent would be every bit as luxurious and adorned as the house is beyond me. This family spared no expense for their little girl's wedding. From the hardwood floors, to the crystal chandeliers, to the fountain of flowing champagne, to the perfectly decorated tables, to the enormous wedding cake —every minute detail has been considered and executed flawlessly.

We find seats closest to the exit and suffer through the funny stories and the touching moments of the bride's and groom's lives. Finally, the DJ announces it's time to break in the brand-new dance floor, and Silas and I prepare to make our move. Only...now we look like living statues with the megawatt spotlight shining directly on us before it moves on to the next table.

"The bride has a special request of her treasured guests tonight. Before she takes the floor with her new husband in their first dance, she asks for all the couples in the room to step out onto the dance floor first. She wants to see love shine all around her on her wedding night. So, come on, friends and family. Make her dream a reality— take your partner by the hand, hold each other close, and let's get it on!"

Marvin Gaye's soulful voice fills the tent, and couples from every direction make their way to the dance floor. Waiters mingle between the tables, encouraging stragglers to comply. Silas stands, takes my hand, and pulls me from my seat to standing.

"You heard the man. Let's get it on." He winks and leads me to an open spot. Then he slides his arms around my waist, pulls my body tight against his, and we start to sway from side to side, keeping time with the music.

With my hands locked behind his neck, our bodies meld into one, flowing with the music and with the beat of our own hearts. His strong arms linked around my waist make me feel sheltered and protected. The spicy scent of his intoxicating cologne makes me feel heady and reckless. Maybe it is from years of living on the edge, from never having someone I cared about other than my sister, or the heavy toll my profession has taken on me, but at this moment in his arms, there is nothing else I want more.

No secret searches for hidden evidence.

No more danger, intrigue, or conspiracies.

No more spying or scheming.

Deep down, a quiet life with someone to love, and

someone to love me in return, is all I've ever really wanted.

When the song finally ends, and the newlyweds take their place for their first dance as husband and wife, Silas and I casually walk out of the tent, up the stairs, and straight into the senator's home office. I watch with sheer admiration as he breaks into the hidden safe as though he were simply opening a cabinet door. The secret drawer wasn't so well hidden that Silas couldn't locate it, open it, and rifle through all the contents.

At the end of the evening, everything I'd hoped to find here eluded me. We leave empty-handed. I don't even have the heart to talk about it on the ride home.

"We'll keep looking, Kira. This isn't the end."

No? Then why do I feel like I just ran headlong into a brick wall on a dead-end street?

CHAPTER 9

Silas

"You know it'll send up a huge red flag if I don't make that dead drop in the morning. My handler has already called to check in, and I confirmed I'd be there. That means I told her I accomplished my mission of getting into the senator's office." Kira slides into the seat beside me at the kitchen table.

In the last couple of evenings since we attended the wedding, Mira and Brad have been coming over to help. It seems the extra company and time spent together has made Kira more relaxed around me. The personality underneath her guarded persona is finally emerging, and even Nick is smiling and talking to her more now. Maybe Nick gleaned more insight into her character the night they went back to her old house to pack her clothes and toiletries.

For Kira to come to me with this request must mean she's starting to trust me.

Part of me wishes the feeling were mutual, because the more I'm around her, the more I like her. But Chuck's "Russian roulette" comment is stuck in my mind. My concern isn't only with Kira, but with who else she works with on the other side.

"And how do you suggest we manage that? They'll be on the lookout for anyone out of place. I'm sure they're trained to spot tails the same as I am, and there's no way in hell you're going alone."

When I lean back in my chair and look in her eyes, I plainly see the regret shining in them. While I feel for her predicament, and I honestly do, I won't make the mistake of giving her a chance to double-cross me. There's too much at stake, just as Chuck so eloquently alluded to in front of her. It was one thing when I personally escorted her to a wedding at the senator's house, but it's quite another to send her out to a dead drop site alone. She's not as adept at this spy business as I am. She's not as cunning and ruthless as she likes to think she is.

But that may be her MO while her every move is being watched.

"I can do it for her." Mira sits in the chair beside Kira and holds her hand.

"No fucking way!" Kira, Brad, Nick, Roman, and I all answer at the same time, with the exact same words.

"Tough room." Mira laughs off our reaction. She's used to us now after all the time she has spent around us while living with Nick's family.

"You've been out of the game for the last year and a half, love. If you put yourself back in it now, even to help your sister, you're risking your freedom. You never know if the drop site is being watched by another agency—or other Russian operatives." Brad could never be a spy—he not only wears his emotions on his sleeve, but his facial expressions give away his every thought.

"He's right, Mira. We won't risk your safety. Kira, why don't you and I head out to your drop site tonight and leave it ahead of the scheduled time? Nick can take your sister back home, where you know she's well cared for and very safe."

"All right. You and I will go late tonight, Silas. You can stand guard from behind cover in case anyone else is watching. If I get caught, at least you'll still be in the clear."

"Just be careful out there, sis." The two sisters look at each other, hesitant to leave the other's side again. "I want you to know I really am happy now, and you will be too very soon. Savannah is like a sister to me, and Nick is the big brother we never had. When this is over, and Silas finds a way to keep you off that airplane, they'll be your family too. That's just who they are."

Mira's eyes cut over to me as she hugs her sister good-bye. "Very subtle message, Mira. No one else caught on to that secret spy message you just sent me at all."

"Hey, this is like 'Spy vs. Spy,' in real life, isn't it?" Brad asks, his face beaming with pride over his corny joke.

"Yes, we're exactly like that." I can't help but laugh and be grateful for Brad's ability to defuse the tension of the situation with such a simple notion. Within seconds, even Nick, with his serious nature can't hold back, and now we're all laughing together.

After everyone leaves, Kira and I sit down at the table and hash out the plan for later tonight. "Where are you supposed to leave the flash drive?"

"Taped under a bench in the pavilion at Armistead Boothe Park on Cameron Station Boulevard."

"Okay, that's not too far from here. We can go late tonight and be back here in no time."

I pull up the map of the park and surrounding area online, so we can walk through our every step before arriving. Before walking into any potential trap, I want to know every possible entry and exit point, the best spot for observing the vicinity, and where we're most likely to encounter trouble.

"I think I'll go try to get some rest before we head out tonight. Do you need any other information from me before I do?" Kira pushes back from the table and stands with her hands clasped together, uncertainty emanating from her entire being.

"No, I think I'm good for now. Thanks."

"Silas?" She stops in the hall before she makes it through the doorway.

"Yeah?"

"I know none of this has been easy for you. I understand the predicament I've put you in—working with me, protecting my sister, and protecting your country. For what it's worth, I am sorry about that, but I do appreciate everything you're doing. You don't trust me, and I don't blame you. If I were in your shoes, I wouldn't trust me either. But you can believe I'd never do anything to hurt Mira, and going rogue now would only expose her. That's one thing I would never do—no matter what the consequences to me may be."

Part of me wants to believe she's being sincere. A small part of me may even put some stock in what she's saying. But the undercover officer inside warns me against it. He reminds me that self-preservation makes people do things they would never consider doing otherwise. Detestable acts that they later regret, but in that split second of decision, they value their own lives over everyone else's.

Including a dearly loved sister.

I've seen the aftermath of family members turning on other family members to save their own skin. It happens more than I'd prefer to think about, and that's precisely why I have to fight the urge to believe she wouldn't do anything to jeopardize Mira or this mission. No matter how much I'd enjoy the luxury of thinking she's actually on my side in this.

That's why I haven't broken my vow and told her about the discrepancies I found in the senator's files. It's why I review the rest of the flash drive contents when she is asleep at night, or for that solid hour locked inside my room while she was busy dressing for the wedding. And why I haven't explained to her all the reasons behind my reassuring her our investigation isn't over. She believes it is because we didn't find anything during our search of his home office—and she's mentally preparing herself to be forcibly removed from the country.

"Thank you for saying that. I appreciate it, Kira. But I really hope your loyalty to your sister is never put to the test."

We remain motionless, staring at each other for several heartbeats. The connection I've felt with her is real—it's like a tether holding me in place near her now. I've had more than a year to watch her from a distance, get to know her intimately without ever saying a word to her, and analyze her every expression, gesture, and mannerism. While I followed her, I memorized everything about her. Not quite at the stalker level, but thorough enough to be effective at my job. But sharing this space with her now, knowing everything I know about her, makes me question how much of my observation was for the job and how much was for me.

The hopeful expression she wore when she pledged her allegiance to me falls as she realizes my trust issues with her run deeper than a few words can bridge. She slowly nods, and a small, sad smile makes a brief appearance. "Our handlers tested our bond every single day since we were first torn from our mother's arms and thrust into this life. My loyalty to her has never faltered in twenty years, and I'm not about to break my long-standing record now. Good night, Silas."

"Good night, Kira."

After changing into my black cargo pants and sweat-shirt, I return to the den and settle on the couch to comb through all the information I've gathered so far. One more time, as I always do. I'm deep in thought, trying to fit two puzzle pieces together that don't want to match when I hear the bedroom door open. I glance down at my watch and realize it's only been forty-five minutes since she left me to nap before our late-night rendezvous in the park.

"Couldn't sleep?"

"No. And there's no use in trying now."

She sits at the other end of the couch and turns her body to face me, bending one leg with her foot under-neath her. She's wearing a pale pink tank top and matching shorts. Her long black hair is pulled to the side, hanging over one shoulder, and she's twirling a strand between her fingers. Seeing her like this, out of her natural element, makes her seem so vulnerable and lost. At the party when I first met her, she was working the scene and identifying her next mark. She was focused on the end goal and confident in her abilities.

In the days since that first meeting, I've fought against the recurring thoughts that she's not the villain I've painted her to be in my mind.

She knows how to get the job done, that's for sure,

but the purpose that drives her to do it isn't anywhere in the same hemisphere as mine. My means and methods may cross lines at times, pushing the regulations and breaking a few rules now and then, but my objective never changes. Service to my country is first and foremost. Period.

Watching her silently fight her fears now, I see her in a different light. Even though we're different, I think I'm starting to unwrap that enigma and understand why she's so hard to read.

First and foremost, she's an actress.

Plain and simple.

In order to survive in this clandestine lifestyle from such an early age, the only way she could keep herself together and focus on one mission at a time, she had to pretend she knew what she was doing and what she wanted out of it. That's the only way she knows how to do this spy thing—it's all an imaginary world, and she's just a player acting out her role on an extremely treacherous stage.

"Care for some free professional advice?"

She stills and raises her gaze to meet mine. "Absolutely." That's a lie in the purest sense of the word, though I'm not convinced she even realizes she's lying. She's still acting, and that answer is the one she thinks she's supposed to give in this circumstance.

"One, if you actually want to be an undercover officer, your heart has to be in it. You have to fight for what you believe in, not what you've been told you believe in.

Two, acting the part will only get you so far. You actually have to become the person you're pretending to be. You have to know her inside and out—how she would react in different situations, how she would handle problems, her entire personality profile—it all has to be ingrained in you. And three, your heart isn't in this, you don't know what you believe in, and you don't know who you are."

"Are you saying I'm not good at my job, Silas?" She arches one eyebrow, daring me to give the wrong answer to her loaded question.

"No, that's not what I'm saying. But I am saying this isn't the life you want, the career you chose, or what you feel is your true calling in life. And to those of us who live and breathe this work, it shows. You've dealt with everyday civilians up until now, haven't you? You haven't been on any counterintelligence missions, have you? Haven't dealt with any battle-hardened soldiers?"

"Yes, all of that is true. My assignments have revolved around getting information out of ordinary people. Executive assistants with loose tongues. Senate staffers with loose zippers. No one who has already been taught the trade, though."

"The man you singled out and almost approached at the fundraiser where we met? He would've read you like a children's book, and we never would've found your body when he was finished with you. Could you not sense that from his carriage and demeanor?"

"I sensed he had connections and could get me into the secure areas. He was right there with several other senators and high-level officials. That's exactly the type of person I needed to complete my job."

"No, love. He wasn't there with them. They were with him. There's a difference. When a man walks into a room and everyone flocks to his side, that man is the one with all the power. Not the followers. He was the center of attention—and they were all vying for five minutes with him. Not the other way around."

"Why are you telling me this? Are you trying to help me to be a better spy against America?" She folds her arms over her chest and tips her head to the side. She's clearly annoyed with me.

"Not at all." I can't help but chuckle. "I'm trying to save you. You're in deep water, way over your head, and you're very close to going under for good. Get out of this business and find something else to do with your life. I would hate to get the news that the wrong person figured out who you really are."

"Thanks for the pep talk. Maybe we should head out to the park now and get this over with before I have time to say the wrong thing to the wrong person and end up dead. It'll be incredibly obvious if I'm killed and you put the flash drive on the wrong bench in my absence."

The smile covering my face as she walks away is genuine. Her false bravado aside, that smartass retort just ratcheted up my respect for her. "Don't worry, love. I'll protect you."

Without a moment's hesitation, she holds up her middle finger, extending her arm as far toward me as it'll reach, just before she disappears into her bedroom. That makes me lean my head back on the couch and release a deep belly laugh. If nothing else, at least the time I have left with Kira will most definitely be entertaining.

WHEN WE REACH THE AREA IN ALEXANDRIA, I PULL INTO a space in the Home Depot parking lot and turn off the truck. A few third shift employees are working, so my vehicle doesn't seem out of place. The park is a couple of blocks from the back side of the building, but we're not taking any chances of being spotted driving around and casing the vicinity.

"We're on foot from here. Stay close to me, Kira, and stay on your guard. We're going out on a limb doing this with no prior reconnaissance and no idea if your coworkers are out here watching, especially the night before a scheduled drop."

Outside the truck, we hold hands as we walk toward the park. We look like any other normal couple out for an extremely late-night stroll. The windows of most of the houses and apartments along the tree-lined street are dark, their inhabitants sound asleep. A small sedan pulls into one of the parallel parking spots, horribly missing the mark. Four young ladies tumble out of a car as we pass by, dressed to the nines after a night out and all walking on wobbly legs and spiky heels. I wrap my arm around Kira's shoulders and pull her face into mine as we pass them, giving the illusion that we're lovers and can't keep our lips off each other. Not that they'd recognize our faces through their beer goggles, but we can't be too careful. I've acted shit-faced drunk many times before when it gave me a marked advantage over my target.

Whistles and catcalls follow us as the girls cheer us on. "Girlfriend! Take that fine specimen of a man home and rock his world!"

"If you don't want him, send him back here! I'll take him!"

Kira rises to the challenge when she stops me, lifts up on her toes, and plants her lips on mine. Her hand glides along my cheek as her soft tongue slides against my lips. Before her actions even register on my shocked brain, my arms wrap around her waist, my lips part, and my tongue slides along hers. Just like that, the sparks I've heard about so many times but never experienced ignite all at once behind my eyes. In a split second, I take control of the kiss she initiated and deepen it. With intentional steps, I back her against a tree and lean into her.

She wraps her arms around my neck and runs her fingers through the hair at the nape of my neck. Her nails trail against my skin with the lightest of scrapes, but the sensation is enough to set my blood boiling. Her breasts push against me, and I feel the rapid rise and fall of her chest from her labored breathing. I brush my fingers along her neck then up to her chin, holding it lightly when I end the kiss and pull back only far enough to look directly into her eyes.

What I'd give to read her mind right now.

Alexandria just experienced a heat wave in the dead of winter.

"Fuck, that's so hot! Now I have to go watch porn and check the batteries in Bob." The girl's words are slurred, but it seems her vision is perfectly fine.

"Who the hell is Bob?" One of the other girls asks, laughing hysterically in her drunken state.

"My battery-operated boyfriend, Sheila. You should already know that—you have one too."

"Oh yeah. Fuck, we need a man to kiss us like that. I think my panties just melted right off me."

All four ladies completely lose their composure, leaning on each other while fighting the fits of laughter overtaking them. The harder they try to stop laughing, the worse it makes their situation. While they're too busy paying attention to each other, Kira and I take the opportunity to disappear around the corner before they compose themselves.

We walk in silence around the perimeter of pavilion area of the park, sticking to the shadows and invisible spots, stopping and listening for any sounds that indicate we're not alone. After several passes around the immediate area and almost an hour of watching and waiting, I'm finally convinced enough that we're alone. I motion for Kira to make her way to the bench then I draw my pistol to cover her, keeping my vantage point in the dark.

She takes the small envelope with the flash drive that contains some real but irrelevant documents, along with some top-secret but doctored documents, and sits on the bench as if she belongs there at two in the morning. She slides forward, plants her hands on either side of her legs, and wraps her fingers around the edge of the bench. Then she stands and walks back toward the way we came in the park, not drawing attention to my location. Her hands are empty…and the package is securely attached to the underside of the bench.

I have to give her credit…that sleight-of-hand trick was expertly executed.

I'd say she's done that once or twice before tonight.

CHAPTER 10

Silas

After I jog around to meet her at the park entrance, we leave the area in the same manner we entered, as a couple completely captivated by each other. With my arm around her shoulders and hers under my coat, wrapped around my waist, we stroll through the empty neighborhood until we reach the truck. I open her door first and help her in, keeping up appearances in case we're under surveillance. She finally looks up at me again, and for just a second, she drops the act, and I get a glimpse of the real Kira Petrova.

The real Kira is beautiful, inside and out.

When our eyes meet for that one moment in time, I feel something more sincere with her than with any other woman I've ever known.

She's shy and unsure and brave and bold. She's

trapped in a life she can't simply walk away from, and she's being used by two competing governments, yet she still puts her trust in me with nothing more than my word as a promise.

An overwhelming and undeniable urge to know her inside and out overcomes me. A call I actively fight against to prevent another impromptu kiss that would be wholly inappropriate this time.

But damn if it wouldn't feel so right.

I stop myself from doing something stupid by closing her door and hurrying around to the driver side. When I'm settled behind the wheel, I start to put the truck in gear, but she stops me before I can drive away.

"Silas? Are you upset with me for kissing you? You haven't really spoken to me since then. That was just part of our cover—because of what those young ladies were saying. If I hadn't reacted that way, anyone watching would've questioned if we were really together."

"No, I'm not mad about that hot as fuck kiss at all. And I'm not still thinking about it until this very second. At all. But if you want to convince anyone else that we're together, all you have to do is say the word." With a wink and a smile, I let her know I'm only teasing her.

She laughs off my harmless flirting. "You'll be the first one to know if we need to convince anyone else that we're hopelessly in love."

Regardless of how passionate that kiss was or that fact that I've only actually known Kira for a few days now, this outing has made us more relaxed in each other's company. Not that I'm ready to give her the Silas Steele badge of trust yet, but I am impressed with how she took my advice about becoming her alias, and how fast she reacted on the fly when we were being taunted. If the circumstances were different, maybe we would make a good team.

THE NEXT MORNING, KIRA IS ALREADY UP AND DRESSED when I stumble into the kitchen in my pajama pants. The aroma of freshly brewed coffee woke me from my deep slumber, but I didn't expect to find her wide awake so early after our late-night activities.

"What's on your mind, Kira?"

"I guess I am pretty obvious, huh?"

"Yep. Up early. On your third cup of coffee. Already showered and dressed. Gnawing your fingernails down to the quick. All very subtle giveaways." I take a long sip of the burning-hot lava from a mug and immediately feel the fog clearing from between my ears.

"How do you know I've had three cups of coffee?" She looks genuinely confused, and I decide to use it to my advantage.

"Didn't I tell you? One of my many abilities is reading minds. I know your every thought." I arch one eyebrow suggestively, and her face lights up like a Christmas tree.

Interesting.

"If you can read minds, you wouldn't have asked me what's on my mind." She crosses her arms over her body and waits for my real explanation.

I chuckle and nod toward the coffee pot. "Half the pot is missing already. You're the only one who could've chugged it this morning. So, let's have it. What's bothering you?"

"We've looked through everything this guy has, but we haven't found any evidence of his collusion. But I know he's somehow tied to this passing of classified information. I've heard his name—I wasn't supposed to hear it, but my handler didn't know I was in the safe house at the time. Something isn't adding up with his connection. I can't put my finger on what's off, and I'm running out of time."

"Tell me why this assignment is so important to you. Help me understand why you need to do this."

"When I was around twenty and just barely out of field training, the Academy sent over a lot of girls who would cycle in and out. I didn't think anything about it at first, other than they had completed the training they needed and were sent out on their assignments. I believed the lies they fed us. Then a couple of years later, I was working in the Miami area, getting insider information from an executive assistant in the FBI office there. I didn't realize how important the files she gave me over lunch were until later that night. By then, I was too late.

"The FBI agents had been watching a massage parlor down there. They suspected the owner of human trafficking. So, I opened the file and started looking through the pictures they'd taken. Some were regular customers, you know? Just going in for a regular massage. But there were several in a row of young girls going in, with notes that they didn't come back out. I stared at one face in particular and I couldn't believe what I saw. It was one of the girls who'd left field training early.

"When I confronted my handler at the time about it, I was severely reprimanded for even asking the question, but she finally relented and told me what they'd reassigned that young girl to do. She'd been abused all that time, moved from place to place to give new men a chance to do whatever they wanted to do to her. After that, I was moved out of Miami and sent here to work. They thought this was far enough away from their activities in Florida for me to forget what I'd seen and focus on my new assignment.

"So, imagine my surprise when all these years later, the same massage parlor name is brought up in a conversation between two handlers—mine and one other. Then they mentioned Senator Hunt's connection to it, and I knew they were still up to their old tricks. So, I did some digging of my own without telling anyone I was looking into him. He has another home in the Miami area, and when he's there, he frequents that very place."

"What's the name of it?" My blood turns to ice in my veins, so cold even my hot coffee can't thaw it because I already know exactly what she'll say. It's like a nightmare that keeps returning to haunt me, even though it's many years later.

"Pure Delight Spa."

The desire to ram my fist through the wall is over-powering, but I find the strength to refrain from some-where deep inside. Knowing this mission isn't finished stays my hand, but knowing a prior mission remains incomplete stirs my blood.

"Tell me everything you know about it." My reaction is more intense than I intended to show, revealing my hand before I've had a chance to process everything.

"You know I'm more than willing to share everything I know, especially if it'll help put an end to the abuse of innocent people. But this feels a lot like a one-sided rela-tionship, Silas. You need to share what you know, too. There may be details I can give you to fill in the full picture. But if I have no idea what you're working on or what you're looking for, we could be running in circles and chasing our tails."

She has a valid point—I'll give her that. But keeping secrets was drilled into me from the start of my career until now. There are very few people I trust implicitly, and I can count them all on one hand. The fact that she already knows about this particular establishment does make me somewhat more comfortable in sharing the rest of the information with her now.

"Several years ago, I was read in on a top-secret assignment regarding that very place. The intel wasn't widely known because the report had been restricted to our eyes only. Russian chatter had been intercepted and decoded by our Signals Intelligence division. The message referred to an international human trafficking ring, and one of the main locations was that very place in Miami." That is the abridged version of the story. The extremely redacted and abridged version.

"Why do I get the feeling you're holding out on me?" Kira rolls her eyes before cutting them sideways toward me.

"Okay, you want the entire story? Here goes. Another officer had a Russian asset he was working for this case. He got a lot of information from her about the next time they were bringing the new batch of girls into the spa— how, when, where, everything. For the entire two weeks before the sting, we took turns driving to the location, parking the car, and walking into a nearby establishment. We'd stay there all day to make it seem like we were working. Technically, we were, but if anyone was casing the neighborhood, our cars had to be easily recognizable as belonging there.

"The day finally came around, and we were more than ready to take down every single person. In the time we were waiting for them to arrive, we were researching their other locations and other illegal activities. They'd set up an extensive network of human trafficking... including a segment of very disturbing offers to sell underage children."

Just the memory of what I saw still haunts me to this day, forcing an involuntary shudder to tear through me.

"Silas, I'm so sorry. That must've been terrible."

"It definitely was. That was one of the worst cases I've ever worked in my entire career. Which made me even more determined to catch the man behind the scheme and take him down by any means necessary. He was so fucking bold. He thought he had everything locked up tight and no one could touch him. When he finally showed up, it was very late at night.

"He, um…" I push the feelings welling up in my chest back down. Now is not the time to dwell on them. "He pulled up in a moving truck, plenty of room in the back to conduct any business he wanted. Before he got the girls out of the back, he chose one to make an example of for the others. I heard her screams from inside that truck, but I was ordered to stand down. We didn't have intel on what else was inside that truck, and the danger to the public was too much to risk for one girl. Or so my deputy director said."

Several moments of silence pass while I mentally relive that dark scene.

"What happened next, Silas?" Kira's voice is soft and soothing. She knows what's next, but she's hoping she's wrong.

"We finally got a visual inside the truck, and I went completely off the rails. I didn't wait for the team to be ready to move. I didn't wait for my backup to reach his vantage point. I just jerked the door open and couldn't believe my eyes. She was already dead by the time we rushed the truck. Instinct and pure hate took over, and I ripped that man apart with my bare hands—just like he did to that poor girl.

"The discussion with the Russian ambassador was a little more civil than mine with the fucker in the back of that truck, but their government got the message, despite the lack of bluntness I preferred. She died because of me. I was there to stop the trafficking, but also to save those young girls. But I didn't do my job—I didn't stop that monster from hurting her, I didn't get her out of that truck in time, and I didn't save her life."

"That wasn't your fault, Silas. You followed orders, just like we've all had to do. That doesn't make you a bad person or any other negative depiction you have stored in your mind. You did what you had to do for your job." She puts her hand on my arm, offering solace and reassurance with the warmth of her touch.

"Yeah. For my job. And what would've happened if I hadn't followed orders? Face being written up for insubordination? Get a week's vacation without pay for disobeying my scene commander? It's not like they would've fired me or arrested me. Even if they did, saving her would've been worth it." I roughly drag my hand through my hair then over my face. The mental images flashing through my mind are enough to choke me out.

"You didn't know that the truck wasn't rigged to explode. You didn't know if you were walking into a trap that would've killed not only you but your entire team.

There's no way to know if the outcome would've been any different."

"Just the chance of saving her would've been better than living with her death on my conscience all these years. They prepared her body, and I escorted her back home to Russia. That's when I met your father at the Kremlin. He was there to apprehend me and throw me into a Russian prison for killing their man—until he saw what all that fucker did to the poor girl. I remember the scene very clearly. He said she reminded him too much of his own daughters, and he was enormously shaken up by all of it. The state of her body, the thought of something like that happening to Mira or you, and knowing his government had a hand in it. But I never realized the Academy was helping by feeding girls to that maniac. I'm glad I killed him."

"Wait. I remember when that happened. That was about ten years ago, right? Our handlers tried to keep us from watching the local news. They said most everything reported about Russia was intentional misinformation to confuse and disarm us. But that specific incident rattled them worse than anything I'd ever seen before. That was you?"

"That was me."

Her brows furrow and she stares hard at nothing, focusing all her brain power on one spot on the table. I've seen that expression before—she's trying to access old memories. Some morsel of information is there on the cusp, waiting to be realized and put into context. Maybe something that didn't make sense at the time, but bringing it out in the open now will answer unresolved questions.

"What is it, Kira? You've remembered something, but you don't want to tell me."

"Silas, you killed Ivan Sokolov. He was one of Russia's most respected foreign relations ministers. What you just told me doesn't match the story released to the Russian media at all. My handler shared that release with me because there was so much buzz about it. She knew I'd hear about it one way or another, so she tried to get ahead of the American version. The Russian embassy claimed he was captured and tortured by the American government because he was falsely accused of spying when he was here on a goodwill mission."

"Typical propaganda to keep the citizens of our countries at odds with each other."

"But when Ivan died, his brother Viktor was alive and well, safely hidden inside Russia. They were partners in everything they did. You didn't see one's name in the Russian news without seeing the other—except when Ivan died. Viktor swore vengeance in a rare outburst to a journalist, but he quickly changed his tune soon after. My guess is the Kremlin silenced him and scrubbed the story."

"His brother? Our research never revealed he had a brother. No names, no mention of any surviving family members, nothing. How is that? What did he look like?"

"Viktor was quite a bit younger than Ivan—maybe a

decade or so. I never saw Viktor's face in the news, only Ivan's. My guess is Ivan kept his brother's name hidden and out of reach of the foreign press for his protection. That way, no one could touch his little brother because no one knew who he was or what he looked like. Then when Ivan died, the Kremlin continued covering him for their own benefit. Someone who never existed is an invaluable resource to the GRU."

"Absolutely. And he'd be a ghost to us, nearly impossible to find."

"Nearly?"

"Nearly."

We have a lot of work to do.

CHAPTER 11

Kira

"Senator Hunt's daughter left last night for her Caribbean honeymoon before heading to Uzbekistan for the next six months. Then Hunt announced he's taking a short vacation at his home away from home in Miami to relax and recuperate from the stress of overseeing the wedding in his home. He'll be there for the next three weeks, possibly longer." Silas beat me to the kitchen this morning. From his bright and chipper mood, I'd say he's already on his third cup of coffee. Seems to be a pattern in this house.

"Well, good morning to you too. I did sleep well. Thank you for asking. And yes, it does look like a beautiful day out there. We should go do something fun for a change. All we do is work, work, work. You know what Johnny says about all work and no play. It's really not a good thing." I grab a mug from the cupboard and fill it full of hot deliciousness to jump-start my brain and hopefully put me in as good a mood as Silas seems to be. "Who's your source anyway? His impromptu trip seems a little too convenient, doesn't it? Maybe he's onto us."

"My source is airtight, so don't you worry your pretty little head about that. And there's no way he's onto us. For future reference, I don't get made when I'm undercover unless I want to."

"Airtight, huh? So who is this magical, never wrong source of yours, and how do I get one?" I join him at the table, sipping my coffee and racking my brain for ideas of how to speed up this waiting game.

He holds up the local newspaper, showing the picture of Senator Hunt watching his daughter drive away in the posh stretch limousine after the wedding. The entire story is about how much time he and his wife have dedicated to the wedding, how stressful yet fun it's been for them both, and how they need a few days away to recharge their batteries before the next congressional session begins.

As if they did any of the actual wedding preparations themselves. They had servants to attend to every single detail for them. All they had to do was be home and dressed on time. They probably even had help with that.

I may be a little angry with that sham of a family right now with everything that's happening right under our noses.

After Silas shared his heartbreaking story last night

and I relived the painful memories from my own past, just the idea of the bastard getting away with his depravity is enough to drive me into a murderous rage. My thoughts and feelings are obviously bleeding over into my disposition this morning.

"Really? Your secret weapon is the newspaper that everyone in a hundred-mile radius reads?" My tone remains deadpan, but I'm fighting a smile and a laugh with everything I have.

I'm trying to hold on to my anger to stay focused on the case. Every day with Silas is muddying the waters, making it harder and harder for me to keep him in his own little box inside my mind. His easygoing personality combined with his muscular build and sexy lips leave me with the most inappropriate thoughts about my jailer.

"Yes, this story tells me everything I need to know. He's not concerned about returning to the scene of the crime, so to speak, so he has no clue he's being watched. If we catch him in the spa while the illegal activity is occurring, we have probable cause to bring him in and question him, even if he is a sitting senator. So, how would you like to go to Miami with me?"

I'm sure I'm hearing things.

"What?"

"Let's go to Miami. My brother has a huge house there. We can crash at his place. Not sure if he's there or at their place in California, but he won't mind either way. If they're in Florida now, you'll love his wife, Brianna. She's the best. We'll be right there at the beach, enjoying the sun, sand, and surf in between taking down bad guys. You said yourself we need to have some fun."

"Silas, I only have a few more days left before your deputy director makes me leave the country. We don't have time to lounge around on the beach and play in the ocean." Has he lost his mind?

"Hmm. You're right, we don't have much of that two-week decree left, do we?" He scratches his chin, pretending to be deep in thought but failing miserably. The ruse only endears him to me even more. "I have the perfect solution. We'll go to Miami, let the clock run out on Graves's two-week investigation bullshit, do our job, and shut this fucker down once and for all. Because, Kira, I can't sleep one more night knowing I left a piece of shit like him on the street because I followed orders. I swore I'd never do that again, no matter what the cost, no matter what line I have to cross. This is more than worth it to me—it feels like a chance to make amends for what I failed to do before. Is that worth the consequences to you?"

"Absolutely. Give me ten minutes to pack, and I'll be ready to go. Are we driving? I'm guessing getting on a plane will be next to impossible for me. I'm sure my face has been distributed to all the airports within driving distance of here." I don't even need time to think about what's right or wrong. We both need this win to help wipe our slates clean again.

"Ordinarily, yes, flying would be a problem. But since my brother runs a very successful security firm, and sometimes has to escort clients on his company jet, I think we can squeeze you past security at the private airstrip just before we board his plane." There's a mischievous twinkle in his eye that is adorable.

"I'm going to pack right now. I've never been on a private jet before. And despite having worked in Miami years ago, I never actually got to go to the beach and get in the ocean." Before I can stop myself, I throw my arms around his neck and kiss his cheek. "Thank you so much for breaking the rules to try to stop him. Even if this doesn't work out the way we want, just the fact that we did everything in our power to stop it means the world to me."

"Since you were denied the complete joy of doing nothing but enjoying the scenery, that's the first stop on our agenda. We have to rectify that wrong as soon as possible. This dreary cold weather here is depressing, and I miss the electric vibe in Miami. You can thank me by packing your bikini and joining me on the beach to soak up some rays."

"Consider this as payment in full, then. I'm packing two bikinis right now."

The change in Silas's demeanor from last night until today is literally dark to daylight. But I'm not complaining or questioning his decision. I'm simply going with it. This case took a very personal turn for him, and I completely understand his need to right the wrongs of his past. Not that I think he did anything unethical— all soldiers are taught to follow orders to the letter. And that's what we've both been, regardless of titles or jobs. We're soldiers at our core. The one deep inside Silas is screaming for justice and absolution.

I'm praying he finds it on this trip because, win or lose, he may no longer have a job when we get back. And I certainly will no longer be allowed to stay on American soil to help him with anything. This is most definitely a now-or-never trip.

All those thoughts flow through my mind as I pack for our trip, stuffing a variety of clothing options into the suitcase since I have no idea what may be needed.

Black clothes? Check.

Dress clothes? Check.

Bikinis? Check.

Although, the only time I've ever even worn one was while working during a pool party, trying to get close to an FBI informant to find out what secrets he held. They've never even been wet, aside from the first wash. Maybe this time, I'll actually make it to the beach and into the ocean for the first time.

When my sister and I were taken away from our parents, the Academy said we were young enough to forget our blood families but old enough not to need coddling anymore. But they were so wrong. I never forgot my parents, not for one second, and the biannual calls home only made my homesickness worse. Even at that tender young age, I had learned to hide my true feelings and only react in the way they expected me to. So I pushed the enormous ball of emotions as far down inside me as I could.

Mira wasn't as agile with her reactions. She learned over time, but she still wore her feelings on her sleeve. From the time we were little kids until now, she's been a hopeless romantic. I've never told her, but I've always admired her for holding on to that piece of humanity. That hope to keep the spark alive inside her that one day she'd have a normal life and a normal family to love. Her beliefs ran counter to our training in every way.

We never were to fall in love.

We never were to care about anyone else.

We never were to put anything above completing the mission.

Any deviation from the rules was considered treason and punishable by watching our parents being shot by a firing squad.

For the first time in as far back as I can remember, I feel a sliver of hope for my future. I'm not naïve or delusional —I fully understand they intend to send me back to Moscow to face my failure. But I'm hopeful my contributions and information will help get my request for asylum approved. And that's a very different feeling for me—to hope, to dare to dream, to want something more for myself.

If I'm completely honest with myself, maybe I also want to explore the attraction between Silas and me to see where it leads us. The desire is mutual, and the temptation is strong. The chemistry between us is real and so tangible, the air crackles with electricity around us. There's no way I'm the only one who thinks it...feels it...wants it.

"Are you almost ready to go?" Silas startles me from my ruminating, making me jump out of shock. Something else I'm not used to—having someone sneak up on me.

"Almost." I stuff another pair of shoes into my suitcase and zip it up. "Now I am."

"What were you thinking about just now, before you realized I was standing here?" He's leaning against the doorjamb, assessing me with those X-ray vision eyes of his.

"If I tell you, it may not come true."

"If you tell me, maybe I can help make it come true."

I have a strong feeling we're not talking about the same thing right now. And just the thought of what he's possibly offering me is enough to make me salivate uncontrollably.

"Um, I was just, um, hoping we'd actually have a chance to enjoy the beach and the ocean. Work always seems to get in the way of the things I'd prefer to do."

"Kira, I personally guarantee at least one day of lounging on the sand and playing in the waves. But just so you know, I don't buy that's what you were thinking for one second." He raises his eyebrows at me, waiting for me to argue or acknowledge his assumption.

But I'm not ready to share my innermost thoughts or feelings with him quite yet. Despite spending twenty-four hours a day with him for the last week or so and getting to know him better than I ever anticipated, I'm more afraid of revealing my feelings and making a complete fool out of myself than facing an army on my own.

"Shouldn't we be leaving now?" I grab my suitcase and start walking toward the door. But he doesn't move to let me pass.

He raises his hand to my face, barely tracing my cheek with his fingertips. I can feel the warmth in his eyes, heating my skin. From no more than a touch, my breath hitches, making my lungs work for every bit of oxygen they draw. "You never have to hide anything from me, Kira. One day, I hope you'll realize that."

He takes the suitcase from my hand and carries it out to his truck. With the house locked up and our plan to fly away to Miami set in stone, there's no looking back now. I'm so excited, I can barely make myself sit still in this seat. Even knowing the wrath we'll face when we finally return…or we're apprehended as fugitives in Florida. Either way.

When we board the private jet without a hitch, I'm literally giddy with excitement. Looking around the high-class cabin, I instantly feel out of my element. I've never experienced anything this luxurious before, and apart from the trip home, it's unlikely I ever will again. That makes this trip all that much more special, so I plan to soak up every second of it. The plush leather chair calls my name, so I take a seat and buckle up.

Silas sits beside me, wearing that same spicy cologne

that makes me want to bury my nose in his neck and stay there for an inappropriate and uncomfortable amount of time.

"Penny for your thoughts."

When I lift my eyes up to his, I realize I've been staring at his neck like a vampire dying of thirst. This is not awkward at all.

"I was just wondering what kind of cologne you wear. You always smell so good."

"If it makes you feel any better, I've wondered that about you a lot."

"Yeah?"

"Oh yeah. When I'm around you. When I'm alone. When you're asleep. When you drink all the coffee and don't leave any for me. I wonder about it a lot."

We're not talking about cologne anymore. I'm certain of it.

"Sounds like we have more in common than we realized. Except for the drinking all the coffee part. Somehow you make sure to leave some for me when you're the first one up."

"I'm a nice guy like that. Ladies should always finish first."

"Good morning from the flight deck. We are preparing for takeoff. For your safety, please make sure your seat belts are fastened, and all luggage is stowed."

If the pilot hadn't interrupted at that exact moment, I would probably already be in Silas's lap right now, covering every inch of myself in his intoxicating scent.

"Noah's house is amazing. You'll love it. There's a pool in the backyard, the whole place is surrounded by a brick fence, state-of-the-art security system, and every amenity you could ever dream of. But when we get there, we're changing clothes, grabbing food and drinks to go, and heading straight for the beach. The rest of the day, we're not giving up our spot in the sand. We both need a relaxing day before we hit it hard tomorrow. Think you can handle that?"

"That sounds like heaven. I'm positive I can handle that. And if anything happens that causes me to say I've changed my mind, you can just handcuff me to the beach chair until my attitude improves."

"With a few tweaks, some minor alterations, that plan has incredible merit. I'll keep that request in mind for later."

What thoughts this man conjures with just a few words…

"So, how did you get drawn into this cloak-and-dagger world? Just from what I know about you, I'd say you could've been anything you wanted to be. Are you an adrenaline junkie? Pathological liar? Functioning schizophrenic?" I'm genuinely interested in what makes him tick. He takes a moment to consider his answer. I can almost see the wheels turning in his head, trying to decide if he should tell me the truth or not.

"You wouldn't know it if you met him today, but my father wasn't always the warm and fuzzy type. He was cold as ice and hard as stone when I was growing up. He expected me to return home immediately after college and follow in his footsteps in the corporate world of business. But I knew before I left for school that I wanted to travel the world and experience life to the fullest, not sit behind a desk inside a plush office all day.

"So, I chose political science as my major and became fluent in several foreign languages. It was really one step at a time. I never set out to become a CIA officer, but the clandestine lifestyle, the worldwide travel, and the constant adrenaline rush of working an asset in the most perilous location in the world were impossible to pass up. I started right out of college and have been doing this ever since. I can't imagine doing anything else now."

"How did your father take your career choice?"

"Dear old dad did not disappoint. He did exactly as I thought he would, confirming my profiling skills were already on point before I even started CIA training. He immediately disowned me and told me never to come home again. I still talked to my mom, brother, and sister when I wasn't deep undercover, but I didn't go back home for many years after that. Turns out, my brother also let Dad down when he joined the Army immediately after high school graduation, leaving my sister home alone with his tyrannical demands. Then Noah and I were both disowned—by our father and our sister, for leaving her."

"Wow. You said he's different now. How did it all get resolved?"

"There's nothing like an unexpected cancer diagnosis to put petty differences into perspective. He retired as CEO of a major insurance company, and they still live in the huge house I grew up in, completely remodeled now. The only difference is, now it's always full of the laughter and pitter-patter of grandbaby feet. I think the grandkids stay with them more than they do their parents."

"What are your siblings' names again?"

"Noah and Chaise. Noah is married to Brianna. Chaise is married to Bull."

"Bull?"

Silas laughs and nods. "Noah and his Delta Force brothers worked together after they left the service. They all still go by their old nicknames."

"Ah, that makes sense. So, what's Noah's nickname?"

"Reaper. The other two guys are Rebel and Shadow."

"Sounds like you have quite an interesting extended family. I'm a little jealous. I've always wanted a large family. You know my family and my history, so you also know that dream was always out of the question."

"At one time, it wasn't possible, that's true. But soon you'll have a chance to start over and make it happen. Don't give up on it if that's what you still want."

I know he means well, but my new start isn't exactly what he thinks it'll be. However, I don't want to dampen the good mood and the fun waiting for us when we land. "Maybe you're right."

The corners of his eyes crinkle, and he cocks one

eyebrow upward. "Kira, let's make a promise to each other right now. This promise can never be broken for any reason."

"What promise is that?"

"We'll be honest with each other, regardless of the cost or how painful the words are to say aloud. No matter what it's about. Just the cold, hard truth. Can you do that?"

"Sure, I can do that. Can you? What about the classified information you're not supposed to share?"

"If it's something I can't tell you, I'll just say that. I won't lie about it. Will that work?"

"That works."

"Good. Now, let's back up for a minute. There was zero conviction in your voice when you said I may be right. Why do you think you'll never have what you want?"

Regardless of how painful the truth is, right? Here goes nothing. "There's no 'maybe' to it, Silas. I'll never have a home, a husband, or any children. When my flight lands in Moscow, I'll be grabbed off the plane and taken to an interrogation site. Once they're satisfied that they've squeezed every last drop of information out of me, it'll be as if I never even existed. They'll destroy anything remotely related to me, including that picture my dad keeps on his desk. In fact, if you can get a message to him to hide it immediately, I'd appreciate it. Just that old picture would probably get Mom and Dad killed too."

He scrubs his hand over his face, leaving it covering

his mouth as he considers my words. I stare out the window to avoid the temptation to try to read his mind through the intensity of his gaze.

"I know I don't have to ask this, but it's too important not to say anything. Mira will have to watch over her shoulder for the rest of her life. She and I worked missions together for years. They know she defected against them, even if she hasn't made it official yet. Even taking her act of treason against them off the table, they know it could be too detrimental to the Academy to leave her out on the lam once they have me in custody. Please help take care of her."

"Let's take this one day at a time. We have a long way to go before we have to cross that bridge. Mira's fine— she's in very capable hands. Today, my only focus is taking care of you. Bikini, beer, beach. Sand, surf, sun. If it doesn't involve one of those, it's not a priority for today. Deal?"

"Deal." I raise my eyes to meet his. "I can't wait to see you in a bikini."

His responding smile is immediate and reaches from ear to ear. "Play your cards right, and you just might."

The rest of the two-and-a-half-hour flight flew by in the blink of an eye. Silas and I spent every moment talking about everyday, normal topics. For a short time, we didn't live in a world entrenched in treachery, buried in lies, or corrupted by enemies. We were just a man and a woman, getting to know each other on a profoundly personal level. We dropped the façade of our cover personalities and let our real selves step out into the sunlight.

There may have even been some harmless flirting, a couple not-so-subtle sexual innuendos thrown around the cabin, and more than a few heated glances.

I've never been so anxious to be seen in a bikini in my entire life. We're wheels down and making a landing now, but my thoughts are already several steps ahead. Silas had an epiphany about rectifying the mistakes of his past. Mine is a little more selfish, but this is the only time I have left. No matter how short or long this Miami trip lasts, I'll live every minute to the fullest. If that means making a complete fool of myself by trying to initiate a short-term relationship with Silas while we're here, so be it.

At least I won't die without checking that item off my new Why Not list. If I don't have much time left, why not do what I want to do—right now? No time like the present.

CHAPTER 12

Silas

We step out of the jet directly into the warm Miami sun, even when it's the dead of winter everywhere else in the country. Kira stops for a moment and soaks it in, with her face tilting upward, her eyes closing of their own accord, and her lips curling into a beautiful smile. The serene expression on her face captivates me, halting my feet and seizing my breath. The slight breeze blows her long black hair away from her face and makes her shirt cling to her curves, leaving me to openly ogle her natural beauty. I'm using all my willpower to avoid pulling her into my arms and crushing my lips against hers before disappearing into the Caribbean with her for the foreseeable future.

"You'll get more sun with your bikini on, you know." I purposely brush my lips across the shell of her ear and murmur the words. A shiver runs through her that has nothing to do with the wind blowing around us.

"I just needed a moment to soak it all in. Now I'm ready." She smiles up at me, her face beaming with bliss.

We cruise away from the private airstrip with the top down on our rental car, heading to my brother's secure estate for some much-needed rest and relaxation. Kira's enthusiasm is contagious as she takes in the sights and sounds of the vibrant city, not having been here in many years. Today is about giving her what she needs, but the selfish part of me hopes she opts for avoiding the crowds in lieu of more private locales.

Now that I have her here alone, I'm not too interested in sharing her with anyone else.

When I pull into Noah's gated driveway, she pulls her sunglasses off her face and openly gapes at our surroundings. He's done exceptionally well for himself with his security business, and his enormous home set behind tall brick fences only reveals part of the picture. With the code keyed in, the gates swing open—and our day of being a South Beach tourist begins.

Kira starts to jump out of the car the second I put it into Park, but I grab her arm to halt her momentum. She whips her head around, looking at me as if I've lost my mind—her excitement is barely contained as it is. Keeping my face passive is nearly impossible.

"Remember my rule."

Her brows draw down, and confusion mars her beautiful face. "What rule is that?"

"You're only allowed to have fun today. Whatever you want to do is fine by me. All you have to do is say the word."

Her face softens, and her lips part on a contented sigh. "Thank you, Silas. Underneath all that hard-as-steel-CIA-badass outer shell, you really are a sweetheart."

I smile in return…then finish my thought. "As I was saying, whatever you want to do is fine by me, as long as you're wearing a bikini the entire time."

She laughs out loud, and I can literally see the tension dissipating in the warm air surrounding her. "Well, okay. There go my plans for skinny-dipping in your brother's pool, though. But you're absolutely right. Rules are rules, after all."

She shrugs her shoulders as she hops out of the car without waiting for my reply—and I eventually would've thought of something to say—once I reeled my tongue back into my mouth and the blood flow to my brain resumed. I swear I hear her evil little giggle as she rushes out of the garage to examine the exterior of the house and yard.

When I catch up with her, she's rounding the corner of the house and heading to the backyard. I know exactly what she'll find back there—heaven on earth. A heated pool for year-round use, complete with a waterfall flowing into the attached hot tub, and an outdoor kitchen that would make any professional chef envious. She stops and lets out an excited squeal.

"Are you sure he doesn't mind us staying here? I'm

afraid to touch anything—I don't want to be the one to break it."

Her modesty is like a rare gem, one I wonder if I'll ever find again. "I'm positive—he doesn't mind at all. As far as breaking anything, don't even think twice about that. If his three rambunctious kids haven't broken it by now, it's completely indestructible."

"Are they here with us?"

"Not for a few days. They'll be back later in the week, along with their rug rats."

"You don't like being an uncle?"

"Are you kidding? I love it. They're awesome kids. We play football in the house. We play cops and robbers, hiding behind furniture and shooting each other with Nerf guns. I get to spoil them, give them all the sugar their little bodies can take, then walk out the door and leave them with their dad. It's the perfect arrangement. Bull and I have our own competitions—to decide who their favorite uncle is."

"Oh yeah? Who usually wins that game?" Kira's shocked expression tells me she never saw me as a family man.

Up until just a few years ago, she would've been correct. But since I've been back in my brother's and sister's lives, my priorities have shifted.

"Who usually wins?" I hesitate to answer for a second. "Shadow does. Which isn't fair, because he's not even related to them. I'm their uncle by blood, and Bull is their uncle by marriage. But Shadow—who's a great guy, but he's technically a friend of the family—always cheats his way in."

She lifts one eyebrow, amused beyond measure over my sulking and irrational jealousy. "This, I must know. How does Shadow cheat to win the title of favorite uncle?"

"He comes up with the best pranks for the kids to play on the family. They get us every fucking time. It's humiliating, really."

"Give me an example." She's trying very hard not to laugh in my face. She's not succeeding, but at least she's trying.

"During the last game, he had them decorate two round pieces of foam with real cake icing, flowers, sprinkles, the whole works. Then they put it on a cake display stand in the kitchen and hid while we each tried to cut a piece without getting caught by Brianna. They even changed the fake cake out so neither of us would figure it out. He videoed us then played the videos for the whole family after dinner. On the big screen."

When she bends over, gasping for breath and wiping tears from her eyes after laughing so hard, I point out the obvious. "You're not even trying to take my side right now. Just so we're clear."

"I'm sorry. I'm just picturing you, trying to sneak a piece of cake from your sister-in-law's kitchen, only to find out it's not really cake. Then, as if that's not bad enough, your entire family watches you hard at work, trying to cut a piece of foam." Then she breaks out into a laughing fit once again.

"Yeah, yeah. It was so fucking funny. Shadow and all my nieces and nephews thought so, too. Now, get your ass inside and get your bikini on. We're late for our appointment at the beach." I unlock the door with the extra key Noah gave me in case I ever wanted to crash at his place and shoo her inside. "Feel free to look around while I grab our bags."

When I join her inside, she's finally managed to control herself.

"This house is amazing. There's absolutely nothing I would change about it. They must love it here."

"It is a great place. Come on upstairs and pick a bedroom. With a record-high temperature, the weather is perfect for a swim in the ocean today."

"How about a swim in the pool and a soak in the hot tub tonight?"

"If you twist my arm really hard, you might be able to talk me into that too." I waggle my eyebrows at her and show her to the available guest bedrooms upstairs. "I'll be back in thirty seconds. You'd better be changed and ready to go by then."

"Yes, sir. So bossy." Her insults are meant in jest from the smile on her face and the twinkle in her eye. "It won't take me long to change—there's very little fabric to worry about."

There she goes again, giving me the best mental images but leaving me speechless in the process.

As promised, she's changed and ready in no time. The only hitch is she's wearing a cover-up over her bathing suit, so I can't confirm she's wearing the required apparel underneath. But since we're burning daylight, I opt to take her at her word and wait for the big reveal when we get to where we're going.

Once we pull into the parking lot at Lummus Park, I'm surprised to find it mostly deserted, but then, it is late January, so it's not exactly high season. We haul our gear out of the car and walk to the beach and set up our spot, and then she grabs the hem of her cover-up and pulls it over her head. If I thought I was speechless before, I was wrong, beyond a shadow of a doubt. The minuscule triangles of fabric on the top and bottom barely cover her luscious body. Her taut, firm stomach muscles perfectly accentuate her perfectly round, perky breasts. Then she turns around, and I nearly groan out loud.

The bottom is a thong, and somehow, the tiny strings of fabric only make the sexy globes of her ass even more appealing.

"I'll race you to water. Loser buys lunch. Go!"

She takes off running toward the water, leaving me standing rooted to the same spot, still panting after her like a man lost in the desert with no water in sight.

Then she rushes into the water, dives into the waves, and comes up on the other side with a huge smile on her face…and now she's wet. Every inch of her luscious body is dripping wet.

Fuck me.

This is going to be a long day.

"Silas, get your ass in here right now," she yells and motions for me to join her.

I jerk my shirt off and drop it onto my outstretched towel, then jog the few feet to the water's edge. It's cooler than I thought it would be, but obviously not too cold for Kira to enjoy it to the fullest. She's swimming and playing in the waves as if she's the sexiest mermaid in the Atlantic, and I have no doubt she'd win that competition.

When I reach her, she surprises me by jumping into my arms and wrapping hers around my neck. I'm acutely aware of her barely covered breasts pushing against my bare chest, the water serving as a lubricant and a stimulant simultaneously.

"Thank you so much for bringing me here with you and for making this day happen. It's so beautiful here—the turquoise water, the beautiful beach, and the bright blue sky. Every single part of this is magical and wonderful and more than I ever expected. I also want you to know, I can't imagine experiencing this for the first time with anyone else."

With little effort, she wraps her legs around my waist and locks them behind my back. I automatically move my hands under her bare ass, holding her in place as the waves slightly jostle us in the waist-deep water. Our eyes lock, and the desire blazing in hers is brighter than the sun above us. Beads of water run down her gorgeous face, some disappearing when she runs her tongue over her lips.

Her gaze drops to my mouth just before she closes the gap and presses her lips to mine. Soft and tentative turns to hungry and demanding in a millisecond. I knead the firm flesh of her behind with my fingers when her tongue glides across mine. She lifts her torso, pulling closer to me, and grazes across my already hard cock. When she releases a needy moan in my mouth, any restraint I had a second ago evaporates into thin air. My fingers dig into her skin, holding her tightly against my body. Her hips undulate, gliding against me—over these fucking swim shorts.

Though I never expected to hear her say those words to me, they affect me more than I want to admit. Relationships have never been my specialty. I've never wanted one for longer than a night or two, and I'm still not looking for one at this moment. Something tells me she isn't either, though, so hopefully, we're on the same page. Because with the sun, water, and a beautiful woman in my arms, there's no fucking way I can resist what she's offering.

Especially when she skims one hand down my chest and stops at the band of my shorts. She drags her nails across the sensitive skin of my lower stomach, teasing and tempting me more than I can resist. Her courage surges again. She slips her hand inside, wraps her fingers around me, and caresses me with soft strokes. I was already hard enough to smash boulders before her soft hand found its mark. Now it's becoming painful in the best way.

While holding her up with one hand, I slide the fingers on my other one along the thin G-string fabric until I reach her core. Her fingers dig into my shoulders, and she presses into my hand, wordlessly urging me on.

But I have to be sure. There's no way to undo what we're about to do.

After I break our kiss, she peers up at me hesitantly. "Are you sure this is what you want, Kira? For the record, I don't expect sex from you. You don't owe me anything."

"I know that—and I completely agree. If knowing what I want makes me a terrible person, then I guess I'm the worst person who ever lived. Because the truth is, I want you more than I can bear, and I can't wait one more minute. But if you tell me you don't want this, that you don't want me, I'll stop right now, and we'll go build a sand castle instead."

"Does what's in your hand feel like I don't want you?"

She crashes her lips into mine again, our tongues clashing like the waves on the shore. She pushes the front of my shorts down at the same time I move the small triangle of fabric to the side and plunge my finger deep inside her, stroking her inner walls and increasing her yearning. She digs her fingernails on one hand into my skin as the other aligns our bodies.

"Now, Silas."

With both hands gripping her ass and the strength of my arms holding her up, I push inside her to the hilt while my hands pull her down on me. Then she takes control, rolling her hips front to back then side to side. The more she grinds her hips, the harder it is for me to hold back. She feels like a tight-fitting velvet glove, made exclusively to mold to and match me. The waves help to hide our movements, but anyone with eyes knows better. Somehow, that makes her desire for me even sexier.

Her inner muscles clutch around me, holding tighter and tighter every time she reaches climax, but she's greedy for more. I'm more than willing to accommodate her, until she screams into my neck the final time, urging me to join her. When her loud cries diminish to breathy whimpers, I pull out of her for my own release. Every muscle in her entire body relaxes at once, turning into a quivering, beautiful mess in my arms.

What the fuck do we do now?

Welcome back to reality, Silas.

CHAPTER 13

Kira

*N*ow that the exhilarating high has subsided, the mortification of what I just did starts to set in. It's time to untangle our limbs and climb down from the large tree of a man I just scaled out of the blue. What I'm feeling isn't regret over actually showing my real desire for Silas, but rather the timing. We only just arrived in Miami, and I'd feel less awkward if I'd allowed a little more time to pass before jumping headfirst into a physical relationship.

Relationship? Is that even the correct word for what this is between us?

Association?

Connection?

Frenemies with benefits?

Silas helps steady me when the waves crash into my back as I find my footing. He wraps his hands around my biceps, keeping me upright in the water…but he's also holding me just far enough away from him to avoid our bodies coming into contact again. The flash of pain through my chest is foreign and unexpected. I was never under the delusion of instant love and marriage proposals from him. I'm not that naïve. But then, I didn't expect him to make me feel like a contagious leper immediately afterward either.

"How about that drink I promised you?" His voice is low and intimate, making me question if I'm overreacting to everything and nothing.

Now I realize I've brought feelings into a situation that was only meant to be for fun—a short fling while we're already crossing the blurred line between us. Today wasn't supposed to mean anything. He wasn't supposed to mean anything. My plan was so simple, but I had to complicate it with feelings and insecurities and doubts.

"Right now, a drink sounds perfect."

He releases me so we can work our way through the waves and onto the beach. After I throw on my cover-up, we make our way to the oceanfront bar and slide up onto the stools. He orders our drinks and a couple of appetizers before looking at me for the first time since I forced myself on him.

"Well, it's official. This is now my favorite beach of all time."

When I glance up at him, he's smiling, and the same warm, friendly, yet mischievous glint is there. In his own way, he's letting me know he won't let our frolic in the water make working together feel weird. We're back to business as usual—teasing, laughing, and enjoying each other's company.

Maybe I'll let him make the next move...if there is one.

Usually, sex wouldn't be a big deal—sometimes it's just part and parcel of getting the job done. But my targets were never anyone I wanted to know or spend time with afterward. The bottom line was I'd get the information I needed, then I'd leave. But getting to know Silas so well first has thrown me off-kilter, and now my head and heart are still reeling from just the thought of our every heated touch and passionate kiss.

"It's my favorite, too. But then, it's also the only one I've been to."

"That sly smile doesn't fool me, young lady. You know exactly what I'm talking about, so don't even try to pretend you don't."

The waiter delivers our appetizers at the same time the bartender sets our drinks in front of us. At least now my hands and mouth will be busy for the next few minutes, giving me an excuse to be quiet and bring my thoughts and feelings under control again. We devour the food and drinks in front of us, then Silas orders seconds, prompting me to raise my eyebrows in silent question.

He shrugs his shoulders. "I'm a growing boy. I need food."

Our drink refills arrive first, and I sip on my piña colada while watching the waves lapping against the shoreline. The roar of the water and the soft breeze are instantly relaxing, making me question why I've waited so long to make time for a trip to the beach. My gaze drifts back to Silas, who is watching me with a curious expression, and the full force of how short life is hits me. All the things I've wanted to do and all the places I've wanted to see have been on the back burner my whole life. Like so many others, I lied to myself and promised I'd check them all off my list one day.

One day doesn't exist, though.

"Do you ever feel like life is just one big blur? Like you're just surviving from day to day instead of really living?" I set down my glass but continue playing with the straw, stirring the frozen drink though it doesn't need it.

"I'd say most everyone feels that exact way at some point in life. It seems to come in stages, as you look back at where you've been and look forward to where you're going. It's all a matter of perspective, though, and depends on your frame of mind at the time. We all only have one life. We all have to work to live. We all have trials and troubles and good days and happy memories. But how we approach every day we have is what makes all the difference. Whether you're happy with what you have, or you think you've been cheated out of having something wonderful, you're right."

"Good points. So, live each day to the fullest, be content with what you have, and keep a good outlook on life. Did I get all that right?"

"You did. I should trademark that and slap it on a bumper sticker before someone else steals it."

"Well, obviously. It's pure gold."

We fall into a comfortable banter over the rest of the meal. Silas finishes off the rest of the food after I've stuffed myself until I'm miserable. I jokingly complain that he'll have to roll me across the sand like a giant beach ball by the end of the week if I go out to eat with him the rest of the time. Resuming our intentional double entendre innuendo and harmless flirting makes the tension from earlier completely fade away.

Which I'm sure is his intention anyway. But the effort he puts into making me feel at ease means the world to me.

"Shouldn't we stake out the spa? See what's happening there today?" I finish off the last drop of my drink just as the waiter leaves the check.

"Not today. I told you—today is all about you having fun. We're going back out on the beach for a while. We can play beach volleyball or swim or rent Jet Skis. If you insist, we can go shopping. Maybe even get you into a luxury spa for a massage—no human trafficking allowed. The world of Miami is all yours, for one day only. So, what will it be?"

"How about…you and I stow away on one of those

huge cruise ships I saw on the flight in? Let's go find our own private island to hide away for a few years."

"You honestly have no idea how appealing that offer is. Can't say it hasn't already crossed my mind at least once or twice today."

His flagrant admission takes me by surprise. He's considered running away with me? Maybe there's a romantic bone hidden in that massive, muscled body after all.

"Then my second choice is Jet Skis. Let's go have some fun on the water."

"Perfect choice. A woman after my own heart." He drops cash on the table to cover the bill and a nice tip. "Let's go ride some waves."

At first, I hop on the back of the watercraft while Silas operates it. The spray of water whips by us as we skim across the top of the water. I love it—the speed, the exhilaration, the beautiful water, the sun. I can't stop the laughter from bubbling up inside me and bursting out every time we jump a wave. He takes us out past where the waves break and stops the engine. We float on the water, enjoying the gentle roll of the waves and the scenery surrounding us.

"You ready to drive now?" He glances over his shoulder at me, and I realize my arms are still wrapped around his waist even though we've been still for several minutes.

"Really? You trust me to operate this water motorcycle?"

"Sure. Climb on up here."

We switch places, and he gives me a quick overview of the controls, then we're off again. After a half hour of proving my mettle, he has another idea.

"There's no doubt you're made for this. Let's head back toward shore. I'll rent another one and extend the time on this one, then we'll cruise up and down the shore and sight-see for a while. Sound good?"

"Sounds perfect. I'm having so much fun." I can't help but gush. Taking time for myself has never been my priority. Now I wonder what else I've missed out on after years of work being my sole focus.

We spend the rest of the afternoon acting as if we don't have a care in the world. Jumping waves on the Jet Skis, snorkeling along the jetties, and soaking up as much vitamin D as our bodies can take while sipping margaritas on the beach. This day excursion is exactly what I've needed, only I never realized it before. When the sun sinks lower in the sky, we pack up our things and head back to the car.

"Looks like you've had enough sun for the day." He nods toward the bikini line already showing on my skin. He leaves the top of the convertible up and rolls down the windows instead. The ride back to Noah's house doesn't take long, but it gives me time to collect my thoughts and consider our next steps.

Today's adventures allowed me to recharge my batteries and refocus my intentions. Now I'm ready to put all my energy into getting to the bottom of what the senator is doing and put an end to it once and for all. No more young girls will fall prey to his hands. At least then, there will be one less disgusting man loose in the world.

"Silas, are we going to stake out the spa tomorrow?"

"In a manner of speaking, yes. A couple of friends are actually watching the building today. When you and I go tomorrow, we're going as patrons. We'll get a good look around inside and figure out how they're bringing them in, where they'll hold them, and how we'll get them out."

"You didn't tell me you had people working today. Now I feel bad for taking the day off and having fun all this time."

"That's exactly why I didn't tell you ahead of time. And you can continue to feel bad for having fun instead of working tonight, because I'm taking you out for dinner and dancing in Miami. There's nowhere else like this city at night—you'll love it."

"You're spoiling me. What if I become accustomed to all this doting? Then I could hold you responsible for maintaining the lifestyle to which I've grown accustomed."

He cuts his eyes over to me, so full of playfulness, and grins. "That would be a shame, wouldn't it?"

Inside his brother's house, he first takes me to the large walk-in closet in the master bedroom.

"Pick out an outfit—whatever you want to wear is fine. Brianna is cool. She won't mind."

Before he leaves me to rifle through her clothes, he shows me where the linens and soaps are located so I can shower and get dressed for a night out on the town. While I try to tell myself that this isn't actually a date, that we're just two friends going out to release some pent-up frustrations before settling into the roles that require our attention twenty-four hours a day, seven days a week until it's over, even I don't fall for that line. This definitely feels like a date. We're getting dressed up.

I mean... I'm wearing heels and a little black dress with long sleeves tonight.

That's definitely only reserved for a date.

When I descend the curved staircase leading to the foyer, Silas stands at the bottom and watches my every step. Hunger burns in his eyes as I approach, heating me from the inside out. The spark between us is still there, and I feel it equally as strongly. He's dressed in a gray suit with a light purple button-down, all exquisitely fitted to his frame. I'm secretly glad I'm not the only one treating this outing as a date.

"You look absolutely stunning. I won't be able to leave your side for a second without every man in the house trying to take my place." He extends his elbow for me to take his arm.

"You don't look so bad yourself, handsome. Don't think all those women won't try to find a way to lock me in the bathroom stall so they can take my place." I wrap my fingers around his arm and step closer to him.

"Guess we'll be stuck to each other like glue tonight, then."

Though part of me knows he means that for the time we're dancing and drinking in the club, another part of me envisions a very different and more satisfying scenario.

CHAPTER 14

Silas

hen she stepped into view, I fought to keep my tongue in my mouth. Otherwise, it would've been on the floor. Not that I haven't found her utterly gorgeous in every other situation I've seen her in, but watching her walk toward me in that tight black dress and those spiky black heels was a full-on fantasy moment.

My plan to take her out dancing until she couldn't walk anymore flew right out the window.

Fuck giving dancing that pleasure.

If there's any reason why she can barely walk later tonight, it'll be because of me and only me. Judging by the way the pulse in her neck jumps from every brush of my fingers and how her breaths become ragged when I lean in to murmur in her ear, I'd say she agrees with me.

We're having dinner at Café Roval, one of the most romantic restaurants in Miami. The Mediterranean food is exquisite, but so is the outdoor seating in the gardens. With the lush green foliage of trees and plants and soft white lanterns lining the path winding around the sparkling pool, we couldn't ask for a more tropical paradise setting. The tables are placed far enough apart to give seclusion and provide us ample privacy. Our chairs are close together, our thighs brush against each other, and our eyes linger on each other's lips for a heart-beat too long to be a coincidence. The fact that we look and act like an enamored couple hasn't escaped me.

Nor has the sickening thought of her being forcibly removed from US soil when this is said and done.

"Silas, this place is amazing. Thank you again for bringing me here." She takes a sip of her wine and releases a little moan of indulgence. She has no idea how much that innocuous noise affects me.

"It's my pleasure, Kira. I hope you have your dancing shoes on. You'll need them." I waggle my eyebrows at her, prompting her to giggle in reply.

"I'm ready to dance whenever you are, big guy. Where are we going?"

"The Copa Room. Heard of it?"

"No, can't say I have."

"I think you'll enjoy it." The wink that follows is entirely automatic, a learned reflex I'm not even conscious of doing most of the time. But in this setting, she may have misunderstood it for something more lascivious.

Not that I mind this small misunderstanding.

"And what exactly is it you think I'll enjoy, Silas?" She folds her hands under her chin and challenges me with her gaze.

"There are cabaret shows and a large dance floor. Loud music and a lot of people. No one sees what you're doing because they're too busy with what they're doing. I'll leave my jacket in the car and roll up my sleeves, then I'll take you out on the floor and spend every minute exploring your body through salsa dancing."

"Holy shit. I don't know which sounds better—salsa lessons back at the house where we'll be alone, or in the middle of a writhing, grinding crowd with loud music and lots of drinks." The flush starts at the base of her neck and crawls upward, coloring her cheeks the perfect shade of pink.

"Why not both? I can always give you all the private lessons you need later tonight."

"Get the check. It's time to go. I'm ready to dance now."

With a chuckle, I signal for the waiter and quickly settle the bill. Then we make a beeline for the club. The bouncer on duty is luckily an old acquaintance, so we walk directly to the front of the line and into the multi-colored light show inside. The music is blaring, the bass is thumping, and all the bodies are grinding on the floor.

Without waiting one more second, I grab her hand and lead her onto the middle of the dance floor.

Our bodies align perfectly as if we were made for this. With one hand on her back and the other holding her hand, I pull her much closer to me than needed for typical salsa dancing. The kind I have in mind is a little more intimate, with my invading her personal space so much we look like one body moving in a fluid motion. Pelvis to pelvis, we begin our dance and use it as a preview to foreplay. Her breasts push into my chest, her mouth is a mere breath's distance from mine, and the way her hips rub against my crotch is making an already impossible situation hard.

Very hard.

Obviously hard.

I glide my hand down her side, relishing her curves as I go, and lift her leg until she wraps it around my thigh, ensuring we're effectively dry-humping on the dance floor. So much about her makes me feel like a crazed man. She's sexy and demure, soft and hard, cunning and trusting—all at the same time. She makes me feel so much—too much sometimes. I shouldn't want her as much as I do. I shouldn't cause a scene in the middle of a crowded danced floor, drawing attention to us rather than blending into the background.

Before we're both escorted away in handcuffs for indecent exposure, the song ends and then the main lights dim. The spotlights draw circles on the curtain, drawing everyone's attention toward the stage. A voice comes through the speakers, telling us to put our hands together and welcome the cabaret performers. When the curtain opens, five beautiful ladies take front and center on the stage, singing and dancing their sultry song. The crowd goes wild before settling down to unite as impromptu backup singers. Kira and I join in, ad-libbing and making up our own dance routine while taking advantage of the darkened dance floor.

Though I would love nothing more than to take her home and rock her world until the sun comes up tomorrow, I know tonight is a rare treat for her. Dates, dinner, dancing, drinks—this atmosphere isn't something she's experienced much outside of working her asset for more information. Simply having fun wasn't in her training manual. For now, we are breaking all the rules and crossing all the lines—even that blurred line that still threatens to keep us apart. The line on the map that prompts my country to say she doesn't belong in it anymore.

I'm not ready to accept that decision, so I'm soaking up the time while we have it.

Since we have no intention of leaving anytime soon, I open a tab and keep the beer coming. We don't leave the dance floor all night, exploring each other through our movements with every song coming from the speakers. When the bar finally shuts down, we stumble out the doors with permanent smiles affixed to our faces and not a wisp of air between us. Taking my state of inebriation into account, I consider calling a taxi to take us back to the house. While doing undercover work, I've had to drive while intoxicated plenty of times. Getting a ride after knocking back a few too many doesn't exactly scream "badass criminal." Though I don't condone it for the average civilian, I have had extensive training in driving under the influence.

Lucky me, I realize I don't have to make that decision the moment we step onto the sidewalk outside the club.

"It's about damn time. You've literally danced your ass off tonight. You have absolutely no ass left now, Silas." Even drunk as I am, there's no way I can mistake his smirk or his smartass remarks.

"Shadow. What the hell are you doing here?"

"What do you think I'm doing here? You have enough people looking for you now to form a regiment. You're not exactly making it hard for them to find you. At least wear a disguise if you're going out and getting caught on every traffic camera from here to Jacksonville." He shakes his head and opens the back door of his truck. With a sideways jerk of his head, he motions for us to get inside. Kira slides in first. "Reaper has your rental vehicle —complete with new tags. And when we get home, you're explaining to my wife why I've been out all night. I'm not taking the fall for this one."

"This is Shadow?" Kira looks between the muscular mountain of a man and me. "The one you told me about?"

"That's him." I nod and shake his hand before sliding into the back seat beside Kira.

"You didn't tell me he's CIA, too." She can't hide the concern in her tone.

"What makes you think I'm CIA?" He closes the driver-side door and starts the vehicle.

"It's not as if you're trying to hide it. If you were with any other government agency, you would've brought a SWAT team and shut down the club to get us. Instead, you're helping us get away. Not many people have the steel balls to pull off something like that."

Shadow throws his head back in laughter. "No wonder you're hiding this one. I like her already. Yes, I'm CIA, but you're safe. Silas, Nick, and Roman are three of the best men I know. The other three men I trust also are waiting to help."

"I don't know what to say. 'Thank you' isn't hardly enough for putting your lives on the line for someone you don't even know." She fights the emotion building in her voice. That small action reveals more than she knows. It tells me she doesn't know what it's like to have a family who supports her regardless of the circumstances.

"We have Silas's back no matter what, darlin'. If he believes in you enough to stick his neck out like this, the rest of us damn sure won't let him do it alone." Shadow glances at us in the rearview mirror as he speaks.

"You know, that's almost enough to make me forgive you for the last time you cheated me out of the 'favorite uncle' title."

"I won that title again fair and square, and you know

that's the truth. It wasn't my fault you fell for that old trick."

"What old trick was that?" Kira looks at me, barely able to contain her amusement.

When I'm silent for two seconds too long, Shadow is more than willing to tell the story. "Whoever plays the funniest prank wins. It's as simple as that. He probably told you about the cakes, right?"

"Yes, he did, and I couldn't help but laugh. Just the picture of that scene in my mind was hilarious."

"It really was great. But this one was even better. When we all crash at Noah and Brianna's house, the kids like to help make breakfast for everyone. So we made a special breakfast for Uncle Silas. We poured the cereal in his favorite bowl and covered it with milk...then we put it in the freezer overnight. The next morning, we put just a splash of milk on top to hide the frozen mixture below, then laughed our asses off when he grabbed a spoon and tried to dig in."

"Yeah, that was really hilarious." I rub the corner of my eye, purposely using my middle finger while staring directly into his eyes.

"The kids voted—they said I'm the fun uncle." Shadow shrugs, not giving a shit that he isn't actually related to them.

"Those are awesome pranks. How do you come up with this stuff?" Kira looks at me and laughs. Again.

"I have a few tricks up my sleeve. I'm saving my best

jokes for when they're older and won't tell their mother what I've taught them."

"You're more afraid of Brianna than Silas?"

"Absolutely!" Shadow and I answer at the same time.

"I hope I get to meet her one day." Kira's smile beams until she realizes time may not be on our side. The somber thought hits us at the same time, changing the mood in the vehicle in a split second.

In a feeble attempt to regain the lighthearted banter, I wrap my arm around her and pull her against me. "Be careful what you wish for, Kira. You just may get it."

"Starting tomorrow, we have a plan to execute. I've done a little recon of my own while you two danced the night away. Something big is going down in the next few weeks. I don't have all the important details yet, but I've squeezed a few of my old contacts to get as much preliminary information as I could."

"What'd they tell you?"

"Only that they've been put on alert to move precious cargo at a moment's notice once it arrives. They're not keeping these new people around to service local customers this time. Sounds like they're getting the buyers lined up and moving the girls out of the area as soon as they sell. My gut tells me they've been spooked by something—maybe even by your noticeable disappearance. But we'll be here waiting for them, regardless."

"How hot is the heat on us right now?" Although I don't want the honest answer, I need to know. "Will we put their capture at risk by being there?"

"The longer you hide, the hotter it'll get, my friend. You know that. I had a chat with the deputy director earlier today and convinced him he's worrying over nothing. We all go dark when we're eyeball-deep in a case. With everything at stake in this one, you needed some time off the grid. He agreed to cool his jets, but we both know that'll only last for so long. If we can keep you both from looking anything like yourselves, maybe we can pull off this mad caper without a hitch."

Maybe. Exactly.

CHAPTER 15

Kira

*W*hen we pull into the driveway, the number of cars parked there is a dead giveaway that the entire team is here. That does give me some peace, though, knowing we have plenty of backup to help us get through this nightmare. The massive show of support by mobilizing at the first sign of a friend in distress from a group of people is largely unheard of these days. It makes me wonder if Silas has any idea how fortunate he is to have all of them by his side. Even knowing the potential consequences, Shadow still stuck his neck out for us in more than one way.

The front door swings open when the truck comes to a full stop, and one of the most beautiful women in the world walks toward us with a determined stride. When I recognize her, even through the beer goggles I'm still wearing, my jaw drops open.

"Is that…Elle Sinclair?" I can't believe my eyes. The famous actress-slash-model is marching straight toward us.

"Elle Kane now, but yes, that's her," Shadow replies before releasing a heavy sigh. "Silas, this is all your fault."

Elle jerks the driver's door open then folds her arms over her body. "Devon, where have you been all night? In what world is it okay for you not to call and tell me you're safe?"

"There is no such world, I know, babe. Trust me. This is actually all on Silas. Since he's gone rogue, I couldn't use my phone and give away our location. I had to wait outside the Copa Room all night while he drank, danced, watched cabaret shows, and had a great time. He closed down the bar. You know I'd much rather have been here with you." Shadow pulls her into his arms and places sweet kisses all over her face until she finally relents and smiles.

"Silas, is that true?" She cocks one eyebrow at him and waits.

"Yes, that's all true. Shadow is covering my ass in so many ways right now that I'll never be able to repay him for all the favors I owe him."

"Then I can't feel sorry for you over what's about to happen." The smile that covers her face is pure evil, and I can't help but laugh out loud in spite of it.

"What's about to happen?" The confused expression

on his face instantly changes when another voice calls out his name.

"Well, well, well, as I live and breathe. If it isn't Silas Steele, in the flesh…and in the country. You told me you were in a remote village in Africa, guarding a king against an uprising, so you couldn't make it to my birthday party. Silas, you look me in the eye right now. Did you lie to me about that? Did you skip my birthday party by lying to me?"

Silas drops his chin to his chest and shakes his head from side to side. "Shadow," he mutters under his breath. "I'm so going to kick your ass for this."

Shadow tries to contain his laughter, but it gets the better of him anyway. He tries to cover it up with a fake cough. "You know what happens if you lie to Liz."

"Liz, you know I would've been at your party if I had any other choice. But I was extremely busy with work and couldn't get away. This is Kira, and I've been protecting her from all kinds of threats. I couldn't tell you about her, and I couldn't leave her with no defense either."

Her eyes narrow, crinkling at the corners, and her hands are curled into fists on her hips. She's not completely buying his story. "You should've called me. I'm a super-spy now, you know. All those tricks and tips you withheld from me have been unlocked and are part of my arsenal at last. I can keep her safe much better than you can. No one would dare mess with me."

"There's no doubt about that, Liz. It's just that I'm

trying to save you from that pesky little law regarding impersonating a federal officer. They really don't play around with that one."

Another beautiful woman with long blond hair and the sweetest smile joins us. "All right, everyone, you know I love a family reunion more than anyone, but we need to wrap this up. It's either really late or really early, depending on how you look at it. Either way, we only have a few hours to grab some sleep before all the fun starts. Last one up after the kids wake will be sorry."

"You're lucky Brianna saved your ass, Silas. Don't think for one second this is over, though."

"Wouldn't dream of it, Liz." The group chuckles at Silas's expense, but it's all done in love and playfulness. Silas envelops the sweet blond lady in a bear hug and kisses the side of her head. "Thank you for saving me. You're my favorite sister-in-law."

"I'm your only sister-in-law, but you're welcome. It's good to have you home again."

Silas turns to me, keeping one arm loosely slung around her shoulders. "Brianna, this is Kira Petrova. Kira, this is Brianna Steele, my brother's wife and the best damn sister-in-law in the world."

I extend my hand to shake hers, but she bats it away. "Sweetie, we hug in this family. You'll just have to get used to it." Then she wraps her arms around me and squeezes me with a gentle rocking motion before releasing me.

"It's so nice to meet you. I've heard so much about

you—all good, I promise. In fact, I just told Shadow and Silas on the way here that I hoped to meet you one day."

"It's great to meet you. Come on in and get some rest while you can. This house will be crazy tomorrow." She hooks her arm through mine and escorts me inside as if we're long-lost sisters. "You look awesome in that dress. It fits you much better than it does me."

Inside is mostly dark and quiet, probably because the children are asleep, and the parents want them to stay that way for a few more hours at least. We tiptoe up the stairs, and she leaves me alone in the guest bedroom I'd chosen earlier. I close the door behind me to get ready for bed, for what little time I have left to sleep. Once I'm changed and comfortably resting in the bed, I feel a large, warm body slide into the bed behind me before an arm snakes over my waist.

"I didn't even hear you come in," I whisper into the darkness.

"I thought you may already be asleep and didn't want to wake you. But I also didn't want to sleep without you tonight. Hope you don't mind."

"I don't mind at all."

"Good, because I'm comfortable now and I'm not getting up."

We chuckle in the darkness, feeling more relaxed with each other than we did even just earlier today. Sleep quickly takes over, wrapping around me like a warm blanket and pulling me under its irresistible spell. The next time I stir, it's morning and we're still in the exact position we passed out in. Silas's body is so warm. It's as if he has a furnace burning on high inside him. That also makes it impossible to get out of bed—I've never had a more restful night of sleep before.

"I smell bacon," I whisper.

"I smell coffee." His morning voice is a deep and raspy murmur near my ear and sends goose bumps fanning out down my arm. "But it doesn't tempt me enough to get out of bed yet. Go back to sleep."

"Won't they be mad we missed breakfast?"

"Nope. My sister is here, and she's cooking. She got plenty of sleep last night. We didn't. Back to sleep now." He curls his arm tighter around me, not really giving me a choice but to relax against him and indulge in extra sleep.

Just as my thoughts settle and I begin to drift back to sleep, the sound of several little feet rushing toward us jars me awake again. Before I have time to lift my head, small bodies pounce on us from every direction, followed by uncontainable and infectious giggling. I roll over onto my back and watch the three little kids, two girls and one boy, climb all over Silas while he pretends to be asleep.

"Uncle Silas, Daddy said it's time for you to get up." The smallest girl draws out his name, only she says it more like "uncky" in her innocent voice. She crawls up to his face and uses her little fingers to pry one of his eyes open, then leans her eye down close to his. "Are you awake yet?"

He remains completely still until the other two join

her at his head, totally surrounding him now. When they're still for more than two seconds, his eyes fly open and he roars loudly as he lifts his head off the pillow. Their shrill shrieks fill the bedroom before they flop onto the bed in laughter. Silas raises up, using his arm as a prop, and tickles them with his free hand.

"Who do you think you are, ambushing me in my sleep like that? When I'm weak and defenseless, even." He grabs one of the girls and blows raspberries on her belly, making her laugh and scream at the same time.

The other two lift their shirts, each taunting him. "You can't do that to me."

"Me either! You can't catch me!"

Of course, he does catch them both with no effort at all and buries his face in their bellies to tickle them. With all three given equal attention, he sits up and pulls them into his lap. Their little faces beam with happiness, making my heart pinch in my chest.

"Amelia, Emery, and Gray, this is Kira. Kira, these are my nieces and nephew. Amelia is the oldest, and as you can see, Emery and Gray are twins. Say hello to Kira, guys."

"Hi, Kira," they say in unison, though the sound of the R is more of a W. They're too adorable for words.

"Hi, Amelia, Emery, and Gray. It's very nice to meet all of you. Seems to me you guys love your uncle Silas a lot, huh?"

"Yeah, we do." Gray nods his head. "But Shadow says not to tell him he's our favorite."

"What? Shadow told you not to tell me that?" Silas asks, clarifying what he heard.

"Yep. Uncle Shadow gives us a dollar every time." Gray's eyes open wide at the mention of the bribe payment.

"Shadows pays you a dollar so you'll say he's your favorite uncle? All three of you?"

"Yeah. We're gonna be rich." Gray smiles and nods.

"Is Silas really your favorite uncle?" I lift my eyes to meet Silas's, waiting for the kids to confirm what I can already see.

"Yes," they all three reply and lean against his chest. He wraps his arms around them, pretending to squeeze them extra hard while their giggles fill the room with so much love, it's impossible to ignore.

"I've lost all three of my kids. Has anyone up here seen them?" Brianna calls from the hallway, her tone betraying her question, though. "They're supposed to be eating breakfast, but they all disappeared at the same time."

"Hurry! Hide!" Silas whispers a little too loudly to be serious. But the kids comply, pulling the comforter over their heads. While they still sit upright in his lap.

Brianna stops in the doorway, smirking at Silas. "Oh my, whatever will I do? I can't find my children anywhere. I guess they're lost forever."

The comforter giggles.

Silas smiles and shrugs. "I'm afraid we can't help you, Bri. As you can see, there are no children in here."

She arches one eyebrow at him, though she can't hide her smile. "I wouldn't go that far, Silas. I think there's at least one big kid in here."

"Don't talk about Kira like that, Brianna. You just met her."

Brianna throws her head back in laughter. "Yeah, you keep telling yourself that, Silas. If you happen to see my kids, tell them I said to get their little butts downstairs and eat, or all four of you will be in big trouble."

"I'll make sure they get the message if I see them."

When we hear Brianna's footsteps on the stairs, Silas pulls the comforter off the top of their heads. "She's gone now. The coast is clear."

Emery, the younger girl, turns around and puts her tiny hands on his cheeks. "I love you, Uncle Silas."

And here I thought my heart already had melted. I was so wrong—that is the sweetest thing I've ever seen.

"I love you too, sweet girl. Now give me a big hug and kiss then go eat before we all get in trouble."

I am pleasantly surprised when all three share their hugs and kisses with me once they've finished with Silas. They're gone just as quickly as they appeared, all rushing out the door and down the stairs. When I glance over at Silas, he's still staring at the doorway with a smile on his face.

"They really do love you. Anyone can see that."

"They're the best. My sister Chaise's kids are too. I can't imagine not being in their lives. There was a long time when I didn't see my brother or my sister. My brother was stationed overseas in hostile territory, and I was undercover God knows where, plus I didn't get along with my dad. But now, you couldn't pay me enough to make me stay away from any of them."

A sobering thought hits me like a two-ton sledge-hammer right in the chest. The risks he's taking by simply being associated with me right now will take him away from his family. After years of being apart, not seeing his siblings grow up or his parents grow older, he finally has them back again. The pure delight on his face when they crawled over him as if he was their human jungle gym was nothing compared to confirming he is their favorite. When little Emery told him she loved him, I saw the first sign of vulnerability in him. He's always kept himself well guarded around me.

Those kids have him wrapped around their little fingers, right where he wants to be.

I can't let him put his entire life at risk for me, especially now that I've seen firsthand that his work isn't his whole life the way mine has been.

He won't like what I have to say, because even though he blurs the lines as a CIA officer, honor and duty still guide his every step. But there's no way around it...no way around what I have to do now.

I pause, knowing what I'm about to say won't be received well. It's just not in his nature—and I can't be the cause of his downfall. "Silas, I need to say something."

"Shoot."

"You have to get out of this investigation. You, your family, and your friends all need to leave. There are way too many people involved, and that means too many people have their necks on the chopping block for me. No matter what anyone does to me, I'll never reveal any names or anything about who has helped me. But I have to get far away from you—to protect you. I need to do this. I'll see it through to the end from here."

One side of his mouth lifts in a sexy smirk before he pulls me into his arms. "No, baby, there's no way you're doing this alone. I've already stepped across that line in the sand, leaving a blurry mark in its place. We're past the two weeks my deputy director gave me to finish this. My family and friends, unfortunately, are accustomed to handling themselves in dangerous situations. They can hold their own in this one, too.

"We're made of Steele, baby. And we know we're stronger with each other, without a doubt. If one person involved didn't want to take the risk, they wouldn't. The fact that they are means they believe you're worth it. You've been inducted into the family, Kira. They'd never turn their backs on you, even if you tried to run away."

CHAPTER 16

Silas

"Might as well get up now. We won't get any more sleep after all."

After we get dressed, Kira and I head down to the kitchen for a quick bite to eat before our brainstorming session with Noah and his team. Chaise stands at the counter, sipping on a piping hot cup of coffee when we enter the room. She sets down the mug and rushes into my arms.

"Hey, big brother. It's been too long since I've seen you. I've missed you."

"I've missed you too, baby girl. You know you're welcome to visit me in DC anytime you want to come." With a kiss on her cheek, I release her and head for the coffee carafe myself.

"Be careful, I just may take you up on that and leave Colton with the kids."

As soon as the words leave her mouth, her husband enters the room and walks straight to her. "What was that about leaving me behind?"

She dismisses him with a wave of her hand before raising up on her toes to plant a kiss on his lips. "You know I'd never leave you, babe."

One thing I can give Bull full credit for is how much he loves my little sister. His protectiveness of her is second only to his deep adoration. I couldn't have hand-picked a better man to care for Chaise.

Bull turns to me and extends his hand. "Good to see you, Silas."

"You too, man." I turn and draw Kira to my side and introduce her to my sister and brother-in-law.

"Now, do you prefer I call you Colton or Bull?" The confused expression on Kira's face is endearing. She's trying to keep up with all the names and faces being thrown at her all at once.

"You can call me Bull. The only person besides my parents who calls me Colton is Chaise."

"That's only because I refuse to admit how stubborn and bullheaded he is." Chaise laughs as she wraps her arm around his waist. "But he knows how much I love him."

Their son rushes me and wraps himself around my leg, holding on as tightly as his hands can grip. When I reach down to ruffle his hair, he grabs my hand with both of his in our standing tug-of-war fight. "And this is their son, Cason. He's six, so only a little younger than Amelia. I'm also his favorite uncle."

Kira smiles and says hello to Cason. He studies her for a second before looking up at me. "Wow, Uncle Silas. She's too pretty for you. She should be my girlfriend. And I'm six *and a half.*"

"Hey—watch it now. We have a guy code around here. No stealing of women. Check the rule book."

"You are such a handsome little man." She runs her fingers through his thick hair. His cheeks lift with a big smile.

"Uncle Silas always says lines are for crossing and rules are for breaking." Cason looks back at me and shrugs. "Your loss, dude."

The room erupts with laughter while Cason and I pretend to have a serious staring contest.

"This little beauty is Chaise's daughter, Lex. She's recently turned a year old. I'm also her favorite." I lift her out of the playpen to cover her little face in kisses. She laughs and puts her little hands on my face. Then she turns her attention to Kira, extending her arms and leaning toward her.

Kira is hesitant to take her at first, but the two seem to form an instant bond. Kira can't wipe the smile off her face as she coos at and talks to Lex. Then Kira's eyes roam around the room, lingering on every face sitting around the table a little too long to be considered casual glances.

Interesting.

"There's one more part of the extended family I want you to meet. This is Rebel and his wife, Heather. Those adorable twins beside them are Kinsley and Elias. They're the same age as Cason. I'm also their favorite uncle."

"Now, Silas. We all know I'm the favorite uncle here." Shadow and Elle walk into the kitchen together, but he has the nerve to smile right to my face after all his games and trickery. At first, I'm tempted to call him on his bullshit, but I decide revenge is better served cold. So he'll choke on it.

"Whatever you say, Shadow. You keep believing that lie."

With introductions out of the way, Kira and I join them at the table and eat until we're stuffed. Kira refuses Chaise's offer to take Kinsley so she can eat in peace. She takes one bite and gives her the next one. One seems to be equally as taken with the other.

"It looks like Shadow and I will both lose our 'favorite' status to Kira any minute now."

"You've both already lost it. You just don't realize it yet." She cuts her eyes up at me and flashes a mischievous grin.

"There's finally someone who can keep Silas in line. I love it," Shadow quips.

As appealing as the initial notion may be, I'm not looking for anyone to keep me in line or keep me anywhere, for that matter. I like my life as it is—uncomplicated with a lot of freedom to do as I please. Roaming from shore to shore or anywhere around the globe at a moment's notice doesn't exactly lend to a happy home. In fact, a serious relationship isn't even anything I've ever seriously considered before.

"I'm glad you're having such a good time at my expense. You'll pay for this later in a very painful way."

He just laughs it off like he does most everything else, then follows up with a shit-eating grin. The bad thing about Shadow is he's a damn good CIA officer himself, with an uncanny ability to see through others, even those who are deep undercover. Knowing he's actively trying to probe my mind through watching my body language is a little unsettling. I don't like being on this side of the equation...and the bastard knows it.

By the time we finish breakfast and head toward Noah's office, we have additional visitors and even more backup for the major trap we're laying for our friendly senator and his partners. Nick, Roman, and Brad arrive with Savannah, Mira, and more kids in tow. We stop in the foyer to greet everyone and chat before disappearing into our version of a war room.

"If all else fails, at least we can build our own army with all these kids around here. They may be more effective than we are anyway. When are you and Elle having kids, Shadow? We may need to start recruiting them sooner rather than later." I turn my attention to my friendly adversary.

A look passes between the couple after my question—

Elle is aggravated, and Shadow is uncomfortable. There is no way in hell I'm letting him off the hook with this one. She's ready for kids, and he's not quite there yet. Time to stoke the fire under his ass and use it to my advantage in every way possible.

"Uh, we're in active, hostile negotiations about that very sensitive topic right now. Let's not muddy the waters by bringing that into our more immediate plans." I've literally never seen Shadow nervous in this way before. I really like it.

"All right, let's get this locked down as soon as possible." Noah nips that conversation in the bud before it can gain traction. "Brad, let's get the blueprints up in my office and go over every inch of the building layout."

"On it, Reap." Brad leads the way, and the rest of us follow.

"Savannah and Mira—bring the babies into the den with the rest of us. The guys have plenty to keep them busy for a while in Noah's office. We girls can all get to know each other in a more relaxing setting." Brianna, ever the gracious host, leads the way for her company. That little lady has never met a stranger in her life.

Kira hesitates for a moment until I take her hand in mine and pull her along with me. "You come with me, love. You're part of this op too. You have more at stake than any of us."

"I wasn't sure how much I'd be trusted in a room full of federal agents and military commandos. Especially when they're all here for recon on a covert and illegal operation."

"Are you kidding? You'll fit right in."

We walk into the office together, and Shadow's eyes immediately drop to our joined hands. He hits me with a satisfied smirk, and I know this is only the beginning of our incessant bantering. So I purposely continue holding her hand so that Shadow doesn't think his taunting is getting to me. I mean, it is—a little—but he doesn't need to know.

"Shadow did some initial recon for us, gathering insider information on the senator and what he does in his free time while he's in Miami. Other than the beach, golf course, and a weekly visit to the spa, he doesn't do much else on the regular. The extended stay of three or four weeks is out of the ordinary, though." Noah boots up his computer and turns on the large TV screen so Brad can display the blueprints for the day spa facility.

"Silas and Kira, we have the original blueprints and an expansion filed later for a building permit, but there's always the strong possibility the new plans don't include everything. You two have an appointment for a couple's massage later today. Get inside, get lost, and figure out what's missing from our information."

"Can I request that we get lost inside the building after our massage? I could really use one and don't want to be kicked out before our appointment." I'm only partially kidding. Now that Noah's mentioned it, I actually am looking forward to it.

"That would probably make more sense anyway. When you get dressed again, just turn the wrong way out of the room and have a look around."

Kira examines every detail of the screen, her eyes slowly moving from room to room. "Okay, that layout is burned into my brain now. We shouldn't have any trouble finding a new door or extra room once we're inside."

"Photographic memory?" I ask. "Nice."

"Yes, pretty much, for as long as I can remember. It has its pros and cons. I'd rather be able to forget some of the things I've seen before."

"Not knowing where or how this is going down means we'll have to take shifts on stakeout so that someone is always close by to make a move if needed. We've already set up a schedule with teams of two. Brad, I need you to stay here and help coordinate the tech piece. If Silas and Kira find undocumented rooms, they can put mole cameras in place if they can get a clear signal. Once you have us linked up, we can rotate watching the inside cameras too." Noah's always been the man with the plan. That shows how brothers' personalities can be in stark contrast—he plans every last detail, while I prefer to wing it and see what happens.

Noah gives us the days and times of our shifts for the week, along with our marching orders. He and Rebel are taking the first night. Our working theory is it's too dangerous to bring the people they intend to sell rather than enslave inside the business during the day. They'll most likely attempt to make all their shady deals at night, with each buyer walking their new merchandise out just as quickly as they walk in.

But experience and common sense tell us this will never happen the way we expect, so we have to stay alert at all times. We review the area around the building once again, identifying the best spots to park and observe who comes and goes, walk and peruse the block, and watch different angles of the building for any signs of trouble. When they make their move, I hope I'm the one on watch so I can tear those assholes apart with my bare hands.

"You two should get going. Don't want you to be late for your massage." Noah opens the door and steps out into the hall. "The rest of us will be around here somewhere. If you don't hear from us in a few hours, send help because that means all the kids have hog-tied and stuffed us into the closets."

"Now that I might even pay to see." I grab Kira's hand again and head toward the front door. "We'll check on everyone later—after our relaxing massage and a long stroll inside the building. That should give the kids plenty of time to stage their coup."

Kira and I walk out the front door with a mixture of laughter and obscenities coming from the group of men behind us. She looks over at me and bursts out laughing. Seeing her carefree side tugs at my heartstrings because I know she hasn't had many opportunities just to relax and be herself. Even though we're still technically working, my goal is to make the next few weeks as fun and special as I can under the circumstances.

When we're in Noah's truck on the way to our appointment, I glance over at her with an intentionally flirty and naughty expression. "You know what?"

"What?" Her bright smile covers her face when she realizes I'm still in playful mode.

"We're getting a couple's massage."

"Yeah, I know. And?" Her eyebrows draw down, and she tilts her head to the side.

"That means we'll be in the same room, so I get to see you completely and totally butt naked. Like, your boobies and everything." I waggle my eyebrows and nod, keeping a huge grin on my face.

When she leans her head back to laugh at my stupidity, her long black hair cascades over her shoulders and down her back. The sheer magnificence of her beauty takes my breath away.

The first thought that fires in my brain is, *How can I ever let her leave?*

Fuck.

I may be in trouble after all.

CHAPTER 17

Kira

Whatever I expected a shady spa that acts as a front for a human trafficking scheme to look like, this isn't it.

This is a five-star luxury health resort with every possible amenity I could imagine, and some I didn't even realize existed. After we sign in and complete the required paperwork, the receptionist brings us each a glass of chilled water flavored with cucumber. Softly in the background, sounds of nature come from the speakers strategically placed around the room. The extra-padded Adirondack chairs instantly put me at ease. The mixture of ambiance and comfort is perfect to create a feeling of serenity.

"Silas and Kira?" A soft voice calls out, and I look up to see an attractive young blonde.

Her hair is pulled back from her face in a ponytail, and she has a welcoming smile. She leads us to the back and shows us to the separate dressing rooms. After explaining how to use the lockers and where to find the robes and slippers, she points out the adjoining waiting room where we'll wait for our massage therapists to come get us.

Nothing about this establishment has raised the first red flag yet, prompting a slight panic attack to flare up in my chest. What if this is the wrong place? What if we've completely misread all the signs? What if this is a wild goose chase, and the very people we're trying to take down have gotten away with everything after all?

After I secure my things in the locker and meet Silas in the posh waiting room, I walk straight up to him, ready to abandon the entire mission. I feel like I've wasted everyone's time and energy on top of putting them all at risk of being arrested just because they wanted to help me.

"Don't say it." His voice is low, and he leans in, his lips close to mine. He rubs his knuckles over my cheek, igniting every nerve ending in my body at once with his simple touch. "We're not wrong. This is a legitimate business, but that doesn't mean they aren't dirty. You have to trust me on this."

"Silas, I do trust you. You have to know that by now." The rest of what I want to say—what I need to say—is on the tip of my tongue. The expression on his face says he knows there's an unspoken "but" at the end of my statement. This is entirely the wrong time to bring it up, though.

His ability to read me like an open book is equally comforting and unsettling. No secrets and no surprises, but that leaves me very few options to protect him…even from himself.

He acknowledges I'm not ready to voice my reluctance with a simple nod. "We'll finish that conversation later. For now, let's suffer through one of the highest-rated massages in South Florida, then we can get lost in the maze of hallways and doorways."

Then he closes the gap between us, and his lips cover mine. The smoldering spark that's always burning just below the surface immediately ignites into an inferno. He slides his hands around my waist, the warmth seeping through the terry cloth robe as if I'm not even wearing it. The tip of his tongue glides across the part in my lips, seeking entry—only he doesn't need to ask for permission. I'm already there, willing and waiting for him when his velvety soft tongue strokes across mine.

I move my hands up his chest, committing every dip and curve of his muscles to memory until I reach the back of his neck. His hair is probably the only soft part of his entire body, and I feel a slight shudder travel through him when I run my fingers through it. My nails lightly scratch his scalp just before I close my fist, gripping his hair with a small tug. His lips leave mine, trailing across my cheek and down the side of my neck. The licks, nips, and bites he scatters across my skin between kisses kick my libido into overdrive. I'm more than tempted to initiate a repeat of our ocean excursion right here in this room—the one anyone could walk into at any moment.

"This is going to be a long fucking day," he murmurs against my skin. "Only one taste of you is cruel and unusual punishment."

"Tonight." My breathy one-word reply is all I can manage at the moment.

"Fucking right, tonight. The first second we're alone, you'll be mine in every possible way."

Is it too soon to say I already am?

Maybe.

But I know, without a doubt, there's no one else who has ever made me feel this way. I never believed in fate before meeting him. Now, I can't imagine our meeting simply being left to chance.

We each take a half step backward from each other when we hear the door open, as if we're a couple teenagers about to be caught making out. Two women in spa uniforms enter, holding clipboards with our paper-work attached. With friendly smiles, they greet us by name and ask what we'd most like to get out of this visit. Two things immediately pop into my mind, but replying my only goal is to finish what I just started with Silas then stop the dirty senator seems inappropriate.

"I carry a lot of tension in my neck and shoulders, so that's my main area of concern." I somehow manage to come up with an intelligent response.

"Same for me." When I look up at Silas, it takes all my willpower not to laugh out loud at his smug expression. He had the same initial thoughts I had.

"We can take care of that for you both. Follow us."

We walk down a long hallway, and I check off the location of each door as we pass, comparing it to the image still clear in my mind. When we reach the couples room, I'm surprised to see a small hot tub in the floor between the two massage beds. Rose petals float on the surface of the water, adding a natural floral fragrance to the room.

"I'm setting this timer for twenty minutes so you two can soak in the tub and loosen up your muscles before we start your massage. When the alarm goes off, dry off and lie face up on the tables. We'll knock before coming in, so don't feel rushed." The therapist puts the timer on the table beside the massage oils before leaving us alone.

"I was only half joking before, but I can't say I'm disappointed at all. Do you need any help removing your robe?" The predatory gleam in his eyes makes my blood boil in the best way.

"Actually, I do need help. This bow I tied in the belt is nearly impossible to untie."

"First of all, let me show you what 'very hard' actually is. Secondly, I'll tear it off you with my teeth if I have to." He grips my hips in his big hands and pulls me toward him, and I go more than willingly. I love his playful alpha side.

Before I even realize the belt is untied, I feel the

warmth of his hands on my skin, pushing the robe off my shoulders until it falls to the floor behind me. Not to be left out, I move my hands under his robe and help him out of it. The heat of his body drives away any chill from the air in the room.

"It was only a few minutes ago when we agreed to wait until tonight. Now I don't know that I can wait. But the ticking of that alarm reminds me why I have to—because there's no way I can do everything I've planned for you in less than twenty minutes. Our first time happened way too fast. I didn't get to hear you scream, so I'm making up for that later by taking my time to touch you, taste you, and feel you. I'll make sure you're so fucking ready for me that you're begging for it. Then I'm burying my face between your legs until I feel your thighs quiver uncontrollably. After I have you all worked up into a frenzy, we'll wake the entire house with you screaming my name."

The words simply tumble out of my mouth without a single forethought. "Fuck me, that's so hot."

He skims his hand along my jaw then he gently grips my chin with his thumb and forefinger. The heat radiates from his eyes as he stares into mine. "That's exactly what I plan to do. All fucking night."

"How long is this massage again? I'm thinking we should go check in to a hotel somewhere instead of staying with your family."

"I like how you think. Now, it's time to get you hot and wet."

"I already am."

He quirks one eyebrow and gives me a sexy smirk. "Oh yeah? Maybe I should check?"

My nod may be a little too enthusiastic. He steps into the hot tub and pulls me toward him, his gaze feasting on me as I join him in the water. We sink down into it, our hands instinctively seeking the other. When he skates his fingers up my inner thigh at a painstakingly slow pace, I know he's giving me every opportunity to stop him. There's no way in hell that's happening, though. His hand stills when mine covers it—but the eagerness returns full force when I quickly pull him to his original destination.

He buries one finger deep inside me while rubbing my clit with his thumb. His tongue leaves a hot trail along my collarbone before he dips his mouth to my nipple. When he adds a second finger, he also increases the pressure and speed of his sensual assault. It's all I can do to keep from crying out his name when my climax rips through me. I cling to him, my fingers digging into his shoulders as I ride the wave until it subsides.

I slide my hand down his body and grasp his rock-hard cock, ready and willing to give him the same pleasure, however he wants it. He wraps his hand around mine then halts my movement.

"Hold that thought, babe. If you keep going, we'll end up fucking right here on the floor. Only, I won't stop when they walk back in. When we leave here, we're getting a room for fucking certain."

"Holy shit. Is it wrong that part of me wants to test you to see if you really wouldn't stop?"

A dangerous, feral expression overtakes his features, and it's such a fucking turn-on. Silas is one heartbeat from losing his calm and cool composure. I've wondered if there was a part of him that he kept hidden away, behind the strict lines he never crosses. Now I know for sure—Silas has a very dark and dangerous side.

"I'll fucking show you right now. We'll get kicked out of here and won't complete our assignment, but it'll be fucking worth it."

The alarm goes off, effectively bringing us out of our carnal haze and putting our priorities back into perspective. He steps out of the hot tub and grabs the towels, holding one out for me to walk into. When he wraps the towel around me, he keeps his arms around me too. Then he kisses me softly, showing a stark contrast to the savage man who just made an appearance. With his own Mr. Hyde safely tucked back in his cage, Silas Steele is back in character and back in his element.

Then he helps me onto the massage table and covers me with the sheet before sliding his towel across his skin and lying on his table.

"Make sure she relaxes all your muscles, Kira. You'll need all the flexibility you can get in a couple of hours." His tone is casual, and his face is passive with his eyes closed and a small smile playing on his lips.

What the fuck? How am I supposed to relax now?

CHAPTER 18

Silas

*A*fter the best massage I've ever had, Kira and I assure the staff we know how to get back to the changing rooms. Once we're dressed again, we meet in the hall and start our search. We move quickly through the corridors, relying on our collective memories of the blueprints to identify anything out of the ordinary.

"Hold on." Kira stops and looks behind us before pointing to the door to our left. "This one wasn't on the newest design."

"By all means, let's see what's behind door number three." Using my undercover skills, I pick the lock. As softly as I can, I open the door and peek inside. "It's a long, dark hallway. I can't tell what's at the end of it from here."

"There was absolutely not a hallway shown on the

plans in this spot. Silas, if they're conducting their side business in a secret room, they could do it at any time of the day or night. How are they moving people in and out?"

"Stay here. If anyone comes back here, just say you got turned around. I have to see what's in here and where it leads."

I creep down the dark hallway, being careful not to make a sound when I move. By the time I reach the door at the end, my eyes have fully adjusted to the dim light. With an easy turn of the knob, I open the door without a creak. The outer door was locked, but they obviously feel comfortable leaving the inner one open.

As I scan the room, the sick feeling in the pit of my stomach grows worse. There's a reason why never underestimating your opponent is drilled into our heads during training. My maxim has always been, "Assume the worst of people and be pleasantly surprised when they don't let you down."

This is what ignoring my training and my gut gets me.

Without caring if I'm heard or seen, I rush back down the hall and find Kira still waiting for me. "Come on. There's someone I need to talk to—I just hope he's still there."

"Who? Where? What's going on? What'd you see?"

"Give me a minute, baby. If I'm right, I'll be able to explain everything very soon."

We reach the door to the men's changing room, and I

calm my pounding heart before rushing in and demanding answers. I'm relieved to find just the man I was looking for still inside, cleaning up after the day's patrons.

"Hey, buddy. I'm glad you're still in here. My teenage nephew needs a job in the worst way. This place is so nice, I thought I'd send him down here to put in an application. Can you tell me a little about working here? Does it pay well? How many days off do you get? Stuff like that."

The alarm on his face tells me everything I need to know. He shakes his head quickly from side to side.

"No, no. Uh, no opening." His broken English nearly breaks me. I've been so blind today, focused on Kira instead of my job, I missed all the signs.

The tiredness in his eyes.

His grim expression.

The way his hands shake when he reaches for items.

How his feet shuffle when he walks because he doesn't have the energy to lift them.

"That's too bad. Do you enjoy working here?" I purposely keep my tone easy and my body language friendly and open. I don't want to spook him more than he already is.

One of the manipulation tactics human traffickers use is to convince their prey that everyone is out to get them. That the police will lock them away forever. Even that ICE is always on standby to deport them to a forgotten prison somewhere offshore. If he thinks I'm anywhere in the neighborhood of being a cop, he'll cover and lie for his captors to save his own hide.

When he looks up at me, I can see the desire to spill all the illegal and immoral secrets he's witnessed behind these walls. He glances around nervously, as if he's waiting for someone to rush in and drag him away.

"I haven't even introduced myself. My name is Silas." I extend my hand to shake his.

He takes my hand, and I sense he's warming up to me more with each passing minute. "Cristano."

"Good to meet you, Cristano. Listen, I know you don't know me at all, but I have a feeling you're in trouble. I can help you if you let me before it gets worse."

Panic starts to set in, and I know he's about to bolt.

"If they said you'd be arrested and sent to prison if you were found out, they lied to you, my friend. That's not how our system works. If your employer isn't paying you and not allowing you any days off, they're not good people, Cristano. They're the criminals, not you. In fact, they're the ones committing illegal acts, but you're not. If they took your passport or your identification, they're definitely using you and not keeping up their end of whatever deal they made with you. Let me help."

He's listening—intently—and I can almost see the gears in his brain turning, putting all the pieces together. But he still doesn't respond.

"Cristano, if you've seen other people come here to work, then all of a sudden, they're gone, that's another bad sign. There are a lot of people who want to help people like you and others who are caught in this unfortunate situation. In fact, a friend of mine has put her life on the line just to stop the bad things that are happening here.

"She found out about it by accident, and her government will likely execute her if she returns home. But it's so important to her, she's willing to risk her life for it. She also found out they're about to bring in more new people. My concern is they'll sell you or someone else who works here to make room for the new people they're taking advantage of.

"If you've seen any of this happening here, I need you to tell me so I can help you. I promise you're not in trouble, and you won't ever be in trouble for trying to make a better life for yourself or your family. We can help you—just tell us what's really happening here."

The aged Filipino man breaks down in front of me, sobs racking his body. Despite the tears and guilt that riddle him, a spark of gratitude still shines in his eyes. Like a dam breaking from too much pressure pushing on a cracked wall, Cristano tells me everything he knows. Everything that's happened. Everything he's seen and experienced in the time he's worked here.

"I will get you out of this, Cristano. You have to trust me. They're bringing in more people to use and abuse soon, and we need to save them, too. Here's my phone number—memorize it or keep it hidden on you at all times. If you're in imminent danger, call me and I'll come rushing in. But if we can save everyone at once, you'll be a hero. Are you with me?"

"I'm with you, Silas." He hugs me, squeezing me as hard as his thin arms will allow.

When I leave, it's with my solemn vow that I'll be back for him. If it's the last thing I ever do, I'll keep that vow to him.

When Kira and I head back to the front desk to pay for our services, I can't contain my disgust for the people who work here, knowing they're helping to exploit destitute people who only want to make their lives better.

"How was your massage, Mr. Steele?" the receptionist asks tentatively. She must sense the fury boiling just beneath the surface.

"The massage was great. Thank you."

When we get in the truck, I relay the entire conversation to Kira. Tears of frustration and disgust well up in her eyes. "Silas, this has to stop. I saw a lady in the women's changing room when I first walked in. She was gone by the time I came out of the curtained area, but now I'm certain she's also being treated like a slave."

"It's going to stop, baby. And the people behind it are going to pay for the shit they've done. We'll make sure of it. Unfortunately, I have to break my promise to you. As much as I want to hide away in a hotel room with you for the next week, this has to take precedent. If we lose Cristano now, I'll never forgive myself."

"Of course. I completely agree. Whatever it takes,

let's do it. What did you find when you went into that dark hallway? What's back there?"

"It's one big room that's lined with beds—one after the other, only separated by half-length curtains to create a tiny room. Many of those beds appear to be new—no sheets, no clothes, nothing to show anyone occupies them. They must be making room to hold their 'precious cargo' until the sale is final. They've been keeping the people there to work for them for free...and who knows what else. I saw a few toys down there too, but I didn't see any kids."

"Did you see how they're bringing them in and out of the building?"

"They don't need a secret entrance to bring workers in and out. They can make them wear uniforms and march them in the front or back door without anyone questioning it. For the kids, they could simply hold their hand and walk in with them. It wouldn't seem so out of place that anyone would notify the authorities.

"I have to get back and share all this information with the team. We need to reevaluate our plan and time-line. My main concern is it'll all happening sooner rather than later. I could be wrong, though—that's happened once or twice before."

We get back to Noah's, and I retrace our every step and conversation for the team, with the exception of our time alone in the hot tub. That memory is only for Kira and me to relive...alone...as soon as humanly possible.

"Okay, then. We work just as well together without a

plan as we do with a plan. We'll watch it day and night. Everyone be ready to move at a moment's notice." Noah calmly removes Gray from the kitchen countertop he climbed up on.

"Daddy!" Gray's little face contorts to show his displeasure.

"What?"

"You ruined everything!"

"Yes, I'm sure I did, by getting you off the counter where you know you're not allowed to climb. But you still have to get down, little man."

"Seems like you have this dad gig down pat."

"Yeah, you should try it. Chaise and I need more nieces and nephews."

"I'm waiting for Shadow to take the plunge first. Then I'll go." I cut my eyes over at him, not bothering to hide the massive grin on my face.

His response is to flip me off, which only makes me laugh out loud.

"Looks like I'll be taking matters into my own hands soon. If I haven't already, that is," Elle says nonchalantly.

Shadow's eyes bulge out of his head, and his mouth drops open. I quickly turn around and snicker to myself. Otherwise, I absolutely will encourage her.

AFTER A WEEK OF ROUND-THE-CLOCK STAKEOUTS AT THE spa and violating the senator's privacy like we're a bunch of peeping toms, we're still no closer to shutting him down than when we started. The man has barely left his house, and those few times have only been to go out to dinner with his wife. I've raised concerns more than once that we're watching the wrong man, but the eyes-only documents he has keep tripping me up.

He wouldn't have those if he were clean.

Unless.

"Shadow, I need you to do me a favor." I find him sitting alone on the deck, staring at nothing while deep in thought.

"It's bothering you too. Isn't it?"

"What, exactly?"

"The idea that we may be focusing all our efforts on the wrong man. But everything we've seen points to him and him alone."

"Yeah, it is. It's a little too convenient, isn't it?" I sit down on the lounge chair beside him.

He nods. "And if my experience has taught me anything, it's not to trust anything that's packaged up all nice and neat. That's a sure sign of misdirection."

"Precisely. Which is why I want you to look into someone else for me. Since I'm technically a fugitive from justice right now, I can't very well call up my friends at Langley and ask for a favor." I hand him a piece of paper. "Find out everything you can on that man for me."

"You got it. Of course, you know this is the first place they'd look if they really wanted to find you, right? Your friends aren't trying too hard to hunt you down."

"You're right. No one is actively looking for me right now. Since I know the CIA has already found me. They're just biding their time right now, in case I'm right about everything."

Shadow nods slowly, weighing my words against his intrinsic understanding of how the agency works. But he doesn't verbally confirm anything.

The door to the deck opens, and Kira calls us both inside. "Brad said he's got something new for us." Shadow and I jump up and follow her into Noah's office.

"The senator is on the move," Brad says from behind his computer screen. "I've got eyes on him, so we're good."

"Just don't lose him. Let's see where he goes and what he's up to, preferably before it's too late." I sit down beside Brad and watch the red dot move on the map.

"They're headed to the private marina," Brad points out.

"I remember reading in his dossier that he has a boat there. Could that be how they're transporting the people into the country?" Kira moves to stand beside me and puts her hand on my shoulder when she leans over to stare at the red dot.

"That's a very good possibility. I'm sure a man of his stature has a large yacht with plenty of holding space." I sit back and fold my arms over my chest. "If he goes out into international waters, that's a sure sign he's up to no good."

"Anyone have an overwhelming urge to rush out and shop for a boat down at the marina right now?" Shadow asks.

"As a matter of fact, I do." I stand and follow him out to his truck. "I've always wanted a boat."

"You're not leaving me behind while you go boat shopping. I'm coming with you." Kira is hot on my heels, refusing to stay here.

The three of us head down to the marina to be there when Senator Hunt's boat docks again. If he unloads his side business of human trafficking tonight, we'll be there to witness it and put a stop to his activities. The haunted expression on Cristano's face still bothers me. Plus, I have no idea what they're doing with the other people they've reserved beds for in that basement. They're not all working inside the spa, that's for sure.

We reach the docks and prepare to spend a long night waiting for the yacht's return. Depending on how far out they have to run to meet their suppliers and the sea conditions surrounding their return, we could be here until sunrise. We stroll around the boats for sale, looking at everything from a small fishing boat to a luxury yacht that's bigger than my house ever thought about being. Kira ventures off into another ship, daydreaming about what it would be like to own one, and Shadow and I hang outside, keeping an eye on the horizon.

"So, what's your hang-up about having kids with

Elle? Why don't you want them?" My casual tone belies the loaded question. Shadow visibly tenses before he answers.

"It's not that I don't want them. I'd love to have kids with her—one day. But we haven't been married that long yet. I'd like to be able to travel more and spend time together as a couple longer before we take that step. Babies will change everything. I've seen Noah and Brianna try to pack up to move across the country for an extended stay at their place in California. There's absolutely no spontaneity—everything has to be planned down to the last snack and nap time."

"Or, you miss being in the middle of danger, chasing bad guys across the stormy seas at a moment's notice. Or jetting off to the Middle East wearing a flak jacket, hunkered down behind a .50 caliber machine gun while cruising across the desert terrain. And you're afraid that having kids will change you."

"Shut the fuck up, Silas."

There's that nerve I've been looking for. Target acquired.

"Convince me I'm wrong." I stop walking and turn to face him.

His deadpan stare is his only response.

"Ah, I see what's really going on here."

"Silas. Let it go."

"Elle doesn't know you never actually left the CIA, does she? You never told her they convinced you to stay on in a specialized capacity when you moved to California. That's why you're avoiding having kids. You're afraid of blowing your cover. You sneaky dog."

"So help me, Silas…"

"Save your threats, Shadow. Your secret is safe with me."

Shadow's phone rings, saving us from an all-out brawl. "That was Brad. He said the boat stopped a short way down the shore. He hacked into the senator's phone camera and verified the senator and his wife are just enjoying some time out on the water. The senator opened a bottle of wine, and the two of them talked about their plans now that the last of their kids is married and off living her own life. He'll check in on them periodically, but there doesn't appear to be anything illicit to their excursion."

CHAPTER 19

Kira

*T*wo and a half weeks.

That's how long we've been watching the spa, the senator, the marina, and combing through every little detail of the senator's life now. Every day, Silas grows more irritated and aggravated. We're somewhat hiding from the government—even though we should've left the country a long time ago if we had any real hope of escaping punishment. But it's his promise to Cristano that weighs the most on his conscience, more and more with every passing minute. Freeing the janitor from his five-star prison is vital to Silas. After spending every minute of the last month and a half with him, I'd like to think I know him reasonably well.

He bends and breaks the rules that don't help with meeting his objective, but there are a few lines he'd never cross. He has a strong sense of protecting the innocent, and failing at that particular mission simply cannot happen. Knowing he's left someone in that precarious position eats him alive inside. Not making any headway on this case makes him a little crazy. But someone beating him at a game where he's usually the victor downright pisses him off.

The only thing that seems to relieve his stress is our time alone, and he uses every precious second of that to work through his frustrations. Night after night, he makes love to my entire body, even my mind. With his whispers and his vows. With his lips and his hands. He elicits feelings and desires that I never knew existed from deep inside me. The licks, nips, and kisses he feathers across my skin in the middle of the night are never enough. He gives until I can't take anymore, but my hunger for him is never fully satiated because I eagerly take him each and every time he reaches for me. When he leaves marks in places that only he and I have seen, it seals a bond between us.

Even if I'm the only one who feels it.

Even if I'm the only one who wants it.

For a long time, I never believed in love. It was only a fairy tale people believed in a hollow attempt to fool themselves into thinking they were happy. I felt sorry for those poor souls, walking around in a self-induced haze until they just woke up one day and realized they weren't "in love" with their partner anymore. Then they left and found the next person they were "in love" with, hoping to fill the hole deep inside them.

Now I have a slightly different outlook.

After watching Noah and Brianna together, hearing their story and seeing firsthand how they never gave up on each other, I'm a believer.

Imagining going back to a life without Silas in it feels empty and pointless.

My instructors back at the Academy never would believe I've turned into a dreamer, trusting in the power of love.

Yet, here I am.

A Russian spy.

Hopelessly in love with a CIA officer.

How can this story ever have a happy ending?

The realization that I only have one ending, and that it's already written in stone, is enough pressure to bear. But every minute that passes with this loving family in harm's way—because of me—nearly destroys me. Watching everyone with their children, so happy, so full of life, and so caring, makes me so envious. I've never wanted that life before. Being trained to never expect happiness beyond what serving my country could bring me set my expectations very low early on in life.

Outside of Mira, I don't remember much about having a family around. I still miss my parents, but my childhood memories were all but pushed out of my mind by the endless drills the Academy put us through. We would whisper our memories to each other at night, trying to hold on to a wisp of our formative years. But we were soon discovered, and they separated us at night, putting us in solitary confinement as punishment until we learned our lesson.

Now I see Mira with Brad, even when they don't think anyone is watching. He's head over heels in love with her, doting on her every need and showering her with affection. She's just as smitten with him, sidling up beside him to steal quick kisses while he works. The way he looks at her when she walks away melts even my cold, black heart. He wants to spend his life with her—that much is crystal clear to me.

I'm afraid to admit, even to myself, that I wish Silas looked at me the same way.

All I really need is a life filled with love and happiness, surrounded by family and friends, with a good man to keep me warm at night. That's my dream life.

Add one more item to that list. I've always wanted a dog, but I was never allowed to have one. A furry, four-legged best friend would complete the perfect picture.

I'm sitting outside by the pool alone, finishing an early morning cup of coffee with only my musings to keep me company, when a voice from the chair beside me nearly makes me jump out of my skin.

"When you went to Russian spy school, did they teach you the art of disguises?" I snap my head to the side, and I find Liz staring me down intently, waiting for an answer.

"Um, yes, ma'am. We were taught how to change our looks and blend in without any distinguishing marks."

"Good, good. And did they teach you other tricks of the trade? Insider secrets that the general public would have no way of knowing?"

"Sure, I guess so. I mean, if everyone knew what to do, it wouldn't be considered a spy trade, would it?"

"Smart girl. Now, here's what you and I are going to do. You'll teach me everything you know, then I'll teach you everything I know, and we'll save the day together." She gives me a long wink along with a sharp nod.

"No. No, no, no, Liz. I've told you a million times. We can't reveal insider practices to you. Stop asking and putting Kira on the spot like that." Silas sits down beside me with two cups of hot coffee and slides one over in front of me. "Keep it up, and I'll slip some sodium pentothal into your drink and make you spill your guts."

Liz stands, leans over the table, and levels her gaze on Silas. "Let me remind you of something, Mr. Steele. You should never make threats to me that you know you can't carry out. They never end well for you. But now that you've thrown down the challenge, I'm thrilled to accept it. The game is on, big boy. I sure hope you're up for it."

She stalks away with a swagger in her step and a scary aura surrounding her.

"She's a formidable foe, isn't she?"

"You have no idea, Kira. No idea. She'd be the world's deadliest weapon if she knew half of what we know." Silas shakes his head, but he can't hide the smile on his face. He loves her, even if she drives him crazy.

"So, what's the plan for today? Since we're not training Liz in the ways of espionage, what else should we do with all our free time?"

"I can think of three or four things that would be a much better use of our time. And a lot more fun for us." He waggles his eyebrows at me. "For one, the pool is heated. We could take a skinny-dip right now."

"Well, if that wouldn't invite the wrath of Liz on us, I don't know what would." I laugh, knowing he's kidding, but the thought is still appealing.

"You have a point there. Although, I'm more afraid of her joining us than anything else." That makes us both laugh out loud. We've grown more relaxed around each other outside of the bedroom, as much as we have inside it. "I suppose we'll have to stick to our standing date of sitting in a car, staring at a building, and waiting for something exciting to happen."

"When it finally does happen, I think we'll have all the excitement we can stand."

"I'm glad you said that. You just jinxed us, so we should have our hands full today."

"It's about fucking time. We should probably get over there in case we just jinxed Nick and Roman."

"Hold up before you two go anywhere." Shadow walks up behind us wearing a grim expression that instantly puts me on alert.

"What happened? Did someone get hurt?" My

stomach drops, and I wait for him to relay the worst news possible.

"No, nothing like that. I need to talk to you both about something Silas asked me to look into for him."

"Oh, okay. What was it, and what'd you find? Will it help us put an end to this once and for all?" Looking on the bright side has never been my strong suit, but I'm trying to find a silver lining to balance the solemn expression on his face.

His long, hard sigh isn't a good sign. "I'm legitimately concerned that will be the outcome, but not in the way you meant."

"Just spill it, Shadow. What'd you find?" Silas doesn't even sound like himself. His tone is cold and distant all of a sudden.

"Do you recognize this man, Kira?" Shadow opens the manila folder and holds up a picture.

"Of course. That's David Groves. He's the senator's aide I picked up in the DC bar to get into the secure office."

"His name isn't David Groves. It's Viktor Sokolov."

"As in, Ivan's younger brother?" I take the picture from his hand and stare at it, trying to find some resemblance to how I remember Ivan.

"The same."

"Oh my god. I can't believe it. Are you sure?"

"I'm positive."

"I don't understand how that can be Viktor. How was I able to fool him and gain access to the senator's computer? That makes no sense. He would've suspected something and been on his guard the entire time."

Shadow stares a hole through me for several long heartbeats. Deep inside, I know what he's about to say, but I still hope I'm wrong.

"Those were my thoughts exactly, Kira. So, I did a little more digging. According to Russian intelligence, you and Sokolov have a long history of working together. You've perfected the divide-and-conquer technique. You knew Silas was tailing you, so you concocted this whole charade of drugging 'David,' breaking into the office, and stealing documents to send us on a wild goose chase. You knew Silas would catch you, taking the focus off your friend 'David,' allowing him to finish his mission undetected."

"No, that's not true!"

"You gave just enough information and just enough evidence to lend credence to an otherwise impossible story. It's no secret the GRU has moles everywhere— from personal assistants to congressional staffers. The GRU also knows way too much about Silas—so 'David' just had to find a document from one of Silas's former cases to rein us in. And you just happened to download that file from the senator's files...from the office 'David' helped you get into. That all seems a little too convenient, doesn't it?"

"I have never met Viktor Sokolov before in my life, so I've certainly never worked with him. I met David that night in the bar, on purpose, because I'd researched my target. The only reason I wanted those documents was to show the senator was selling secrets to the Russian government. I didn't even put all the pieces of the puzzle together until Silas and I talked about the human trafficking racket. Even though I know I'll be sent back to Moscow to face the firing squad, I still only want to stop them from abusing more innocent people."

I turn my attention to Silas, who is uncharacteristically quiet.

"Silas, you know I'm telling the truth. You were there. Tell him this isn't true."

"Your involvement with Viktor would explain a lot of things. Like why we haven't found one shred of evidence against the senator when you're the one who implicated him from the beginning." Silas's response cuts me to the core. "And playing on our emotions over sending you back to your death would be an effective ploy."

"Are you serious? You're doubting me now? Yes, I thought Senator Hunt was behind it. But if Shadow is right and that's really Viktor, it makes just as much sense that he's behind it since he has an all-access pass to the senator and all his files, whether Hunt knows it or not. That means Viktor is running the entire operation his brother used to run, only under someone else's name. He's stepped into his brother's shoes and has been doing it right underneath the government's nose."

Silas and Shadow exchange a wordless glance, but the message comes across loud and clear.

I'm once again the enemy.

A seed of doubt has been planted, and they no longer trust me, even though I've done nothing but share what I know and help every step of the way.

"And your documented involvement with Viktor? How do you explain that?"

"Oh, I don't know, Shadow. Maybe if your government found out one of their main operatives went rogue and joined forces with the enemy, they'd conjure up some fake mission reports to discredit her and cause the rest of the team to doubt her motives. Sounds a lot like what we do for a living, doesn't it?"

"Unfortunately, so does that answer, Kira. You could be playing all of us right now. Telling us what we want to hear so your partner can carry out whatever plans he has. With him working in the senator's office in DC, I can't imagine his main objective is to sell slaves in a Miami day spa. He has something much more nefarious going on, and we're a thousand miles away. That takes a lot of heat off him to do whatever he needs to do in Washington, doesn't it?"

"I suppose it would. That is, if you're sure he's still in Washington. Do you know for sure he didn't come down here with the senator? Do you have someone with eyes on him in Washington right now?"

Shadow draws in a deep breath, straightening his back so that he towers over me even more.

"I'll take your silence as a 'no.' I've been nothing but honest about my involvement in this since day one. I've told Silas everything remotely related to this. I've answered every question he's asked of me with honesty, even to my own detriment. I've never lied to him.

"So, to address who can be trusted here and who can't, let me ask you this one question. Does your wife know you're working undercover with the CIA right now? Does she know that while you're helping your friend with your right hand, you're reporting his activities back to the Agency with your left? What happens to Silas when this is over—and how much blood will be on both of your hands that day?"

CHAPTER 20

Silas

The silence inside the truck we borrow from Noah is deafening, and the tension is stifling. The rapport we've developed over the last several weeks seems to have dissipated, along with all the trust we'd built between us. One seed of doubt planted in my mind by Shadow, and it's almost as if the past several weeks with Kira never happened.

Well, not exactly Shadow, but being the bearer of bad news makes him guilty by association. Even though I know he was only sharing information he'd uncovered in the investigation I asked for, that doesn't make it easier to swallow. The Russian government could've altered the mission information to cover their tracks after their agent went rogue, or she could be guilty of everything it said.

She could've been playing me the entire time, keeping me from identifying their real endgame. One scenario is as likely to be the truth as the other.

"You know, you can't keep shutting me out like this. When we get back to Noah's house tonight, are you planning to sleep in the other room away from me?"

For once in my career, I honestly haven't thought that far ahead. I'm just trying to get through the current minute before planning what I'll do in the next one. My thoughts are still circling the drain, trying to maintain some semblance of professionalism through my internal battle. Do I follow my head or...that other organ that shouldn't be involved at all?

"Great. That's just fucking great, Silas. I'll tell you what. Since you're so unsure about me and can't make a decision for yourself, I'll make it for you. I won't be in that bed tonight, so it's all yours. Don't bother looking for me either. If you show up anywhere near me, I'll get up and move to another part of the house where you're not. After all this time, you doubt me now. What happened to your fucking lie detector test? Do you think I can beat a system I don't even know about?"

"Are you saying you'd be willing to take that test to prove you're not lying?" The moment the words leave my mouth, I know they're a mistake. I didn't mean it the way it came across, but there's no way I'll convince her of that now.

She surprises me by not answering at all. I expected a

smack upside my head. When I glance over at her, the crushed expression on her face and the tears glistening in her eyes do the talking for her. My regret is instantaneous. The sharp pain that shoots through my chest, clawing at my heart like a steel trap, is my own doing.

She swallows hard, regrouping and getting her emotions under control before speaking. Her voice is aloof and distant, not the warm and affectionate Kira I've grown to…know…over time. "No, I'm not willing to do that at all. Go ahead and turn me in. I have nothing left to prove to you."

"Kira—"

"Don't. Just don't. Keep whatever lie you were about to tell me to yourself. It's amazing you're even wasting your time on this stakeout since I'm a complete liar and only diverting your attention to a nonexistent threat. But don't worry. I'll be gone after tonight, and you can drop this case completely. Of course, when it turns out I was telling the truth, you'll look like an even bigger incompetent moron, but that won't be my problem. You can be the one to explain it to Cristano."

Thankfully, we aren't far from the day spa building, and we'll have time for a more rational conversation when I'm not driving and distracted by the road. I know she only lashed out at me because she's hurt, but I don't think she realizes I need time to process everything that's transpired in such a short time. Admittedly, I could've avoided this entire confrontation if I'd just spilled my guts to her, but sharing my feelings never been my style. I've already spent more time with her than all my previous dates combined. Complicated feelings were never part of the equation before now.

But what I don't want to admit is even I know that excuse is utter bullshit. I'm a grown man who can use big words and everything. I'm stopping shy of calling myself a pussy…but the voices in my head are screaming it loud enough anyway.

When I find a parking spot that gives us a line of sight to the back of the building, I put the truck into Park and turn off the engine. Just as I turn in the seat to face Kira and hash out this bullshit once and for all, she jumps out of the passenger door. There's a stronger than usual breeze stirring today with a storm brewing just off the coast. Her long black hair whips around with a mind of its own when powerful gusts come up out of the blue. She takes a seat on a retaining wall in front of our parking spot, pulls a hair band out of her pocket, and pulls her hair into a low ponytail. With her sunglasses in place, she looks like a normal Floridian, enjoying the bright sun and mild late-February temperatures.

Only, I know who she really is.

Or do I?

"Fuck it." I reach for the handle to climb out of the truck, but I stop when I see her perk up.

But she's not paying attention to me. She lifts the pocket-size binoculars toward the spa building across the street. Her back remains straight as a rod, and her muscles are tensed and ready to pounce. I follow her line of sight and recognize a familiar form slinking around the back door. I move swiftly and silently to her side, keeping my gaze trained on the target.

"Isn't that Viktor?"

"Yes, it is. Give me a gun, Silas."

"No fucking way, Kira. You know I can't do that. You're not even supposed to be here."

She lowers the binoculars momentarily to look at me. "But I am here. And so is Viktor. But your rules and laws won't stop him. Obviously. There are laws against human trafficking in this country, right? But he's a criminal, so he doesn't care about your laws because what he's doing makes him money. He's willing to take the risk regardless of what your rule book says." Flames flash in her eyes when she yanks her sunglasses off her face and glares at me.

Seems she's genuinely upset with me, and this isn't just a passing spat.

"I'm trained, licensed, and a US federal agent. I'll subdue him while you help the victims get out of there safely."

"You're impossible. So, just in case you've read me wrong and this is a setup to take you out, you want me to walk into that devil's den unarmed. Is that it?"

"I can't take that chance, Kira." Plain and simple, that's what it boils down to.

"Even if you don't believe I actually have feelings for you and also want to stop this monster, do you honestly believe I could betray my sister like that? She'd be the one who'd be left behind to take the fall for me."

This is but one more reason why I shouldn't have allowed any feelings to become involved in this affair. That thought never crossed my mind. I've been so focused on Kira betraying me, I didn't stop to consider she'd never do that to Mira. I realized how strong their bond was after seeing them together the first time, and that has only amplified over the past several weeks of constant contact. Her sister is the only real family she has left. She'd die before she let Mira pay for her sins.

She turns her face away from me and lifts the binoculars again, hiding her own hurt and anger. But I can see she's at the tipping point—even more so than before.

"It's happening now. They're on the move. Oh my god...that man just shook hands with Viktor, and now he's dragging a little girl away. We have to stop him!"

Kira flings the binoculars to the side and takes off like a bullet, sprinting across the way without alerting the other team or waiting for backup. I race to catch up with her, calling Roman and Nick on my way to get them in place. Viktor rushes back inside the building. We can't risk him escaping through any other door, so I order them to search the building while I follow Kira to the back. Roman cautions me to hang back since this could be the perfect setup to lure me into an ambush once and for all. Pretending a child is in danger definitely would be an effective trap, and the cost of not taking the risk is too high.

When I finally catch up with her, Kira grabs the little girl from the man's grasp. "Hi, sweetheart. Do you know this man?"

The sheer terror on the little girl's face when she looks up at the man in question is enough of an answer for me. Huge tears well up in her eyes as she nervously glances between him and Kira. She wants to answer, but she's obviously been coached and coerced into staying silent. She can't be more than five years old, and that alone is enough for me to empty the magazine into these fuckers.

"It's okay, sweetie. You can tell me. If he's not your daddy, I won't let him take you anywhere. I'll protect you. Have you ever seen him before today?"

The little girl finally shakes her head, indicating no.

"Has he hurt you, sweetie?" Kira's voice is controlled and reassuring as she tries to soothe the little girl.

The heart I deny having shatters in my chest when she nods.

"You sick motherfucker. I should blow your fucking head off your shoulders right now so I can stuff it and mount it on my wall for target practice." The sights at the end of my barrel are set directly between his eyes. With just a twitch of my finger, the leftover pieces wouldn't even resemble a head.

"Who the hell are you?" He somehow thinks he can bluff and bluster his way out of this.

"CIA."

"Then I know you're full of shit. You can't shoot me

—I'm unarmed. You are required to arrest me and take me in. I'm entitled to a lawyer." He puffs out his chest, thinking he's won this round.

I laugh in his face, but it's a humorless chuckle. "You obviously have no clue how we work. Get that little girl out of here. She doesn't need to see this."

Kira lifts the girl into her arms, holding the child tightly against her body, and walks briskly toward the truck. I keep my sights steady on him until they're out of sight.

"I have rights. I'm an American citizen. You can't just shoot an unarmed man and get away with it. I'm entitled to a lawyer and due process." His bravado is waning, as it should be.

"Not today, you're not. You're a member of an undercover Russian terrorist cell, putting the lives of millions of Americans at stake. You're a traitor, committing treason against the United States of America of the highest measure."

"That's not true. None of that is true."

"Funny, that's how my report will read. And that's exactly what will be in your obituary." The round leaves the chamber and strikes him before the meaning and weight of my words have time to fully register in his brain.

His is the most satisfying death of my career.

One less piece of shit running loose in the world, preying on innocent children while pretending to be a human being.

Roman and Nick rush through the door with their weapons drawn then quickly put them away when they realize the threat has been neutralized.

"All clear inside, Silas. Viktor got away somehow. There must've been another exit we didn't know about because Roman and I checked every room, every closet, and under every massage table. He gave us the slip."

"What?" I can't believe my ears. We combed over the blueprints and checked the interior ourselves.

"I'm sorry, man. We're thoroughly pissed too. Let's go track him down. He couldn't have gotten far. We'll ground every plane and shut down every mode of transportation out of the county." Roman begins to walk away, ready to be in hot pursuit.

But my feet are rooted to the concrete beneath me. I can't breathe. It feels as if my lungs are filled with water, preventing me from inhaling the oxygen I need to survive. I've never experienced a full-blown panic attack before—nothing even remotely close to it. But I know, beyond a shadow of a doubt, the exact transportation Viktor will use to leave the area.

Because I drove here in it. And I sent Kira and that little girl to wait for me in it.

"He's already gone, Roman. And he took Kira and a victim she rescued with him as bargaining collateral—or human shields—whichever comes first."

We rush back to the parking area, and my worst fears are confirmed.

The truck is gone, along with the two people I should've been protecting.

Approaching sirens grow louder until many different organizations surround us, including my brother and his team. When Shadow and I explain our involvement to the FBI Special Agent in Charge, we're immediately released with his promise to ground all commercial and private flights out of the area. Even though this only took mere minutes from start to finish, I know we're too late. Grounding other flights will only be a nuisance and inconvenience to innocent travelers.

That fucker is a trained GRU agent. His emergency credentials will list him as a visiting dignitary with diplomatic immunity, resourcefully putting him out of our reach. Along with Kira. He'll take her back to Russia to be executed for helping us. God only knows what he's done with that little lost girl.

"Who has my security camera videos? Traffic cameras, ATMs, local businesses. I want them all on my computer in the next thirty seconds!" the special agent in charge bellows to his team, looking for immediate answers.

"I need to see those too." I'm not asking.

The first available footage shows Viktor emerging from a small window at ground level. He must've had his exit planned ahead of time and climbed out before Nick or Roman found him. When we're finally able to see him from a different angle, I have the perfect view of him running toward the truck, climbing inside with Kira, and holding a gun to the little girl's head to make Kira cooperate.

If any lingering doubt remained, it is completely squashed now. Kira was right about one more fact as well. I absolutely am an incompetent moron, and I've left no room for doubt or debate.

CHAPTER 21

Kira

"*V*iktor, take me but let the little girl go. I can stop and let her out at a hospital or something. She's been through enough. Besides, she'll only slow you down." I don't bother keeping up the "David" charade. We both know who he really is.

"You know, this whole situation is pretty amusing when you think about it."

"I don't think any of this is funny."

"Oh, but it is. I've lived in the DC area for years. Decades. I've worked my way into the office of one of the most powerful senators ever elected. I have access to everything the Intelligence Committee sees. Do you know how important my role is to our government? But everything I accomplished wasn't enough to quiet the storm inside me.

"No one in DC seems to question whatever Senator Hunt wants—he's just trusted implicitly. So, I had one of the senator's CIA contacts locate Silas Steele and share all the information that could be found on him. It's amazing to have that kind of power, so I used it to my advantage to find the one man whose name is still on my list. Do you know what it's like to have the person you're closest to suddenly ripped out of your life?"

"I know exactly what that's like, and you know very well I do."

"Yeah, I guess that was a stupid question to ask you. Anyway, even though we were thirteen years apart in age, my brother and I were very close. When he was murdered, it changed me in ways I never realized until I matured more. I tried to push past the need for vengeance, I really did. But I've accepted that's just not in my DNA. At first, I planned to kill his siblings and be done with it. That would've made us even.

"But while I was watching him one day, I realized he was watching you. Then you started working me, and I realized you had no idea about my true identity. I've never believed in the whole 'it was fate' bullshit. Until that night. There was no other explanation for it. Silas's attention was so laser-focused on you that he never even noticed me. I could've picked him off with a single shot to the head, and he never would've seen it coming.

"That's when I realized just watching him die wouldn't be enough. He would've been a hero, a martyr, and I would've had to hear about it for years to come.

No, he has to know he's been beaten, but more importantly, who beat him. The great Silas Steele will be blamed, shamed, and convicted while I have a front row seat to watch all his hard work unravel around him. It's the perfect scenario."

"I don't understand. What do you mean exactly?"

He turns his head and meets my gaze with a sadistic smile. "This may sound odd coming from me, considering I'm not only going to ruin the man but annihilate him completely. I respect you for trying to protect him regardless of what you're facing yourself. But you can stop recording me with your phone now. Where you're going, you'll never be given an opportunity to get it to him. To address your earlier request about the little girl, the answer is no. She'll prove useful to my overall goal. She comes with us."

"Where are you taking us?" He's too forthcoming with information. That's never a good sign. We're trained to be uncrackable vaults, but he's singing like a canary.

"Home, Kira. You're going home. How long has it been since you've visited Moscow?"

"The last time I was there was during my training. I haven't been back for a visit at all."

"Wow…so, about twenty years, then? So much has changed over there since then. It's not the same place you remember. You won't believe the differences."

Somehow, I doubt that. A new coat of paint only hides the repulsiveness underneath for so long. It's bound to rear its ugly head soon after our plane touches down. I turn my head to look out the side window for a moment, hiding my true thoughts and feelings from him.

"And your plans for her?" I motion to the terrified child sitting beside me, so close that she's almost in my lap while I'm driving.

"I have a question for you."

"Okay." My response is drawn out much longer than usual.

"Are you aware that Silas is in love with you?"

I can barely find my voice to reply. "He's not in love with me. Our relationship is just...convenient."

"You really don't know, do you? I'm sorry I have to be the one to tell you this instead of him, but you're wrong about that. I've seen how he looks at you. I've watched you two together when neither of you knew I was there, following your every move. That day at the beach was hot as fuck, by the way. You're in love with each other, but you're both too proud or stubborn or both to say it."

"You're wrong, Viktor. We haven't even known each other long enough to fall in love."

He laughs at that. "Kira, tell me something. Who is this wise and all-knowing person who set a time limit on how long it takes for two people to fall in love? Did they share the rules of love with the rest of the world and get a stamp of approval before making up these ridiculous laws? No, my dear. The people who subscribe to that are sheep—blindly led off a cliff without asking a question. I've seen it happen myself with people I've respected. I was shocked, no doubt, but it was just as real as if they'd spent ten years dating first."

"Why are you telling me all this? You're suddenly a romantic?"

"Hell no, of course not. Don't be ludicrous. I'm telling you this because your death will be much more poignant and impactful to Silas than anyone else in his life. Sure, he'd miss his brother and sister, but he'd move on. But I don't think the man has ever been in love before. And after he loses you, he will never fall in love again." His maniacal laugh sends shivers down my spine.

Part of the reason why he's telling me all this is for psychological torture. If he can break me mentally, he'll revel in that accomplishment more than my physical death. There's a reason why the Academy strongly discourages getting attached to others in our line of work. They can and will be used as pawns against us, putting them in harm's way and compromising us as both agents and informants.

Time to change the subject. I don't want his focus on Silas.

"Everything you did pointed to the senator as the culprit. The leaked confidential documents, the human trafficking through a spa close to his home in Miami, even getting my handler to send me on that mission. That was you, wasn't it?"

"It was, indeed."

"You knew I needed a way in, and you volunteered. Didn't they question why?"

"Of course. I told them I had my doubts about you and your dedication to the cause. One grain of doubt was all it took for the GRU to test you. But I'm the one who let you pass. When I went to the bar for your refill and you spiked my drink, I took the antidote the Academy made for our special compound. When I 'passed out' in the office, I wasn't actually asleep. After that, Silas was attached to you like a tattoo, which made my job easier."

"You resumed your brother's business since you knew where Silas was at all times and that his attention was on me. You used me as a diversion."

"I played you like a bass drum, girl. You fell in line perfectly. When you disappeared, that only affirmed my suspicions to the GRU. I know you're in love with him the same as he is with you. When I turn you in, the general will take care of you, but Silas's fate will be much worse. You'll probably get a swift and painless execution. Silas will be put through the wringer by his government and publicly disgraced. Once the shitstorm dies down, the CIA will eliminate him and put him out of his misery, and the public will think he's rotting in some federal prison."

"Sounds like you've got it all planned out."

"I've thought about my revenge for a very long time. You're just the first woman Silas has ever shown any attachment to, outside of his family members."

He tells me to pull into a parking garage, and we ditch Noah's truck, forcing the little girl and me into another car nearby. I'm sure Noah has a state-of-the-art tracking system on all his vehicles, but we'll be long gone by the time he gets here. With the barrel held flush against her back, I can't fight back and risk him killing her. I know his training, and I've seen his kind too many times to count. He'll do it in a heartbeat and never look back. Inside the car, we head in the opposite direction, almost doubling back to the area we just left.

He turns down a dead-end street then slows when we reach the water. We pull into the driveway for a private marina, and he opens the gate with a remote he retrieves from his pocket. Boats of all shapes and sizes fill the covered slips along the multiple docks. He forces us out and through the gate toward the ships.

"They'll be watching the airports the most. Private boats leave the docks all the time without any paperwork or tracking at all. Pretty smart, huh?" He's genuinely proud of himself.

"Brilliant." My deadpan response is lost on him. He takes it as a compliment. His only answer is a huge smile, showing he's very proud of himself. I have to physically restrain myself from rolling my eyes. The art of a sharp, sarcastic jab is lost on so many. "You never told me what you're doing with her, though."

He looks down at the little girl for a moment before replying. "I'll give her to the program. The Academy will train her well. You were really too old when they took you—they've figured that out in the last twenty years. Younger is better. If she never knows a different life from the one that we teach her, she'll never betray us like you did. Her mother died tragically, and her father was some low-life thug who traded drugs for sex with her mother. She'll have a better life with the Academy than she would in the foster care system here."

Over my dead body.

I don't voice the words, because that outcome is inevitable, but I'll find a way to get her out before they get their claws into her. She's had enough pain and heartache already in her short life. That needs to end now. Viktor is obviously a sociopath who thinks he's genuinely doing her a huge favor and saving her life with this option.

"Get in." He waves the gun, motioning for us to climb onto the speed boat and into the cabin. He takes my phone from me and throws it overboard, smiling as he watches it sink in the salt water.

He locks the door, leaving us inside, and I immediately look for any communication devices. Marine radio, ham radio, satellite phone, flares, walkie-talkies, anything. But he's thought of that ahead of time because the cabin has been stripped of all radios—even for music. The refrigerator is stocked with food and drinks, and there are clothes in the small closet that will fit me but not the child. Guess he didn't account for every possibility after all.

When I look down at the little girl, her big blue eyes are wide, staring at all the food. That squeeze in my chest is my heart cracking in two for her.

"What's your name, sweetheart?" I kneel down in front of her and brush her long blond hair from her face.

"Amber."

"Hi, Amber. My name is Kira. Are you hungry? Do you want me to make you something to eat?"

She nods enthusiastically, so I start pulling out items out of the cupboard and refrigerator. With all the provisions he stocked in this cruiser, I wonder if we're sailing all the way to Moscow. I know better, but this is somewhat overkill considering what's about to happen. Makes me wonder if this is his boat or if we're just stealing someone else's. Neither would surprise me at this point.

While Amber eats, I check every inch of the cabin, looking for anything to help us escape. Life vests, rope, a net bag, knives—I start making a small stockpile of anything useful I can find. I'll only have one shot at this, so I have to make it the best I can. The windows have already been boarded up from the outside, so I can't even get Amber out one of the small portholes. There's only one way out—the locked door where Viktor is waiting on the other side.

It's either pick the lock...or eat all the chocolate on the way to wherever he's taking us. I hear the engines fire and feel the boat start to move out of the slip just as I being to work on the door.

"You're very resourceful, Kira. But you're not going anywhere. You don't think I've already taken every precaution, knowing your abilities? I suggest you enjoy the time you have getting to know little Amber. We have a long night ahead of us. The bed in there is for you—I have my own out here."

He's watching me. Of course, there's a camera in here. Secured door. Provisions. Bedroom. Bathroom. No way out.

We're stuck inside here until we reach our destination.

CHAPTER 22

Silas—One Week Later

"*A*re you shitting me right now?" I'm about to crush this fucking phone in my hand. "You know I'm still working this case. You know what has happened here—you've been updated every fucking day. And I know you have because Shadow has been staying here with me, and he never stays here when he's in town. He has his own place."

I'm pacing back and forth, about to wear a hole in the marble floor of the foyer, arguing with my deputy director about his unreasonable demand.

"No, I'm not flying back to DC when he took her from here in Miami, and he could still have her here somewhere. If you want to see me in person, you can come down here. If I haven't found her by the time you get here, I'll gladly talk to you. But just so we're clear, you are not my priority right now." I end the call before I throw the phone against the wall in a fit of sheer rage.

"He wants you to fly to DC now, knowing what's going on? What the hell, man?" Shadow stands beside me, regret etched in his face.

"Don't even go there, Shadow. You were only doing your job by reporting the information back to them. I have nothing to hide. I blatantly kept her in the country past the two weeks he gave me. Then I brought her down here to catch the bastard. My eyes are wide open—I did all of that knowing the consequences I'd face because of my actions. And if you hadn't done your job, you'd be in trouble now because of me."

"Let me talk to the deputy director and tell him I have it under control. See if I can convince him to stay out of it for now and let me handle it."

"He won't, but I appreciate the offer. He'll say we let Kira get away with Viktor and that it was her plan the entire time. Then he'll say you and I look like dirty CIA officers now, so the whole agency looks bad."

"You're probably right." Shadow runs his fingers through his hair, aggravated and irritated with the circumstances. "He should know us better than that by now, but he'd use that just to tear us a new asshole."

"He'll say *what*?"

Shadow and I whip around at the same time to face the angry voice demanding answers.

Oh shit.

"Elle." The color drains from Shadow's face, while Elle's quickly fills with red-hot rage.

"The deputy director of the CIA will say you're a dirty officer, Devon' Shadow' Kane? Is that what I just heard?"

Oh shit. She used his full name.

Shadow doesn't answer right away, but his guilt-ridden expression says enough. "Let me explain, darlin'."

"Don't you dare 'darlin" me right now. How long have you been back with the agency?" She folds her arms over her body and burns a hole through him with her eyes. "What the fuck, Devon? You never left, did you?"

"Elle, wait just a second before you fly off the handle and say something you'll regret later." He holds up his hands in mock surrender, trying to calm her down before it escalates out of control.

My opinion? Her temper is already out of control.

"Too late, Shadow. You've lied to me this whole time. I've always supported you and your career. I even waited months on end for you when you were undercover. But we're married now. We're building a home together, and I'd hoped one day soon we'd start our own family. But after everything we've endured, you decided you didn't trust me enough to let me into your life fully. This secret isn't like you spent too much money on your hobby, or, surprise, you came home with a brand-new motorcycle. You intentionally chose to leave me out of one of the biggest parts of your life, as if I'm not affected at all."

"It's not that I wanted to leave you out of anything.

No officer can share what they do with their families. You'd have to be part of the operation or have a need to know—with security clearance—for me to tell you anything."

"Don't try to pull that agency bullshit with me. I've never expected you to tell me anything top-secret. But you could've told me you were working for them. As your wife, I have a right to know that. What if you were out on a mission and didn't come home? Did you ever consider what that would do to me—not having a clue you were still in that line of work?"

Elle walks away and leaves Shadow with his head hanging low in shame. "She's right. I tried to protect her from my life but only ended up shutting her out of it instead."

"You should've known she'd support your decision to stay on the same as you'd support her if she decided she wanted back in front of the camera."

"Is the world's most eligible bachelor giving me relationship advice?"

A knock on the front door interrupts our conversation. Our eyes meet, and I know we have the same questions. Who's here, and how did they get past Noah's security gate?

When I open the door, I'm hardly surprised to find the deputy director standing on the doorstep.

"Graves. Come on in." I step back and let him enter. "Brought your own equipment, I see."

"Sure did. Don't trust yours one bit. Where do you want to do this?"

I show him to Noah's office and make room for the high-tech machine and brain scanner that will tell him if I'm lying.

"Have a seat, Steele. We're going to settle this right now."

"Fine by me. The quicker, the better."

"Kane, you can leave now." Graves arches his eyebrow at Shadow. Being the true friend he is, Shadow looks at me for confirmation before leaving us alone.

"It's fine. Go take care of your business. Graves knows I can take him out with a snap of my fingers. He won't try anything underhanded with me."

Graves doesn't crack a smile. Typical.

After he straps me in, measuring all my vitals along with my brain wave pattern, he pulls a large brown envelope from his briefcase. "I received some interesting documents in the mail today. It's a full dossier on you, actually. I'm going to ask you questions about yourself, the work you've done with the Russians, and the black-market business you've set up here in Miami. I also have a few questions about your girlfriend."

"The black-market business I've set up? What business would that be?"

"We'll get to that."

Over the next two hours, he grills me about every single encounter I've had with anyone of Russian nationality—whether they were an asset, a spy, or a dignitary.

When he brought up Dmitri, the explanations were more complicated than a simple yes or no answer. I gave him more ammunition about our interactions, so we spent a good thirty minutes on my relationship with Dmitri and his wife.

"Are you in any way involved in a human trafficking business operated anywhere in the world?" Just the mere accusation makes my blood boil, but I cool my jets before my temper sets off a false positive.

"No."

"Did you assist in any way with setting up a human trafficking business here in Miami?"

"No."

"Have you visited the spa where a suspected human trafficking ring conducted business?"

"Yes."

I explain the nature of my visits and what occurred each time, including all the days and nights on stakeout time while we waited for someone to make a move. I even tell him about the little girl we rescued from that sick fucker and the bullet I put between his eyes on her behalf.

"Since you passed all the questions for that part, I'm going to tell you what the official documents I received from the Russian embassy contain. You're not going to like it, Silas."

"Go ahead. I need to know."

"Through his work with the CIA and the network he

has established in the numerous countries he has worked over his career, Silas Steele has created a virtually undetectable human trafficking ring. One of his main hubs is an unassuming day spa in Miami, Florida. We have a five-year-old girl currently in our custody who was a victim of Mr. Steele's activities. Our agent, Kira Petrova, rescued her and fled the country, as she feared for their lives.

"Silas Steele, in conjunction with Senator Hunt, is passing top-secret information to North Korea regarding every government with which he has ties. The data to substantiate these claims can be found on Senator Hunt's private server in his Miami home. Attached you will find copies of some of these documents, along with the IP address from where it originated and where it was ultimately transmitted."

Graves hands the documents to me for review, but my dark chuckle holds anything but humor. "You know what's really fucking funny about this? A week ago, Shadow received intel alleging Kira and Viktor Sokolov were in league together, and that she concocted this whole scheme about Senator Hunt selling secrets so her partner could finish his Miami human slave sale without me catching on.

"Now, this intel alleges that I'm the mastermind behind the business, working with Senator Hunt, while Kira and Viktor narrowly escaped the country with their lives. How convenient that the intelligence coming out of this case points the finger all around, and we automatically run after it, like we're a fucking cat chasing a laser light."

"Touché. The next part, I actually believe part of it to be true." He pauses and watches me for a moment before continuing to read from the report. "Kira Petrova has returned to Moscow. Due to the sensitive nature of her position and the grave threat Silas Steele poses, no further communication with her will be possible. If you have specific questions to validate this information, please contact me directly." He finishes reading the ambassador's name and lays the document on the desk.

"So, she's back in Moscow. I knew it, but I didn't want to admit it. I tried to get a flight scheduled under one of my old aliases, but it bounced back. They must have it flagged."

"I'm sure they do."

"Do you think they've executed her yet?"

"My contact says no. She's still being held in an interrogation facility for now. Her father has used every bit of his influence to keep her alive, but his persuasion is waning."

"I have to get to Moscow and break her out."

"You're going to fly to Moscow, break into a secure facility, find an enemy of the state, break her out, and fly back here with her? Do you have some kind of magical powers I'm not aware of?"

"Yes, as a matter of fact, I do. I'm a master of disguises. I'm fluent in Russian. And I'm a man in love."

"You love her?"

"Yes."

"Did you tell her?"

"No."

"Because you're too chickenshit to say the words? Remember, you're still obligated to tell me the truth. Don't start lying to the lie detector now."

"Yes." I grit my teeth and spit out my answer at him. Fucker laughs at me.

"Do you think it's too soon to fall in love?"

"Yes."

"Amateur. I asked my wife to marry me on our first date, and I'd only met her the day before. Finally convinced her to say yes three weeks later. We've been married twenty-seven years now. I haven't regretted it one day of my life. When you know, you know."

He unhooks all the wires and turns off the machine. Then he pulls a smaller envelope out of his bag. "Here are your new passports. Two for you, one for her. Your Russian military uniform and access card are in my car. Get in, get out, and get home. Don't start World War III in the process."

"Yes, sir."

Graves walks out, taking all his equipment with him, and his driver hands me the disguise to get me into the facility. The uniform is freshly dry-cleaned, still covered by the plastic to keep it in pristine condition, and the shoes are buffed to a glossy shine. This will be hard enough to pull off with the full outfit and the keycard to get in. Getting out with her in prison clothes and apparent signs of interrogation without being seen will be impossible.

But damn if I won't give it my best shot. If I die, at least I'll know I died trying.

I close the door as they drive away and turn to find Shadow bounding down the stairs. His eyes are wide, his face is pale, and he's mumbling to himself.

"Shadow, what's wrong?"

"Elle packed her things and left while I was working. She didn't say a word. Didn't say where she was going. Won't answer her phone. Disabled her location services. She just left me."

"I'm sorry to hear that, man. I hate that you got pulled into this because of me."

"It's not your fault, Silas. I've worked on other cases before yours. This is all on me." His eyes finally focus, seeing the uniform draped over my shoulder. "Oh shit. You're breaking in the Kremlin interrogation dungeons, aren't you? Did they leave a uniform for me?"

"No, Shadow. You're not going with me on this one. It's likely to be a one-way ticket, but I've got to try. You should go find Elle, talk to her, and fix your marriage right now. Don't let any grass grow under your feet. You'll regret it if you do."

"It's a pity I have to use my CIA skills on my wife and take relationship advice from my unattached friend." A small smile plays on his face before he gives me a quick, manly hug. "Be careful over there. You don't let any grass grow under your feet while you're rescuing Kira either.

We need you back here as soon as possible, to keep us all in line and to save us from Liz."

"Maybe I should take her with me. Those boys in the Kremlin wouldn't stand a chance."

We share a good belly laugh over that vision, but our parting glance holds more sentiment than words can express. Our friends are our family, the people we choose to keep in our lives and share so much of ourselves with. We're all brothers and sisters. The loss of one would be devastating to all.

"Elle and I will see you when you get back, Silas. If you need me while you're there, send a message through Brad's secret system, and I'll be on the next plane out."

"The four of us will go out for dinner and dancing when Kira and I get back. Keep a Saturday night open on your calendar for us."

CHAPTER 23

Kira

"What did you tell the CIA about our operations?" Igor grips my hair near the scalp and yanks my head backward with a forceful tug. "You'll eventually break—one way or another. You can stop all this pain now with a simple answer."

He's lying. Anything I say will be viewed as weakness and used against me in much harsher methods. There's no way for me to win this game he's playing. It was designed to be a lose-lose outcome for anyone sitting in this chair.

"Have it your way, then." He nods to Vlad with a sadistic grin. Igor loves his job.

I'm strapped to a chair in a grungy, dank room in a basement somewhere in Moscow. Viktor knocked me out before we landed. When I first came to, I asked anyone and everyone about Amber, but no one would answer me. I'm a traitor, so they can't be seen speaking to me.

A sharp pain suddenly cuts through my back. I barely had time to hear the crack of the whip before I feel the lash tear into my skin. With strike after strike, I scream and wiggle, trying to shrink away from the agonizing stings. The chair I'm in topples over from my excessive movements, and I try to crawl away, moving like an inch-worm across the floor with the chair scraping the concrete since it's still strapped to me.

Igor stands and stomps on my hand, stopping my movement with his wicked smile in place. "She thinks she can get away, comrade. Maybe you should show her what happens to bitches who try to run."

"With pleasure."

Vlad approaches me with slow, measured steps. He swings a pair of pliers in his hand, taunting me with what I know is coming. Igor holds my hand in place with his boot while Vlad clamps the pliers onto the end of my fingernail. His hesitation is a textbook torture tactic— build up the anticipation of the moment, make the victim cry and beg before carrying out the ploy regard-less, let him get his rocks off with all the power he holds.

I refuse to give him the satisfaction. With my eyes squeezed shut and the fingers of my opposite hand grip-ping the arm of the chair as hard as I can, I prepare for the horrible pain that I already know is coming. But I can't stop the scream that nearly splits my throat in two when he rips my fingernail entirely off. Blood pours, my entire hand throbs, and the intense pain almost takes my breath away.

"That's enough!" The stern voice echoes in the concrete block room. "You disobeyed direct orders. Wait for me in the hall."

Vlad's smug smirk disappears as he drops the pliers on the table and scurries away with his tail tucked between his legs. My only consolation is knowing the same will be done to him for not following his commander's orders. He knows what's coming, too. Only he'll have to wait longer for his than I did mine.

"Sasha, get her cleaned up and bandage her hand. Igor, you come with me. Right now." I glance over to see who entered the room and recognize General Krupin. He's one of the few men my father trusts.

I also recognize Sasha from my early days at the Academy. She's an older woman who never quite made it as an undercover operative, but she was always very supportive of everyone who came through the program. She helped Mira and me when we were forced into the program against our will as children. She comforted us every night when we thought we'd drown in our tears. She's the one who helped convince the headmistress to put us back in a room together. She pointed out how much of an asset twins would be when working a complicated case. We could literally be in two places at once, but we had to stay in sync with each other. Over the years I lived in that hellhole, she made it as bearable as possible.

After Krupin and Igor leave the room, Sasha unties me and helps me up before she begins gathering the supplies to wash and bandage my injuries. When she returns to me, the concern in her eyes for my physical state is palpable. She pulls up a chair in front of me and begins wiping my face with a warm, wet washcloth. Her touch is gentle when she cleans my wounds. I think it hurts her worse than it does me. This is why she washed out of the program. She had too much compassion for others, and her every emotion was prominently displayed on her face, giving away her thoughts and intentions every time.

"Sasha." My voice barely reaches a whisper to keep any microphones from picking it up. "Where's the little girl?"

She continues dabbing at the abrasion on my cheekbone, acting as if she didn't hear me. "Dorm."

The dorm—the bedrooms used by the Academy. So, Viktor was telling the truth about putting her in the program and using her as an operative one day.

"Take her to my father."

She stills, pretending to examine my cut closer for anyone watching, but her eyes are solidly on mine. "This one is almost impossible to fix."

I understand her hidden message.

"Saving even just one from the infection is worth all the pain."

She understands my cryptic reply. Save the child from the diseased life we've been forced to live. Give her a chance to be a kid—to run, play, laugh, love—to live. The conflict in Sasha's eyes gives me hope that she's at least considering my request. If she's caught, it'll mean certain death for her. But giving Amber the opportunity we never had would make everything I've endured worth every ounce of pain.

"Don't let them do to her what they've done to us, Sasha. Tell my father she's his daughter now." In a rare moment of showing my own emotions, I feel tears form in my eyes as I wait for her reply. Whether she reports me or consents to my request, I know I've tried to help that baby girl live the best life I can give her under the circumstances.

"Try not to worry. I'll do my best to keep the infection at bay."

I've never wanted to break down and sob in my life as much as I do right now. If anyone can help Amber escape the dorms, it's Sasha.

"Thank you. You have no idea how much I appreciate your help."

She gives me a single nod in response, her throat muscles working hard to swallow the ball of emotion that's threatening to choke her while she continues putting medication and bandages on me. When she works her way down to my hand, her disgust with the process and their tactics is released in a string of curses and obscenities hurled at the two men in particular. After cleaning the area around where my fingernail was, she slathers it with Vaseline before wrapping it with nonstick bandages and gauze. She takes so much time to give me her full attention and care, but I can't help but wonder why. So that I look more presentable when my father identifies my body?

"Tell my parents I love them and that I don't blame them for anything."

She nods and wipes away a stray tear from her eye.

"It's okay, Sasha. I know what's coming. Thank you for everything you've ever done for me. I haven't ever appreciated the people in my life nearly enough. Before it's too late, I want you to know you were always special to me."

"Thank you for saying that, Kira. I've often wondered if my job mattered. It's nice to hear that it does." She stands abruptly, moves to the small wardrobe, and returns with a clean prisoner uniform. It's a very dull and lifeless tan outfit—far from fashionable while remaining utterly functional at the same time. "Let's get you out of those dirty clothes and into some clean ones."

She gasps when I pull my shirt over my head. The bruises and burns I've endured are still relatively fresh, but the recent lashes left the worst marks. Before helping me into the clean shirt, she takes the time to apply ointment and bandages to the raw areas. When I'm finally dressed, she pulls me into her arms and holds me for several long seconds. After the last—I don't even know how long I've been here—however many days it's been, this little bit of warmth is enough.

General Krupin opens the door and starts to say my

name but stops when he sees us in an embrace. After a few moments, his patience is worn thin. "Kira, come with me."

We walk down the long, dark corridor and turn left when we reach the end. A few doors down on the right, light filters into the hall from under the door. He opens it and extends his arm into the room, indicating for me to enter. Inside, I find a twin bed, a small desk and chair, and an en suite bathroom.

"As a favor to your father, I've arranged to let you stay in here for the next few nights. No more questioning. Absolutely no more techniques to encourage you to talk. Make yourself comfortable—this is your room now. Your dinner will be here in about an hour."

"Thank you, General. I appreciate your kindness."

Sleep is the last thing on my mind, but as my thoughts drift to Silas and the last interaction we had, my body decides to shut down after all the recent trauma. The darkness pulls me under, my muscles relax, and my mind finally calms. When the need for rest surpasses my desire to stay awake until my execution, I give in and let my dreams take me to the places I've left behind.

The beach with Silas.

Noah's house in Miami.

Our nightly routine of falling asleep in each other's arms after hours of exhausting escapades.

These are the images my dreams are made of.

The next couple of days are much of the same. Rest, recuperate, and refuel with the large meals they bring three times a day. But that all changes the third day in my new room. The guard's personality is entirely different when he delivers breakfast. He refuses to make eye contact with me and acts slightly nervous.

At lunch, the tray is left on the floor outside the door, and he only alerts me with a knock. When I open the door, he's already gone.

He's completely avoiding me.

That means today is the day.

Execution day.

After I finish eating lunch, I stroll into the bathroom and take a long, hot shower. Then I dry and style my hair after rebandaging my hand. There's no reason why Mom and Dad need to see that exposed. There's no makeup in here, so the au naturel look will have to do. Just as well— it's the way I came into the world, and it's the way I'll go out.

Morose. Morbid. Depressing. But true.

A light rap on the door draws my attention just before the doorknob slowly turns. When the door swings open, General Krupin waits with a sad expression on his face.

"I'm sorry, Kira. I argued for a stay of execution, but I was overruled. There's nothing more I can do, my dear. It's time."

The long walk to the execution room simultaneously feels like it takes forever and is over in the blink of an eye. Thick plastic covers the floor, making the cleanup effort an easy job. General Krupin moves to stand behind the desk on the back wall as the lone judge, jury, and witness to the execution. My executioner stands behind me, his hands firmly gripping my biceps to hold me in place.

He knows the drill all too well. He knows what's about to happen.

My knees buckle underneath me from the fear and anxiety coursing through my veins at over 200 miles per hour, and my captor prevents me from crumbling into a heap on the floor before my time. My heart is no longer beating, only fluttering in my chest as it tries to keep up with the adrenaline that's been dumped into my bloodstream. My face is wet from the tears streaming down my cheeks like a raging river during the spring thaw. Strange, since I didn't even realize I was crying until just now.

"I'll leave you to it, then. Goodbye, Kira." In the back of my mind, I hear General Krupin's voice, but his words don't register. All my focus is on the plastic on the floor underneath me.

"I've got you. It's okay now." Strong arms wrap around my waist from behind me and pull me against a hard chest. With virtually no effort, he twists me around, slides his arm under my knees, and cradles me against him. "We're getting the fuck out of here right now."

He jumps to his feet with me secure in his arms, and the whiff of air that envelops me pulls me out of my haze. I know that scent. I recognize that voice. When I peer up at him through my teardrop-covered lashes, the face I see doesn't match who I know the voice belongs to.

"Silas?"

"Yeah, baby, it's me." I've never loved being called that term of endearment more than I do at this moment.

Two men enter from the other end of the room, carrying a limp body to the spot where Silas just stood. She's dressed in the same prison uniform I am. Her hair and build match mine. They lay her down on the plastic and roll her tightly inside.

"Who is she?"

"Her name is Kira Petrova. This lady was an enemy of the state for the murder of the Minister of Health. She injected him with poison after he raped her. Her execution was scheduled to take place today, but she decided to take matters into her own hands and not give anyone else control over her fate." He places soft kisses all over my face, hugs me tightly to him for several long seconds, then helps me to stand on my own again.

The confused expression on my face quickly morphs into understanding. According to all official records, Kira Petrova died in this prison today. That's all that matters to them—that I'm dead and gone. I nod slowly, feeling guilty for being grateful to a woman who took her own life. "Who am I?"

"You're Nadia Utkin, attaché for the Canadian Ambassador. You're here on a diplomatic goodwill assignment to help orphaned children."

The two guards carry Kira Petrova out of the room, and Sasha walks in with a garment bag. "Here you are, Miss Utkin. Your change of clothes just arrived." Tears glisten in her eyes as she passes the packet to me. "I hope you have a safe trip home. I'm sorry you were in a car wreck during your first trip to Russia." She lightly strokes the still visible wounds on my face.

"Thank you." I can barely choke out the words.

She leaves us alone, and Silas turns to face me now that we're alone. "I'm so sorry, baby. I'm sorry I had even one doubt about you and your intentions. This is all my fault—everything you've been through over the last week. If I'd had my head screwed on right, this never would've happened."

I step toward him and put my finger over his lips, shaking my head. "Viktor played us both from the beginning, Silas. He made sure our paths crossed then took advantage of our connection. Since he held all the cards, there wasn't much we could've done to change the outcome. If it wasn't here, it would've happened somewhere else. And I forgive you for questioning me. The story he told was a good one, and you're trained to be suspicious of everyone. It's part of who you are now."

He bends over and places a soft kiss on my lips. "I'll make it up to you, I promise."

"Don't think you'll ever get away with that shit again, though. You used your one free chance. If there's a next time, you'll pay dearly for it." I narrow my eyes at him, but I can't contain the smile that immediately follows. I'm just so happy and relieved and elated and grateful to see him again at all.

"Never again, baby. Let's get you out of that prison uniform and into your regular clothes. We have to move quickly now." He sheds his uniform and puts on a tailored suit in record time.

He doesn't have to tell me twice. In seconds, I'm out of the lifeless tan garb and dressed in a beautiful blue shell dress and matching jacket. Silas clips the required Kremlin identification badge on the lapel of my coat before pulling more tricks out of his pocket.

"So I get a facial prosthesis too?"

"Yes, we can't look like ourselves when we walk out of here. Too many people in this building can recognize both of us on sight." After a couple minutes, he completely changes my facial features, making me unrecognizable as Kira. "Can I escort you out, Miss Utkin?"

I glance at his badge and smile up at him. "Yes, Mr. Fedorov. You do know what that name means, don't you?"

"Absolutely. It's Greek for 'gift of God.' I think it fits me perfectly, don't you?" The teasing, playful glint in his eyes is back.

"Of course. Most days anyway."

"Most days? How about today?"

"Most definitely today, without a doubt." My knight in shining armor. The crazy American who broke in a Kremlin-run prison to free the woman he…what? What am I to him?

"Yes, I love you, baby. With all my heart, I do, and I've never said those words before to a woman outside of my family in my life. I'm afraid you're stuck with me for the rest of yours."

"If you insist. Let's hope that's a long life, with too many years ahead of us to count…and not only the next few minutes while we're escaping from this building."

When we step off the elevator on the main floor, the buzz of workers hurrying from one place to another is a stark contrast to the dungeon we just left. No one even bothers to pass a glance our way. Our indistinct features and visitor passes don't draw the kind of interest and respect the high-ranking officials here do. We head straight for the door that leads outside and to freedom. Every half second that passes only increases the panic rising in my chest. We're so close but so far away.

Stepping out into the sun has never felt as wonderful as it does now. After the last week of torture, waiting to die, and trying to live, my emotions are all over the board. Silas puts his hand on the small of my back and leads me to the waiting car and driver. He's arranged the entire setup and ensured every detail is authentic to our cover. When we slide into the back seat, he tells the driver to get us to the airport immediately. Then he hands me a passport with my new name and picture on it.

"How'd you get a current picture of me?" I'm wearing the prosthesis in the passport photo.

"I'm hurt that you doubt my skills like that, Nadia."

Hurt, my ass. That smile is one of pure pride.

When we get out of the car at the airport, I use all my willpower not to run straight out onto the tarmac and hop on the first plane out of the country. Silas gives no outward indication of being rushed or worried whatsoever, but his eyes scan the area for possible threats more than usual. He's ready to fight our way out if necessary.

He reaches for the door leading into the airport terminal to open it for me but pauses for just a second. "I have a surprise for you before we leave."

"Silas, I appreciate the gesture, really I do, but can't it wait until we get home? I've had enough excitement for one day."

He offers me a small smile, but there's a hint of sadness in his eyes. Then he pulls on the door, and I start to walk through. My feet suddenly stop moving, and my lungs stop working. My eyes bug out of my head, momentarily unable to comprehend the sight directly in front of me. I cover my mouth with my hand to prevent the squeal that's building inside me from erupting.

"Mama? Daddy?" I rush to them. Arms wrap around me from everywhere, squeezing me with all the love my parents have in them.

"I couldn't let you leave without saying goodbye this time. The good news is they'll be able to visit us now that Kira is gone." Silas stands beside us, watching our family reunion after too many years apart.

Daddy holds me with one hand and grabs Silas with the other, pulling him into our tight circle. Through his tears, he somehow manages to speak. "Thank you for this, Silas. I thought I'd never get my little girls back."

Mama cries and repeatedly kisses both Silas and me. We're causing a scene in the middle of the airport, but

I'm not even worried now. These few minutes are worth the risk. Then a different kind of panic grips me.

"Mama, Daddy, what about Amber? Did Sasha get her out?" I search their faces, praying Sasha was able to pull off one last miracle for me.

"See for yourself." Silas points toward the security line.

A beautiful little girl waits with her small suitcase, sitting in a chair beside the security checkpoint agent. Her eyes land on mine and a bright smile covers her face.

"Sasha brought her to our house a couple of nights ago. We explained she'd be reunited with you soon, but that you'd look different because you had to hide from some bad men, too. She understood that and promised she wouldn't tell anyone who you are," Mama explains. "She's not your daughter, though?"

"She is now," Silas replies while watching Amber. Then he looks down at me. "She's our daughter."

I jerk my eyes up to meet his. On the one hand, I'm shocked at his declaration, then I realize I shouldn't be. The man only has one weakness, and that's his love for children. I've seen it in the way he loves his nieces and nephews. In how he competes with Shadow and Bull for the honor of being the favorite uncle. In the way he spoils them and dotes on them with complete ease.

"Ours?" Tears again... I thought I'd have run out of them by now.

"Ours."

CHAPTER 24

Silas

*W*e've been back in the US for two weeks, staying at my brother's house for a little rest and relaxation now that we've closed the case against the congressman. Senator Hunt was more than willing to work with us on tracking Viktor's digital fingerprint through his files. But Viktor himself is like a ghost in the wind—he's out there, but he's hiding.

Most of Kira's wounds have healed, all except her hand. That'll take several more months before her fingernail is back to normal. Every time I even glance at it, I'm reminded of how narrowly I made it there in time to stop her execution. A few men who were still loyal to her father agreed to help get her out of the country.

If they hadn't agreed, I would've shot them all on the spot so they couldn't stop me and still gotten her out. Of course, her father didn't take much convincing at all. I sensed he was ready to storm the dungeons himself.

Kira has asked several times about the woman who took her place. Survivor's guilt still bothers her at times, but I've assured her what I told her about the woman was true. She retaliated against a cruel man for the hell he'd put her through, and the officials sentenced her to die for her actions. She didn't regret what she'd done, though, and chose her own path out of this life. She has my respect for sticking to her guns the way she did. And she has my eternal gratitude for giving me a last-minute Hail Mary to save Kira.

"Here's a question I haven't asked you yet." Kira has peppered me every day with one question after the other about how I got there, how I found her, and how I was dressed in a Russian military uniform.

"There are no questions left in this world you haven't asked me. I'd bet my life on it. This is worse than a hostile interrogation."

"Don't bet your life on it—you'd lose. I don't want to lose you again."

"Fine. I'd bet my truck on it, then."

"Does that mean I get your truck when you're wrong?"

"No."

She laughs, shakes her head, and rolls her eyes at me. "The last thing I remember is being locked in the cabin of a boat. Amber and I lay down on the bed to get some sleep, but I was on a plane bound for Moscow when I woke up. How did that happen?"

"The best we can piece together from our contact in Havana is Viktor introduced an aerosol sleeping agent into the boat's cabin to make sure you didn't fight. Then he had Amber and you transferred to the plane."

"Told you I hadn't asked that question before."

"I'm pretty sure you have. Maybe even twice."

"Liar." She swats my arm playfully. "Our vacation is almost over. The real world waits for us to rejoin it. I have to figure out what I'll do for a living now. My Russian spy career is over, you know, since I'm dead and all."

"Do you have any idea how hard it was for me to convince Graves of that? That man is way more distrustful than I am. But he does have a job offer for you if you're interested. You wouldn't have access to any of our files, just to be clear. But he's willing to give you a chance."

"That's amazing, Silas. What's the job? Not that beggars can be choosers, but I'm obviously curious."

"Linguistics. Translating documents and verbal conversations for us. Detecting any hidden messages or ciphers."

"Sounds like that's right up my alley. I can't wait to find out more about it."

My family walks out the back door, joining us on the deck. Noah walks straight to the grill and fires it up, while Brianna and Chaise try to corral the younger kids.

Amelia and Amber dash out of the house, running as fast as their little legs will carry them, and dive right on top of me. I pretend to be hurt, as if those little girls could do any damage to me, and I wait until they check on me to reveal my hand.

When they squat down level with my face, patting my head, I suddenly fly up with a roar and grab them in my arms. They squeal and laugh, only pretending they want to get away from me while I act like a monster. Then they settle into my lap, each in the crook of my arms, and lean back against my chest.

"My double A batteries." I kiss each of them on the head.

"We're not batteries, Uncle Silas," Amelia says then cackles.

"You could've fooled me. You have way too much energy. You're always running. You never slow down. You two sound just like batteries to me, little girl."

"Big brother, you look good with two kids on your lap. I bet you'd look even better with two more." Chaise sits down beside us with her daughter asleep in her arms. "You're behind the rest of us. You're the oldest—you're supposed to be setting the example for us youngsters."

"You're so funny, Chaise." My deadpan expression only makes her laugh harder at me. "Hey, where's Shadow? I've only seen him once since we've been back."

"Oh, he's still in the doghouse with Elle. He hasn't been around as much lately." Noah tries to suppress his grin, but it's still there, bright as the sun anyway.

"Did he ever find her?" I look over at Noah to gauge his reaction. He coughs to try to hide his laughter.

"Um, no, he hasn't. The infamous CIA officer who has ways of finding someone in the WITSEC program halfway around the world can't find his own wife here in Miami."

"He knows she's still in the area?"

"Yeah, he's isolated and analyzed every single background noise he hears—when she'll take his calls, that is. He'll think he has it figured out, but she's never there when he arrives." Noah shrugs but doesn't seem overly concerned about her whereabouts.

"You know where she is."

"I have an idea. But she doesn't want to be found, or she'd tell Shadow where she is. I'm giving them time to work out their problems without interfering."

"You're watching him squirm. You should feel bad— he has helped you out of all kinds of problems." Then I think about what I just said and realize it doesn't sound like my brother at all. "Oh, I get it. She asked you not to say anything, didn't she?"

"She made me swear. It's killing me that I can't even give him a clue or a hint."

"You better not, Noah, or you'll find yourself in the same situation. You know I love Shadow like a brother, but he's put Elle through enough. This time, he gets to see what it feels like to be left out." I love my sister-in-law. She keeps my brother in line better than his commanding officers ever could.

"Yes, ma'am. You know I'm not going anywhere, and neither are you. The food's ready. Come and get it before it's all gone."

We gather around the grill and table, piling food on our plates as if we'll never eat again. When we're all settled in and enjoying our meal, Kira's phone pings with a text message. She picks it up mid-bite and glances at the screen before dropping her fork and choking on her food.

"It's Viktor. He sent a picture of the dead woman from Moscow, Silas. He knows." Her hands shake, and she's breathing so fast, she'll hyperventilate soon.

"Kira, calm down, baby. Listen to my voice right now. He won't get to you again—I won't let that happen. You're not going anywhere either."

Her phone vibrates in her hand with another text, and all color drains from her face. She drops her phone on the table, and her hands fly to her mouth. From her reaction, that's the only way she's containing a scream. I grab the phone and look at the picture on the screen.

This picture is of Sasha. She's been brutally murdered.

Working on autopilot, I grab my phone from my pocket and call Dmitri. "Get Nat and get out of your house right now. Take her to the place no one knows about. You remember the place we used to talk about, right?"

"Yes, I remember. We're leaving now." He disconnects, not wasting time asking questions. He knows I would only mention that in a dire emergency. This situation positively qualifies.

"Kira, your parents are okay. They're going into hiding now until we can get them out of the country. If they make it to our secret place, we can extract them without Viktor or anyone from the GRU ever knowing." I hold her hands in mine, waiting for my words to sink in and make sense to her.

"Okay," she stutters, her teeth chattering. "Sasha. Oh my god, he mutilated her."

"I know, and I'm so sorry, baby. We tried to get her to come with us, but she refused. She said that she was home. She was born there, and she would die there. She knew the risks she faced, but she wanted to give you the best life she could because she loved you."

"Mira? Is Mira okay? Find my sister."

"I'm here, Kira. What's wrong?" Mira joins us, walking hand in hand with Brad. She rushes to her sister's side and wraps her arms around her. We give Mira the abbreviated version of what's happening.

"We have to kill him, Kira. He won't ever stop coming after us if we don't. You, me, Mom, and Dad—and anyone else we love—will always be targets." Mira hugs Kira and tries to quiet her tears.

"You're absolutely right. I'll do it—I'll find him and kill him the same way he killed Sasha." Kira's fighting to regain control of her emotions and think somewhat rationally.

"You're not doing anything of the sort. If you get

involved in anything to do with this again, we'll both be exiled to Siberia. You'll have to trust me to handle it once and for all. Now that he's contacted you, I'll find him. Don't you worry, baby."

She nods and leans against me. I wrap my arm around her and hold her against me. We quickly change the subject so that the kids don't get overwhelmed with our stress. Kira picks at her food, not really eating much but also not wanting to appear rude. Plus, Amber encourages her every couple of minutes to eat because the food her uncle Noah made is so good.

Kira can't resist that little girl.

When Brianna brings out the dessert, Shadow lumbers in, looking like a shell of his former self. He's in pain, suffering every day without his better half. I know a little about how he feels. The week that Kira was missing and I didn't know if she was still alive was pure hell, and we hadn't even been together for long at that point. Shadow and Elle have a long history together, one he likely relives every night without her.

"There's my brother. How are you today?" Brianna turns and hugs Shadow.

"I'm a miserable fucking fool. That's how I am today."

"Watch your language around the kids."

"Fuck. I'm sorry, Bri."

"Call her, Shadow. Tell her how you feel instead of trying to play the CIA officer investigating your target. She told you what she wanted—for you to open up to her and let her in your life. Listen to her and do what she's asking you to do. You're suffering for no reason."

Shadow considers her advice for a minute before finally surrendering. "Okay, Bri. I know you're right."

He sits down at the table and dials her number on his cell. We all hold our breath while it rings, pretending we're not all eavesdropping on his private conversation.

"Elle? Don't hang up, darlin'. Just hear me out. I've said I'm sorry a million times, but I want to tell you what I'm sorry for this time. You've been my life for as long as I can remember now. But I realize that by trying to protect you from what I do, I've excluded you from being in my life. I know I hurt you by leaving you out, by not telling you the truth about everything, and even by lying about some of the things I did.

"From now on, I want you to be involved in everything in my life. If that means I have to share top-secret information with you so that you'll believe I mean what I say, then so be it. If I need to quit my job and learn to love another line of work, then that's what I'll do. I only want you to come back home to me, be my wife, my best friend, my lover. What would make you happy and make you love me again?"

"I've never stopped loving you, Devon. I had a crush on you as a kid when you were my brother's best friend. I fell in love with you years ago. And I love you more today than I did yesterday." Elle steps out of the kitchen onto the back deck, shocking the hell out of Shadow.

He drops his phone and rushes to her, wrapping his

arms around her and squeezing her so tightly, she can hardly breathe. "I've missed you so much, darlin'. I'm so glad to see you and hold you again. Where have you been?"

"That's not important. What matters is that you understand how it feels to be completely excluded from my life. Not knowing where I am, what I'm doing, who I'm with, or if I'm okay. We either make a life together, or we'll be apart for good. Make up your mind right now and stick to it, Devon. Because if you ever do this to me again, I'll make that choice for you, and I won't change my mind again."

"You always have been and always will be my entire life. I understand exactly how I made you feel, and I'll never hurt you like that again. I love you, darlin'. More than you'll ever know. In fact, I'm so in love with you, I'm ready to give you a baby right now. I want a little girl who looks exactly like you."

Tears well up in Elle's eyes as she draws in a ragged breath. She places his hand on her stomach and keeps her eyes locked on his. "I can't promise you it'll be a girl, but we're definitely having a baby in about seven months."

Shadow changes from a downtrodden, beaten soul to an elated and exhilarated man right before my eyes. He lifts her off her feet and twirls her around with the biggest smile plastered on his fugly mug.

"I can't believe I'm going to be a daddy." Shadow's

voice is full of excitement. He's so loud, I wouldn't be surprised if the neighbors heard him.

I feel a hand slide into mine and squeeze, so I look away from the happily reunited couple to find Kira watching me with an odd expression. This is one of the rare times I'm unable to read her mind.

"I love you, Silas. I just realized I've never said it, although I should've already told you a million times over. I love you like I've never loved anyone in my life."

I press my lips against hers, relishing the softness there while also wishing I could satisfy the yearning I feel in them. She rubs her fingers along my jaw then into my hair as I deepen the kiss. It's still amazing to me that I can't get enough of this woman, no matter how hard I try.

The urgent tapping of a little hand on my arm ends the tender moment I'm sharing with Kira, and I look down at Amber with her big blue eyes staring up at me. "I love you too. Are you my daddy now?"

Stick a fork in me. I'm done.

CHAPTER 25

Silas

*W*hen we returned from Russia, the first thing we did was contact the authorities and the Department of Children and Families about Amber. We were fortunate to have contacts—thank you, Senator Hunt, for your influence—to get an emergency custody order to keep Amber with us while the formal paperwork to foster her is finalized. Fostering is just the first step, though. We've agreed to co-adopt her and raise her as our own. She's already stolen our hearts, and we've proven we're willing to go to the ends of the earth for her, so her assigned social worker was more than happy to keep her out of the normal process.

I fully realize we're blessed beyond measure. Most people who want to adopt don't experience the same speedy service. But just looking at that precious little girl, I know I couldn't have given her up even if they'd said no.

Now that I feel responsible for two beautiful ladies, taking out Viktor is more important to me than ever. After we located him when he took them to Havana, I never actually lost tabs on him. I've just been biding my time. His handler has been protecting him inside the Russian embassy in DC, but a man like him could only take being locked behind the walls of that building for so long.

He's accustomed to moving around freely and playing his games at will. Inside the embassy, he'd be held to their strict rules and code of conduct. Without autonomy, a spy can only drive a desk and do what his superiors tell him to do. The very concept of thinking on his feet flies out the window, and he's left with the memories of the "good old days" when he could make his own decisions.

I know all too well how that scenario would work out for me... It wouldn't. Same line of business, same circumstances, I know it won't work for him. And I know he'll never be content with sending those lame texts like the pussy he is. He'll crave a more hands-on approach to his taunting and mocking, but he'll never have the chance. I'll make sure of that.

Which also concerns me that the job Kira's been offered won't work for her when we get back to DC. Will she be happy working in an office, behind a desk, and shuffling papers? Or will she be bored to tears and looking for something else to fulfill the thrill of the chase?

One major hurdle at a time, Silas. There's one thing we need to focus on at the moment.

When I slip into bed with Kira, I slide my arm over her waist and pull her back against my front. "This is our last night here. Back to DC in the morning. Are you going to miss Miami Beach?"

"Absolutely. I'm not sure I'm mentally prepared to face another DC winter after spending so much time in South Florida."

"Do you think you'd ever want to move here permanently? My parents live nearby. Noah and his crew are here frequently. Chaise and Bull and their kids follow when Noah comes back. Actually, so do Rebel, Heather, Shadow, and Elle. And Brad, of course. They all work together and count on one another to get shit done."

She turns and looks at me, the moonlight caressing her face through the blinds. "If we did, Amber would get to grow up with a huge family. Aunts, uncles, cousins, and grandparents to make all the bad memories disappear and replace them with only good. That would be perfect."

"Yes, Amber would have that...and so would you. This extended family loves you too, you know?"

"The first time you told me you loved me, I wasn't sure if I'd imagined it or if you'd really said it. That day was the worst. But I realized you made me feel the words long before you spoke them. The way you've protected me, helped me, trusted me, and saved me.

"You risked your own life to save mine. I mean, you came into the Kremlin dressed as a Russian officer in uniform. If you'd been caught...well, I don't even want to think about what they would've done to you. I still can't believe you did all that for me."

"I'd do it all again—and more, Kira. I realize my timing couldn't have been worse, but I knew there was a chance neither of us would make it out of there alive. I couldn't let that happen without telling you how much you mean to me first. Now that I've accepted the fact that I can never go back to being the bachelor who's content with being alone, I'll tell you how much you mean to me every day. It's amazing how much real love can make someone want the things they never wanted before."

"I know exactly what you mean because I feel the same way."

"I don't think it'll be a problem to convince Roman to move back here. He's originally from Florida, so I think he feels the same about the cold and snow as you do. I'm not sure about Nick and Savannah, though. If nothing else, we'd just rely on video conferences for our meetings and cases. We don't have to be in the DC area all the time to do our jobs."

"Just think, if we can convince the entire Scooby gang to live in the same area, we can start our own cult.

Noah's house can be our compound." Then she bursts out in uncontrollable laughter, and I join her.

Hearing her laugh, seeing her relaxed and playful, and knowing she's safe and sound in my arms gives me more happiness than I ever imagined possible. Guess it just took meeting the right person, at the right time, and under the right circumstances to change my mind about marriage, love, and a happily-ever-after ending.

Thoughts of a happy ending give me more immediate ideas. With my lips pressed to hers, I roll her onto her back and cover her body with mine. The feel of her body against mine is like pouring jet fuel on the open flame of my libido. After I peel off her clothes, I take my time and give every inch of her body all the attention she can take. With my lips, with my tongue, and with my fingers, I give her my full devotion. When I slide into her, she fits around me as if she is made only for me. The sensation of my every powerful thrust and the sound of her every sexy moan only make me want her more. When we reach the peak of our desire, we tumble over the edge together, our bodies slick with sweat, her nails digging into my back, and our eyes locked in the final throes.

"Just so you know, I'm never letting you go. You're stuck with me now, baby."

"You're the one who's stuck with me. If you ever try to leave me, I'll just follow you."

∿

WE SAY GOODBYE FOR NOW TO MY EXTENDED FAMILY AND head to the private airstrip for our return trip to DC. Nick, Savannah, and their small kids board the plane while we help stow all their luggage. Then Roman, Brad, Mira, Kira, Amber, and I all take our seats. Now is as good a time as any to broach the subject of relocating. As I predicted to Kira last night, the only holdout is Nick, with his meticulous planning and need for order. He won't make that decision without having time to discuss it thoroughly with Savannah, but I can see the wheels turning in his mind. He's thinking about all the same points I had—so many members of our family and friends would be close by, making life easier for all of us.

"What do you think about the prospect of moving, Savannah?" Mira asks.

Mira is Savannah and Nick's live-in nanny as of today, but I have a feeling that'll change soon anyway. Her relationship with Brad seems to be taking on a life of its own. He's as crazy about Mira as I am about her sister. Since the two ladies have been separated for more than a year now, they'll definitely want to live close to each other.

"I'm very intrigued by just the thought. Staying with Brianna for the last few weeks in Miami have completely spoiled me." Savannah looks over at Nick and grins, essentially giving away her final answer.

"Honestly, I think if I said yes right now, she'd have all of our belongings packed the minute we get home." Nick smiles at the thought. "We don't have any family in the DC area. Savannah's best friend and her husband would be welcome to stay with us whenever they wanted. Since she works from home, moving wouldn't affect that either."

"That's a good point, Nick. What about you, Kira? That job proposal was only in the office. You wouldn't be able to do that from Miami. Are you sure you want to give up that offer?" I turn to Kira to gauge her reaction.

"That doesn't bother me. Sitting in an office from eight to five isn't my idea of fun, but I was willing to do it for the opportunity. There are plenty of other jobs I can find, so I'm honestly not worried about it. Besides, according to the government, I'm Nadia Utkin now, and she doesn't have a sordid past. As long as we're all together, I'll be fine." She leans over and kisses my cheek.

We land in DC, and I stop Nick and Kira before we reach my truck. "Nick, I need a favor."

"Of course. What's up?"

"Can Kira and Amber stay with you and Savannah for a while? I have some business to take care of, and I won't leave them alone yet."

Kira looks at me as if I've lost my mind. I offer an apologetic shrug, but that's the most she'll get from me on this. She almost died once—I won't knowingly take her back into a situation where that could happen.

"You got it. Kira, Mira, and Amber are welcome to hang out with Savannah and me for as long as they need. Brad, do you have plans for dinner tonight?"

"Nope, none."

"Good. Join us for dinner. Savannah will love having a house full of adults to talk to for a while longer, and the three of you can finish convincing her to move to Miami."

We get a good laugh out of that. "Chickenshit."

"Hey, I just know who takes care of me. Let's go—the Tucker train is leaving the station."

Kira wraps her arms around my waist and looks up at me with worry in her eyes. "Why do I have a feeling you're about to do something I wouldn't like?"

"I don't know, baby. Maybe you know me a little too well." I smile down at her and place a soft, lingering kiss on her lips. "Don't worry. I'll be by Nick's to pick you up late tonight."

"Please be careful. If you don't show up, I'll hunt you down and make you regret it."

"Yes, ma'am."

Small arms wrap around my leg and squeeze as hard as a five-year-old is capable of. I lean over and lift Amber in the air until she's sitting comfortably on my forearm. She leans her head over on my shoulder and wraps her thin arms around my neck. She doesn't have to say anything because I know exactly what she's thinking. She knows we're going in separate directions, and she wants to hold on to our little family.

"Don't worry, sweet girl. I'll be there to pick you up, too. You believe me, don't you?"

She nods her head, but she still clings to me. When I

finally hand her over to Kira, a big piece of my heart goes with her. The sadness on her face at our being separated almost changes my mind.

Almost. But I'm doing this to protect her too.

They all pile into Nick's SUV, and Kira and Amber wave at me as they drive away. Roman is still standing beside me, acting casual but knowing something big is about to go down.

"What's the plan, Silas?"

"I know where he is. I'm going to kill him."

"What do you want me to do?"

"Cover the exits so he doesn't slither away again like the snake he is."

"You got it."

We climb into my truck and head to my place to coordinate our movements. When night falls and it's pitch black outside, we make our way to the rendezvous point. As I suspected, Viktor has been sneaking out of the embassy to frequent his favorite watering holes and go home with whatever willing woman he can find. Tonight, I'm helping him out with a sure thing.

I wait silently in the darkened room for them to get inside the house. She comes in first with her keys still in her hand. He's hot on her heels, holding on to her hips and kissing the side of her neck. She promised him a night he'll never forget, and she didn't lie.

"Oh shit. I left my purse in the car. I need to grab it before someone steals it out of the backseat. We've had a string of car break-ins lately. I'll be right back—make yourself comfortable on the couch." She nods her head toward the sofa, and he takes her up on her offer.

Fucker should've offered to get it for her at the very least.

She closes the door behind her with a smug smile on her face. When she turned the lock on the way in, she activated an automatic mechanism that locks the door from the inside. He won't be able to run out that door when he realizes something is awry. And that realization will hit him in three...two...

"What the fuck?" He jumps up when he hears the car engine start. He's still staring out the window when the car headlights flash across him as she drives away.

He darts to the door to open it, only thinking about getting his rocks off tonight, but the door won't open. The knob only spins freely in his hand. "What the fuck is wrong with this door?"

"Nothing's wrong with it."

He jumps about a foot high and twirls around toward the sound of my voice. His back is pushed against the door, and his eyes are wide with fear.

"That doorknob is working exactly as designed. It's locked and can't be opened from the inside without the right tool. It's keeping you in here with me, where you need to be. No more hiding out in the Russian embassy. No more using the consulate as your errand boy. No more sneaking out of the building at night to grab some pussy. That doorknob's sole job is to make my job of executing you easier." I step out of the shadows and directly into the stream of light coming in through the windows.

I want him to know I'm the one who ends his life.

I want him to die knowing that he lost and Kira won.

I want him to know he's as much of a piece of shit as his older brother was.

"Silas Steele. I have diplomatic immunity. You can't touch me." He juts out his chin, daring me.

Challenge accepted.

With a quick jab, I bust his nose and deflate his puffed-out chest. "Funny, I just touched you. Guess your diplomatic immunity superpowers don't work in here."

"You know what I mean, fucker!"

"I know exactly what you mean. But you don't have that immunity anymore, Viktor Egorov."

"My name is Viktor Sokolov—not Egorov."

"Not according to this passport, it isn't. You're here illegally, and you attacked an NSA agent."

"You work for the CIA."

"Some days, I do. Some days, I work for the NSA. Today, I'm an NSA agent. Guess you're shit out of luck, Egorov. Be sure to tell your pedophile brother I said I hope he's rotting in hell beside you."

Before Viktor can respond or even attempt to run for his life, I draw my handgun and leave a trench in his head wide enough to drive a car through.

"Roman, do me a favor? Call for a clean-up crew."

"You got it, Silas. I'll take it from here. Go pick up your woman and your new daughter. They've waited long enough for a happy home."

"Thanks, man. I'll talk to you later."

CHAPTER 26

Kira—One Year Later

"r. Steele?" I call out from the veranda.

"Yes, Mrs. Steele?" Silas replies with an unmistakable smile in his tone. I'm aware a sound can't smile, but somehow, Silas pulls it off, regardless. What can I say? The man is multi-talented.

"I seem to be out of lemonade. Do you mind fixing that little problem for me?"

"Not at all. I'm on my way." My hunk of a man slides up beside me, shirtless, wearing his swimming shorts and flip-flops, and refills my glass.

"Service with a smile. I love it, Mr. Steele."

"I'll service you with a smile any time you want, Mrs. Steele." He waggles his eyebrows at me, making me blush.

"For the love of God, please stop with the Mr. and

Mrs. Steele bullshit. You two have been saying that every day for the last month since you got married." Noah shakes his head as he passes by us, but I see the huge smile on his face despite his words.

"The new hasn't worn off yet. We'll stop saying it when it gets old," Silas retorts.

"So, you mean, never. You're never going to stop."

"Exactly." Silas smiles broadly, showing how proud he is of his witty reply.

The past year has held so many changes for us, it's hard to keep up with everything sometimes. We moved from DC to Miami. We left the cold and snow in favor of sand and surf. Our friends and family were all too excited to move with us, even Nick and Savannah. Spending time with them without the constant threat of danger surrounding us made it a much more relaxed atmosphere.

Now I completely understand why everyone loves Savannah so much. She's so giving and caring, but she's also strong and resilient. She had a rough time with a former flame, and she gives Nick all the credit for saving her. He disagrees—he insists he only provided the muscle and she did the rest.

Mira and Brad married soon after we returned to DC. I'd never seen her so excited before. She ran into Nick's house while we were visiting, crying and laughing at the same time, to show off her engagement ring. Brad followed behind her with a red face and a huge smile. He promised me he would love and care for her for the rest of her life. I promised no one would ever find his body if he broke that promise.

I'm positive he believed me.

The adoption of Amber was finalized, so she's officially a Steele now. She had her name changed before I did. She was thrilled to write her new last name on all her school papers. I'm officially Mama, and Silas is officially Daddy. My parents are officially thrilled for all of us and visit as often as they're able, doting on their granddaughter and spending time with Mira and me. In the months between visits, we have weekly video chats so we can all share our lives. They hid in a remote cabin until Viktor was neutralized. Silas wouldn't take any chances of Viktor's associates getting to my parents. When the smoke cleared from that fiasco, Dad returned to work and announced his retirement. They moved to Zurich immediately after and haven't looked back since.

Amber had nightmares when we first brought her back home. We spent a lot of very late nights calming and soothing her and a lot of days talking to child psychologists about how best to treat her anxiety. She has more good days than bad now, so we're making substantial progress. Oddly enough, it's her daddy she wants when she wakes in the middle of the night. The therapist warned us his imposing male figure may frighten her more after what she experienced, but it seems to be just the opposite. She's comforted by how he protects her because she knows she can trust him. He'd never hurt her or abandon her.

She's definitely a daddy's girl.

"Where'd you go?" Silas sits down beside me and lightly strokes his knuckles across my cheek.

"Just thinking about how different everything is from just a short year ago. We were only here for two weeks last time, detoxing after my stint in a Russian prison and your elaborate prison break scheme, and now we're all closer than ever. Everything we've endured has brought us here, and I wouldn't change our life now for anything in the world. It's perfect. You're perfect. I love our little corner of the world."

"It only gets better from here, baby. I promise you that."

When the sun begins to set, Silas takes my hand and helps me up from the lounge chair. We help clean up the area after our impromptu pool party with the kids and head inside as the night air cools.

"Thanks again for letting us stay here with you while the painters are working on our house. I don't want Kira or Amber sniffing paint fumes all night." Silas puts a stack of dishes and cups in the sink and rolls up his sleeves before loading them in the dishwasher.

"It's no problem at all. You're always welcome here, even if they're not painting. You know we love having you." Brianna pats him on the back on her way to the refrigerator with the leftover food.

"I'm going upstairs to take a shower, babe. Can you keep an eye on Amber? She's a little daredevil, and I'm afraid she'll jump in the pool when we're not watching." I wrap my arms around him from behind and squeeze him tightly.

"Shh—don't give her any ideas." He chuckles. "I've got her, baby. Go enjoy your long, hot shower."

I do exactly that—my shower is long, hot, and thoroughly relaxing. After I towel off and put on my nightgown, I dry my hair and finish getting ready for bed. After thirty or so minutes, I finally emerge from the bathroom and stroll into the bedroom, expecting to find Silas already sawing logs.

What I find instead is unbelievable. And almost indescribable.

Silas is lying in the middle of the bed, on top of the covers, sound asleep. He's wearing a French maid uniform, his swim shorts barely peeking out from under the frilly skirt. The fishnet hose that covers his legs from his thighs down to his toes are clipped to the hem of his shorts. Heavy makeup coats his face, complete with bright-blue eye shadow I thought had stopped being made back in the 80s. His lips are painted with very bright red lipstick. Topping it all off is a tiny cap decorated with lace and netting, held on his head with bobby pins.

"Oh, there you are. I couldn't find you earlier, so I had to get my friend Victoria to help me out with this. Be a dear and stay out of the frame for a minute, will you?" Liz saunters by me in a full tuxedo, complete with tails, a top hat, and white gloves, as if it's the most ordinary scene to walk in on.

She climbs up on the bed next to Silas and extends a riding crop toward him until it touches his leg. Victoria snaps picture after picture from every angle while Liz changes her position to show she's the dominant in each frame. When Victoria's tears of laughter flow so hard she can't see to take more pictures, Liz decides they have enough photographs. Then they're simply done—they start to walk out of the room together with no explanation.

"Um, hold on. What the hell is going on here? What did you do to Silas?"

Liz pats my cheek. "Oh, my sweet girl. I'm sorry if you had any plans to get frisky with him tonight. I'm afraid he'll sleep soundly until morning. He's perfectly fine—there are no dangerous side effects, other than he'll be hard to rouse until he's had time to sleep it off. He's probably forgotten the way he threatened to use sodium pentothal on me last year, but I never forget a thing. He has to pay for his crimes."

The two ladies saunter off together, scrolling through the pictures on Liz's phone and discussing which picture they will send to whom.

Noah passes them in the hall on the way to the master bedroom. He stops at our guest bedroom and glances inside. He doesn't appear fazed at all. Then he meets my questioning gaze and shrugs. "Guess he disrespected Liz again, huh?"

"This has happened before?"

"Not this exact payback, but close enough. Whatever

he did to her, he absolutely knew better than to do it in the first place. He'll find no sympathy around here. Good night, Kira."

Just like that, Noah's gone too.

Silas told me stories about Liz, but I thought he exaggerated for the sake of storytelling. Now, I think there's no way in hell he told me everything. He left out a lot of crazy details he obviously never thought I'd believe. Before I saw this entire scene firsthand, he would've been one-hundred-percent correct—I wouldn't have grasped the full magnitude.

But now...I can't let this moment pass without snapping a few pictures of my own. This is the perfect inspiration for ending possible future marriage spats.

I grab a blanket out of the closet to drape over him before sliding under the covers next to him. As soon as my head hits the pillow, I'm out like a light and sleep straight through until morning. When I wake, it's to my husband yelling obscenities and screaming Liz's name... in between trying to unzip the dress he's wearing.

I have to remember to ask Liz where she found his size...

"Kira?"

"Yes, dear?"

"Do you think you can stop laughing long enough to help me out of this getup?"

"I can't promise I'll stop laughing, but I will help you out of it."

"Ha-ha. Very funny."

After I unzip it and help him out of the dress and fishnets, he stomps into the bathroom across the hall, and the cursing resumes full force. He just realized he's wearing full stage makeup.

"Holy hell. This shit doesn't come off with soap and water. What kind of makeup did she put on me? Get the turpentine!"

Liz appears in the hallway with a devious grin on her face. "We're fresh out of turpentine, Silas."

He steps out of the bathroom to face Liz head on. "Then go to the store and buy more."

"The store is sold out of it too." Her tone is casual, unaffected by his mounting annoyance. She huffs on her fingernails then rubs them on her shirt, buffing them to a glistening shine.

"All of them?"

"Tragically, yes. There's a shortage of it in all of South Florida." She folds her arms across her chest. "Every single store is sold out of turpentine."

I feel like I'm watching an old Western movie with a showdown at twenty paces between two gunmen. It's not even high noon yet, so anything could happen before this feud is over. I still can't look away, though. It's all too fascinating to leave before it's over.

"All right, Liz. What did I do?"

"Do you remember threatening me with truth serum to learn all my secrets? You threw down the challenge, and I simply answered it. Of course, I won, as I knew I would."

"I don't recall that specific moment. All I can think is I must've been especially stressed at the time and didn't realize what I was saying." His reply is clearly made under duress, considering the way he's clenching his jaw and gritting his teeth as he speaks.

"Apology accepted. Do you promise never to dis me again?"

"Dis you?" He raises his eyebrows, and it's all I can do to keep from laughing out loud at the bright-blue eye shadow. "Yes, I promise never to do that again."

She hands him a small bottle of makeup remover from her pocket, explicitly designed for the product she applied. He disappears back into the bathroom to shower and scrub all the skin off his face to remove any traces of her artwork. When we finally join the others downstairs for breakfast, everyone's phone pings with text messages simultaneously. When we all look...except for Liz...I know what's inside.

Victoria has pieced the still pictures together to make a movie of Liz's dominatrix cosplay. Silas drops his fork on the plate and covers his bright red face in embarrassment while everyone else laughs, points, and makes crude jokes. I keep my eyes glued to my plate, but I can't stop my shoulders from shaking or the tears from pouring out of my eyes from my stifled laughter. When the replies from Bull, Rebel, and Shadow start pouring in, I completely lose it.

"Nice legs...you should get a job as the poster boy for Nair."

"That dress is fucking sexy. Does it come in men's sizes?"

"I'll never look at a French maid costume in the same light again. Or in any light, for that matter. Ever. Again."

"Liz. You coerced a surrender without telling me about the pictures?" It's not really a question, obviously. I think he simply needs a second to digest everything.

"You didn't ask about any pictures. Our agreement wasn't contingent on anything."

The stare-down occurring across the table tells me this competition isn't over by a long shot.

Looking around the table at this crazy bunch of people, I realize this is the family I never knew I wanted but always needed. They give love so freely, accepting and embracing one another's differences and similarities. When one is down, the others rally around until the situation passes. When one is in trouble, everyone takes it personally and doesn't walk away until the job is done, regardless of the personal costs. Their lighthearted banter is the perfect complement to the stress of everyday life.

I couldn't have picked a better man, husband, or best friend to spend my life with. Our love continues to grow stronger every day, with every passing hurdle we clear, and with every failure we overcome together. Our daughter is healthy and happy and keeps urging us to give her a little brother or sister. We're not quite ready for that yet, but we know it's in the cards for our future.

We somehow finish breakfast without further incidents then make plans to spend time with my in-laws for the rest of the day. The whole family will be there—that includes friends we've claimed as family.

Just over a year ago, this would've been more than I'd ever dared to dream about, to hope for, or to expect.

Today, I'm living my dream life to the fullest.

EPILOGUE

Roman—Three Years Ago

"*I* can't do this anymore." Tawnee places her hands on her hips and burns a hole through me with the anger in her eyes.

"You can't do what anymore?" I know she isn't saying what I think she's saying.

"Us, Roman. I can't do us anymore. This isn't working for me. I've put up with too much, and I can't do it one more day. I'm sorry, but this is over between us." She snatches her bag off the bed and starts toward the door.

"You're breaking up with me? Are you fucking kidding me right now?"

"No, I'm absolutely not kidding you at all. I'm done. I'm so done."

"What do you expect from me, Tawnee? I mean, I gave you a drawer and everything."

Ah, shit. That was the wrong thing to say apparently. She's seriously considering drawing her gun and shooting me right now. She's weighing the pros and cons at this very second. I can see it in her expression and the way her muscles are tensed. I don't know what I've done this time to piss her off so badly. All I know is whatever we fight about always ends up being my fucking fault.

"You gave me a drawer? Yeah, let's talk about that drawer, Roman. Let's examine that gesture for a minute. One, it's the smallest fucking drawer in the whole house. Two, why the hell would I put a few items of clothes in that drawer when I still have to go back home for all the rest of my shit anyway? And, most of all, three." She walks over to the drawer I gave her and yanks it open. "You haven't even noticed I've never used the fucking thing!"

She releases it with a jerk, and it crashes to the floor as she walks away, leaving it where it landed.

We'd been dating on and off for a while before that eventful fight. I don't even remember what started the fight now. It was probably something stupid, like I said green is a better color than blue. Who the fuck knows or cares? The point is, she left me and said she was never coming back. I gave her two days to change her mind and her attitude. When I didn't hear a single peep from her within that time, I decided it was time to move on.

And that's exactly what I did. I went out the next night, I met someone new, and I enjoyed the pleasure of her company. Repeatedly.

I haven't seen the same girl twice since the day Tawnee walked out, and I haven't regretted one minute of living my life to the fullest.

~

Present Day

"ROMAN, I SWEAR TO GOD, IF YOU TELL ME THAT fucking story one more time...I'm going to take this plastic knife I just used to smear cream cheese on my bagel, and I'm going to slit my wrists with it." Blake holds the knife at his wrist and pretends to saw his skin.

"I've told you that story before?"

"Only once or twice...a week...for three fucking years, man. Listen, I'm going to tell you this one last time as your friend. If you're my friend, you need to listen to what I have to say because I'm as fucking tired of repeating myself as I am of hearing you repeat yourself.

"One. It's time for you to face the truth.

"Two. You are not over being dumped.

"Three. You're not over her moving halfway around the world and never calling you to say goodbye when she left the country.

"Four. You are nowhere near being over Tawnee.

"Five. You're in love with the woman. Still. To this very day. If she walked into this bakery right now and said she wanted you back, you'd jump for fucking joy. And so would I, because at least you'd have a new fucking story to tell." Blake bites into his bagel, tearing it with excessive force, and glares at me over his coffee cup.

"That's ridiculous. How do you get that from what I just told you?"

"Because I'm not a fucking moron, Roman. Unlike you. That's how."

"You're so full of shit. I don't give second chances, Blake. One and done—that's how I manage my relationship issues. Plain and simple. No fuss, no muss. No complications. No baggage. No unresolved issues."

"Yeah, I got it, man. You're still full of shit, for the record. I stick by my original statement and assessment of you."

We walk out of the restaurant and stroll down the street, keeping our target in sight without giving away our position.

My phone vibrates with an incoming text, so I fish it out of my pocket and quickly glance at the screen. My attention is on my mark, but when I glance down at the screen, I forget all about my mission.

I forget about my job.

I forget about my mark.

I forget why I'm following him.

After three long years, Tawnee has sent me a

message. But it's not just any message. To anyone else, it appears to be a string of letters and numbers with no discernable pattern. But I know better. I recognize the secret code on sight. With a quick copy and paste into our own software program and our specific key, I decode the message and nearly let my phone slip through my fingers when I read what it says.

Send help immediately. Assassination plot. Extraction needed.

Her life is in imminent danger, and she's reaching out to me for help...from Dubai.

How can I not answer this call?

"What's wrong? Did you just see a ghost or what?" Blake looks over his shoulder at where I've stopped walking in the middle of the sidewalk.

"Something like that. Tawnee just texted me using Brad's secret message system. I haven't heard from her in three years, Blake."

"Yeah. Funny how I got that from the conversation we just had not three seconds ago. What did her message say?"

I hand Blake my phone and take his out of his hand. In seconds, I have my CIA partners, Silas Steele and Nick Tucker, on the phone and I'm relaying the message from Tawnee.

"What do you want to do, Roman?" Silas asks.

He knows damn well what I want to do, but he's testing me in more ways than one. It's not just my commitment to carrying out my duties as a CIA officer he's questioning. It's my commitment to her—someone who once worked alongside me at Steele Security. Someone who slept beside me, almost lived with me, and loved me. And someone I should've treated better than I did.

"I want to drop everything and leave a blazing trail on our way out of Dubai with her safely in my arms." That's probably the most honest statement I've made regarding her in the last three years.

"Have you done any research into what's going on and why she's involved in an imminent assassination attempt?" Nick asks, ever the level-headed hero.

"No, Nick. I just got the text and immediately called you two." I grit my teeth to keep my impatience under wraps.

"So, we could be walking straight into an ambush. It could all be a ruse to get you there for some reason. Or Silas. Or me. Or all three of us, for that matter. You have nothing but a simple text that could be from anyone pretending to be Tawnee."

"It came through Brad's encrypted system. Only Tawnee would know what secret key to use so I could decode the message. She sent it to me—not you and not Silas. Me. She needs me, and I'm going with or without you two."

"That's what I wanted to hear. Get your shit together, Roman, and screw your head on straight. If she's in a volatile situation, what do you think is waiting for us? We have no idea what we're walking into, so you need to check your emotions at the door and think logically. What is she working on? Who is she working with? Who are their friends and enemies?" Nick has been in so many dangerous situations in his career, this line of questioning has become second nature to him.

He's right, though. I saw her plea for help, and I was ready to run headlong into the fire, no questions asked.

Maybe Blake is right after all.

"Tell Blake to pack his gear. He's going along for the ride, too. I'll contact Langley and get all the intel we have on the situation. There's a flight leaving Miami today at 5:35. Let's meet at the airport and prepare for the long-ass flight to Dubai. Leave your guns at home. You'll never make it through customs with a weapon." Silas is the most seasoned CIA officer of us all.

Even though we're assigned to a joint task force with the NSA and CIA, we mostly perform under CIA rules. Meaning, there are none. This should be an interesting trip.

Tawnee

"RAFAEL, IT'S TIME TO GO. WE'VE CLEARED THE hallway." I approach my handsome Latin employer and try to urge him out of the luxury hotel suite for the third time this morning.

"Tawnee, you have to relax. You're far too pretty to

be so stressed all the time." He finally stands from the overstuffed sofa and slides his sunglasses over his eyes.

"Unfortunately, my looks have no bearing on my stress levels. Ensuring your security does. You not taking your own security seriously also does. Why hire me and make me travel around the world with you if you don't listen to me?" I turn and walk back to the entrance to check the hallway before letting him pass through the door.

"There's nothing I have to worry about. I know you've already worried about it a thousand times over before I've even considered it."

"I don't doubt that's true. Not even for a second. Which makes me even more stressed since, again, you don't take your own safety seriously. We're caught in a vicious cycle, you and I. So I need you to help me out here and don't make me old before my time. Stay close to your security team, be vigilant about watching your surroundings, and do exactly as you're told to do."

"I love it when you're bossy like that. It's so sexy."

"I'm serious, Raf."

"So am I. And your ass looks awesome in those pants. You should wear those every day."

I stop and turn to look him dead in the eyes. "Rafael, I do wear the same style of pants every single day that I'm with you. They're basically my work uniform. And you can't possibly watch your surroundings if you're watching my ass."

His dark chuckle makes me smile. He knows he drives

me crazy—that's why he does it on purpose. He's a shameless flirt, but he's also harmless. If he thought for one second his comments offended me or made me uncomfortable, he'd apologize profusely and buy me a mega yacht to make up for it. But then, he can afford to be so lavish since he's one of the richest men in the world. As the owner of a very profitable holding company, he controls the majority of shares in a lot of very high-powered, high-profile companies. Those businesses have made him an extraordinary amount of money, but he's still the same down-to-earth man he was before the cash starting rolling in.

All the money he has made is why I have a job today, albeit one that makes me crazy more than anything else in my life at the moment. Buying the controlling shares in companies whose owners aren't ready to give up control hasn't made him the most popular man on the Forbes Top 100 list. Corporate enemies can be ruthless. Kidnapping is a real threat for someone who is worth so much. Then there's the matter of his life insurance policy—it requires him to have private security in most circumstances…like when he leaves his house for any length of time, goes out on dates with unvetted partners, or when he's traveling to Dubai for both business and pleasure.

We're in the UAE for both reasons on this trip.

He's taking a tour of a recently built high-rise condo building as he considers expanding his interests. Not that he needs more income, but he's bored with managing his life against where the stock market closes or how a company performs. Expanding into real estate in one of the most popular destinations in the world makes good business sense to him.

Buying the entire building in this destination mecca isn't something many people would be able to afford.

But Rafael Cruz isn't just anyone.

We finally make it to the waiting car and get him inside without incident. On the way to tour the high-rise, Raf makes another business call while I watch our surroundings.

"Tony, change lanes abruptly." Our driver, Tony, is used to my obsessive behavior by now, so he does as I ask without question.

All the hairs on the back of my neck stand at attention. I speak into the comms, alerting the rest of the team in the other cars. "We have a possible tail. White Nissan Altima. Two males. Two cars behind and speeding up fast to catch up with us. Tony, make an unexpected turn, but not down a dead-end street. Make sure there's an easy out."

Tony's more alert now. His eyes are glued to the rearview mirror when he identifies the turn he'll make. Rafael, on the other hand, continues his conversation for a few more seconds before disconnecting the call as if nothing out of the ordinary is happening around him. The other car is traveling too fast in an attempt to catch up with us, so they're unable to make the same turn. They slam on their brakes, and the tires screech against the asphalt. Then they turn, and the front wheel jumps the curb before they speed up again, racing toward us.

"Tony, get us out of here. Now."

We race through the crowded city, drawing way too much attention in a culture that doesn't appreciate such outrageous behavior. But these guys aren't stopping. If anything, they're becoming more aggressive.

"Raf, you need to get down out of sight."

"Don't you have your gun? Shoot their tires out." He slides down in the seat, snatches his shades off his face, and looks at me with fear in his eyes for the first time since this chase started.

"Do I have a gun in Dubai? No, Raf, we're not residents here. We can't carry firearms without a special invitation from the sheik himself. Even you don't have that kind of clout here."

"Then how exactly do you plan to protect me?"

"By losing them and getting you to a safe place until we can work with the police to identify the owner of the car and the men inside."

Suddenly, another car appears out of nowhere and rams us from a side street. While we were watching the car behind us for the last several miles, they coordinated a sneak attack. Our car spins around in the middle of the street and slams into the side of a building. The initial shock of the crash takes me a few precious seconds to clear my mind, then I check on Rafael to make sure he isn't hurt.

He assures me he's fine, so I immediately survey our

surroundings to get my bearings. Tony and the second car of security guys surround our car, ready to fight off our attackers. Raf's door is pinned against the building, so I turn and shield him with my body since there's no way out and nowhere to run. The ruckus outside the car is fierce, with aggressive yelling in Arabic and English. The men start to scuffle, leaving me exposed inside the car. Arms reach in, grabbing at me, trying to pull me out. But I plant my feet against the side of the vehicle and push with all my might, staying between them and Rafael.

Tony dispatches the man who had distracted him then rushes back to help me. Two other members of our detail soon join him, effectively beating back the attack with fists and brawn. The entire scene lasts mere seconds, but it feels like it takes forever. The next thing I see, the attackers run back to their cars. One turns to look at me again before he slides into the passenger seat. He angrily yells something in Arabic...but I distinctly hear my name right in the middle of his rant.

Now I'm not so sure Rafael was the intended target after all.

Haven't read Nick Tucker's story yet? Get it now in *Fine Line*.
Roman's story is coming soon in *Hard Line*.

Want more of Nick Tucker? Read ***Her Dom*** and ***Her Dom's Lesson***!

Want more of Nick, Silas, Roman, Reaper, Bull, Rebel, and Shadow? Find them and more the ***Steele Security series***: ***Wicked Games***, ***Wicked Ties***, ***Wicked Nights***, ***Wicked Intentions***, and ***Wicked Shadows!***

ABOUT THE AUTHOR

A.D. Justice is the award-winning USA Today bestselling author of the Steele Security Series (Wicked Games, Wicked Ties, Wicked Nights, Wicked Intentions, Wicked Shadows), the Crazy Series (Crazy Maybe, Crazy Baby), the Dominic Powers series (Her Dom, Her Dom's Lesson), the Immortal Obsessions series (Immortal Envy), and a few stand-alone romance novels, such as Saving Grace, Completely Captivated, Just One Summer, Intent, and Mistletoe Not Required.

When she's not writing, she's spending time with her own alpha male character in their North Georgia mountain home. She is also an avid reader of romance novels, a master at procrastination, a chocolate sommelier, a twister of words, and speaks fluent sarcasm. An avid animal lover, A.D. Justice has two horses, three cats, and two very spoiled dogs.

While the primary focus of her books has been romantic suspense, she has expanded into different sub-genres of romance. Stay tuned to read what she has in store for you!

Connect with her online!

Newsletter
Facebook Reader Group
Website

facebook.com/adjusticeauthor

instagram.com/adjbooks

bookbub.com/authors/a-d-justice

amazon.com/author/adjustice

BOOKS BY A.D. JUSTICE

Steele Security Series

Wicked Games (Book 1)

Wicked Ties (Book 2)

Wicked Nights (Book 3)

Wicked Intentions (Book 4)

Wicked Shadows (Book 5)

The Crazy Series

Crazy Maybe (Book 1)

Crazy Baby (Book 2)

Crazy Love (FREE Short Story)

Dominic Powers Series

Her Dom (Book 1)

Her Dom's Lesson (Book 2)

The Vault

Warning, Part One

Warning, Part Two

Warning, Part Three

Crossing Lines

Fine Line

Blurred Line

Hard Line

Immortal Obsession

Immortal Envy (Book 1)

Stand-alone Romance Novels

Saving Grace

Completely Captivated

Intent

Just One Summer (Novella)

Mistletoe Not Required (Novella)

ACKNOWLEDGMENTS

Writing a book is much harder than one would think. The finished product only takes a few hours to read, but months to agonize over every single word, plot point, and character action. Only speaking for myself, I can honestly say I put my heart and soul into the story, taking time away from family and friends (and cleaning house....oh, the messy house!) to write just one more chapter.

When I finally reach those two little magical words, a weight is lifted from my shoulders and I'm able to breathe again. Until I start the next book. Which is usually while my editor works on the recently completed one.

My writing journey includes chatting with several people I trust and admire to give feedback and suggestions. There are also people who encourage and support me along the way, taking a chance on a new type of book or a storyline outside the norm. Those who aren't afraid to step outside the box and give "different" a chance. These are my people—my tribe—whether they realize it or not.

Acknowledgments are hard to write because I never want to leave anyone out or make anyone feel their place in my life isn't important. If you've ever read my books, you hold a special place in my heart. There are a few special people I want to recognize for helping make this book special to me.

First and foremost, I thank my Lord and Savior, Jesus Christ, for his unending love, mercy, and forgiveness of a sinner like me. Without Him, I am nothing. Yes, when I say I fall short, I realize I fall way short, but thankfully, there's no such thing as being too far from Him. He knows my heart. Someone recently called me a hypocrite for adding this to my acknowledgments. Since I openly admit I'm a sinner, I don't see it the same way she does. To me, a hypocrite implies someone denies any wrong-doing WHILE actually doing wrong. Adding this is my way of sharing my belief and thanking Him for the many blessings in my life, even though I'm well aware I don't deserve them.

Michelle Dare, you've been with me since the beginning of this crazy journey. All these years later, it's very clear that you're stuck with me. FOR.EV.A. Sorry for your bad luck. ;)

Victoria Renteria, you are an AWESOME alpha reader! Thank you for your time, feedback, and belief that I could actually finish this book. Silas was quite the

PITA, but you made it feel much easier with you wittiness and awesomeness!

Lisa A. Hollett with Silently Correcting Your Grammar, my editor and my friend, thank you once again for working through this book with me and polishing it until it's as perfect as possible.

Wander Aguiar, the photographer for the covers in this series, is always wonderful to work with—although he does make choosing one photo very difficult. Fortunately, I was able to find three that perfectly fit this series.

Sommer Stein with Perfect Pear Creative Covers, thank you for creating these awesome covers. I'm always in awe of your amazing talent.

To the readers, whether you love, like, or hate this book, thank you for taking your time to read it. Thank you for your reviews, even if all you say is you liked it or not. Thank you for your support—you have no idea how much every little bit means to me. You are the best!

All my love to you,
Angel